SUMMER NIGHTS IN WILD HARBOR

GRACE WORTHINGTON

Summer Nights in Wild Harbor by Grace Worthington

Copyright © 2021 by Grace Worthington

All rights reserved.

ISBN: 978-1-7334110-5-9

Published by Poets & Saints Publishing

Cover Design: Kristen Ingebretson

This novel is a work of fiction. Names, characters, and incidents are the product of the author's imagination or are used fictitiously. Any resemblance to actual events or persons, living or dead, is entirely coincidental.

Visit graceworthington.com for a free bonus wedding scene.

CHAPTER ONE

MEGAN

Megan Woods slumped in the seat of her roommate's car, staring out the window as the lake came into view.

"It's not like I don't want to be married. I do." She turned to her roommate, Aspen. "I just don't want to date to find Mr. Right."

In the past, blind dates had been awkward and had always seemed to lower her self-esteem. She was still reeling from the last one, a disastrous night out with James, a waterskiing instructor. When Megan had confessed to him that she was afraid of the water, he had recoiled like someone had stabbed him in the eyeball with a fork. He hadn't even wanted to hear her story explaining why the lake had triggered her panic. He casually dismissed it, his attention flitting around the room, counting down the minutes until he could politely excuse himself.

As Megan observed James, she jabbed her baked potato with a fork and stuffed a chunk in her mouth. The writing was on the wall. There was no hope for this night to end well.

After that, she'd put a moratorium on all blind dates. She was weary from meeting strangers, exhausted from trying to fit into their tightly constructed boxes of expectations. One date didn't like dogs. Another expressed concern that she was a fake news reporter. A third man confessed he preferred blondes. Apparently, he hadn't stalked her on social media to see that her hair was nearly black.

She needed a year off from dating. Maybe five. Perhaps forever, at this rate.

She brushed stray dog hairs off her pants as her roommate listened. "Why can't he show up on my doorstep, like a box from the mailman?" Life with her golden retriever was sounding more appealing by the day.

"Nice. So you want a mail-order husband?" Aspen glanced at Megan.

"No, I want him to sweep me off my feet without all the awkwardness."

Aspen furrowed her eyebrows.

"Why are you looking at me that way?" Megan asked as her friend gripped the steering wheel, her knuckles turning white.

"What way?"

"Like you just committed a crime."

"No reason." Aspen raised her shoulders and took a deep breath. "Okay, so maybe a teeny tiny reason. Remember how you recited that poem from your diary as a thirteen-year-old? The one inspired by that cheesy Christmas romance movie?"

Megan nodded.

"First it was me.

Then I met you.

Now it's you and me, forever."

Megan leaned her head against the seat. "I hadn't figured out yet that the Hollywood version of love is a bunch of over-romanticized baloney." She had stopped watching movies like that. The kind where the couple always ended up together. A happily ever after was expected. Demanded, even. But real life didn't work that way. Or at least, her life didn't.

"Well, I met someone." Aspen pulled up to a stoplight on Main Street and turned to Megan.

"For you?" Megan's phone dinged with a message. A selfie of a couple posing on the beach popped up. Newlyweds in Hawaii. They appeared to be having the time of their lives.

"No, for *you*." The light turned green, and Aspen stepped on the gas. "Jeff at the computer store. He saw you in the car and recognized you from the paper. It's time for you to try again."

"Absolutely not. I do not want to be fixed up. I don't need a man to be happy. How do I know he's not some weirdo?"

"It's not like meeting someone anonymously on the internet. He knows you from the paper. It's about time you returned to the dating scene. You can't let a few bad dates keep you from trying again."

"Then why don't *you* date him?"

Aspen waved away the suggestion. "Not my type. I don't date guys like him. He's got an outstanding personality though."

"People only say that about unattractive men." Megan narrowed her gaze. "What's wrong with him?"

"Nothing. There just wasn't chemistry, you know? Not to mention he was interested in you. I thought he was quite charming."

"Even narcissists can be charming. Besides, I've officially called off dating. As in, hit the road, Jack. Sayonara."

"I can't tell him no." Aspen chewed her lip, a habit that only emerged when she was extremely nervous. "Don't kill me for this."

"What did you do?"

"I told him you'd go out with him." Aspen clenched the steering wheel, waiting for Megan's reaction.

"What?" Megan shook her head in disbelief. "No . . . no, you didn't."

"He seemed so cute with his hound dog eyes . . ."

"I'm not going out with a puppy."

"For me . . . please?"

"No. Case closed. Tell him I canceled. I'm not doing it."

"Go out with Jeff. He's perfect for you!"

Megan raised her eyebrows. This time she was serious. "No, Aspen. No matchmaking."

Aspen's face fell. "I'm not giving up so easily."

∾

A FEW DAYS LATER, Megan's phone buzzed with a text from Aspen.

Aspen: Cancel your plans. Meet me at Brewster's at seven after work.

Skipping lunch had been a good choice. Now she could indulge in a cheeseburger without guilt for girls' night.

The Wild Harbor burger joint was known for their loaded double cheeseburgers and buttered buns, a favorite stop for locals. She headed home to change into jeans and a pair of heels and then walked to Brewster's from her apartment.

Aspen sat on a barstool next to a muscular guy with a full beard. She gave Megan a little wave.

"Hey, Megan." Aspen's voice cracked. Smoke from the grill permeated the room. After tonight, she'd go home smelling like a well-done hamburger, which would probably make her hungry later.

"Hey, what's up?" Megan nodded toward the guy and mouthed the words, "Who's that?"

"Please take my spot." Aspen hopped off her barstool, her blonde curls bouncing, and patted the seat. "I actually had something come up and need to leave, but I wanted you to meet

Jeff." She tapped Jeff's arm to pull his attention from the baseball game on the TV.

"Wait, did you say *Jeff?*" Megan looked from Beard Man to Aspen, and the horrifying reality hit her. The guy from the computer store. Aspen had set her up. No, no, no . . .

Her mouth fell open. Jeff wiped his hands on his pants, then held out his palm for a handshake. "Howdy."

She had failed to mention to Aspen that she wasn't partial to beards. She didn't dislike them, but kissing a hairy man was like getting a facial with steel wool.

Aspen took a step backwards, but Megan was too quick.

"Hey, hang on a sec." She grabbed Aspen's sleeve. "You're leaving? What about girls' night?"

Aspen pulled away. "I can't stay. You remember me mentioning Jeff, the guy who fixed my computer, right?" Aspen's smile froze as her eyes pleaded, *Don't kill me for this.*

Megan shook her head. This was a total setup, and she had fallen for it. Hook, line, and sinker. "No, you can't leave yet."

Aspen backed away. "You'll have fun. Promise."

"I told you I wasn't doing this." Megan followed Aspen, trying to grab her arm. "You can't abandon me—"

Aspen dodged her and then waved quickly. "You two have fun getting to know each other. Bye!" She nearly knocked down a server as she sprinted toward the door.

Megan exhaled and slumped onto the stool. Like it or not, she was stuck with Mr. Beard Man.

Jeff cleared his throat. "I'm a big fan of your articles. To be honest, I'm nervous. Usually, people say I can't stop talking. But I'm downright tongue-tied tonight." Jeff grinned. He had a nice smile under all that hair.

"I'm really flattered, but I'm afraid there's been a mistake . . ."

Someone turned the TV louder, drowning out her words.

"What did you say? You wanted a steak?" He motioned the server over.

5

As the redheaded woman approached, he scanned the menu. "We're ready to order. This lady wants a steak." He pointed at Megan.

"We don't have steak here. Just burgers."

He looked crestfallen. "I'm so sorry. You okay with a burger?"

Megan nodded. She wasn't okay with any of this. She wanted to go home, but her stomach painfully rumbled. One little burger couldn't hurt. Plus, he was nice looking. Maybe she could be swayed about the beard.

Jeff pointed at his menu. "I'll take a cheeseburger and onion rings, please. If it's not too much, add an orange soda to my order. Thank you, ma'am." Apparently, Jeff was on his best manners tonight. He seemed unusually chirpy. It was like eating with a child who'd just learned how to say please and thank you.

"Anything to drink for you?" The server scribbled Jeff's order onto a notepad.

"A diet soda, please," Megan added. "And fries. Thank you very much." She couldn't be one-upped by Jeff's manners.

"Coming right up." The waitress left them alone in awkward silence.

Jeff fixed his stare on her. "You play any sports?"

She squirmed in her seat. She ought to enjoy herself. "Yeah, I played soccer and basketball. How about you?"

"I'm so glad you asked." Jeff brightened. "I was a linebacker for a high school in Lansing."

She paused. Either her silence was an invitation for more details, or something miraculously healed Jeff from his shyness, because he launched into the complete history of his high school football career. He seemed to remember every score and statistic from his senior year. She wondered if he kept a football spreadsheet that he reviewed on a semi-regular basis.

Her phone buzzed in her purse. Jeff was knee-deep in the

final epic football game of his senior year as her phone vibrated again. He'd never notice if she took one little peek.

Aspen: How's the date going? What do you think about Jeff?
Megan: He is quite the talker.
Aspen: I thought you'd like a guy who talked a lot? You're a journalist. You love stories!

Stories, yes. One-sided conversations where the other person dominated? *No.*

The waitress hustled over with their hamburgers and sides. "You guys need anything else?"

Jeff's face twitched as she interrupted his story, like he was slightly annoyed. "Haven't even finished my first round of soda." He held up his full glass and took a sip, staring at the server with a message to get lost.

He had been so friendly before, but now his manners were slipping.

"I need a refill." Megan handed the glass to the waitress and offered an apologetic smile.

Jeff eyed the gigantic bite she'd just taken. "Wow, you eat fast for a girl."

"My brother and I used to have food races. He usually beat me, except for when I was ten, and he choked on a hot dog."

Jeff's forehead wrinkled, like he hadn't known girls behaved like that. Megan wasn't about to pretend she was a fragile flower. More like a rose. Beautiful, with sharp edges.

Growing up with two sisters and one brother, she had always been game for competition, from debate team to running. Perseverance was her superpower, thanks to her belief that if she achieved enough, people would like her. It was the reason she was good at her job. If she worked hard, she'd earn people's approval. Success was such a potent drug.

Suddenly, the clammy touch of someone's hand on hers catapulted her back to the present.

"How about a movie next? Please?" Jeff squeezed her hand.

Her stomach churned. "Uh, it was nice to meet you, but I'm exhausted tonight." She slid her hand away from him and hid it in her lap. Surely he would get the hint now.

Jeff frowned and turned to his plate of food. A sulky expression passed over it as he stared at his onion rings.

A guy next to Jeff, sitting two stools down, glanced over. Long lashes, thick brown hair, chiseled jaw shadowed with whiskers, sculpted muscles underneath his T-shirt. He checked all the boxes. Not that Megan noticed. But she wished, for a second, that he was her blind date instead of Jeff. She could look at that face forever. Or at least for one night.

He pushed away his food and sat straighter on his stool, casting sidelong glances at Jeff.

Until now, he had been another stranger in the restaurant. But now he zeroed in on Megan. Why hadn't she noticed him before? A smile played across his lips, like he found their interchange amusing.

Jeff dug into his cheeseburger, swallowing half of it down in a few quick bites. What had happened to Mr. Manners?

Next, he attacked his onion rings, stuffing the greasy circles in his mouth. Apparently, rejection caused him to stress eat.

He paused mid-bite, holding an onion ring in his fingers. "You just need to get to know me a little better. I don't think you've given us a chance." He put down his last limp ring and brushed her arm with his greasy fingers.

She instinctively recoiled, then cleared her throat. The handsome stranger tilted his head her way.

She had tried to be nice about it, but the message wasn't getting through to Jeff. She lowered her voice so that the stranger couldn't hear. "I'm sorry, but I'm not sure you heard me the first time. I'm heading home after dinner."

"But, princess, we're perfect together. I knew it from the moment I saw you."

Megan hated being called princess or any cutesy name. It made her feel like she was five. "First, don't call me princess. Second, I'm not interested."

She threw down her napkin and swiveled off the stool, but he grabbed her arms and locked his grip on them.

"Hey, we've hardly had time to get to know each other. I'm a great guy. If you take some time to get to know me, you'll really like me." He narrowed his eyes and smiled. Flecks of onion ring batter clung to his beard.

She couldn't believe that the man who had been so painfully shy was now singing his own praises while holding her hostage. *Lucky her.*

She leaned away from him and tried to wriggle free from his hands, which were slick from onion ring grease.

"You want me to finish my drink first?" she asked.

"Yeah, just stay and talk awhile and maybe later we can . . ."

"We can what?"

"You know . . . see if my kiss makes you change your mind."

The suggestion was too much for Megan. "As much as I'd like to, I'm really not interested." She picked up her drink, and dumped the ice in his lap, letting the frigid cola hit his seat, soaking his pants.

He stood up with a jerk, the ice sliding off him. He looked like a toddler who'd wet his pants.

Megan dashed from the restaurant, trying to make it to her car before Jeff followed. As she fled out the door to the dark parking lot, a firm hand gripped her arm.

"Wait a minute," a gruff voice barked.

She barely had time to register that he'd followed her.

He jerked her around. "You can't leave yet. You haven't paid for your dinner."

"What?" The realization hit her: Dinner was on her. "I thought you were picking up the tab."

"Only if my date leaves with me. Otherwise, you're on your own."

If that's what was keeping him from leaving her alone, she'd foot the bill. It was worth it to get rid of this guy.

"Fine." She fiddled with the clasp on her purse before handing him a twenty. "Tell the waitress to keep the change."

He frowned at the bill in her hands. Apparently, he hadn't expected her to relent so easily.

"Listen, Megan, I'm really attracted to you. I think you'd feel the same if you'd just give me a chance . . ."

Before Megan realized it, he leaned forward to kiss her. Her instincts screamed to pull back as quickly as possible. She tried to dodge and weave, but he was too quick and landed his sloppy lips on her ear instead. Without thinking, she gripped her purse, ready to wallop him with a forceful blow.

As her purse came down, someone from the shadows stepped between them at the last minute, pulling Jeff off her. Instead of hitting her blind date, the metal clasp on her bag smacked the stranger across his cheekbone. He winced and grabbed his cheek.

Jeff fell to the ground as the man doubled over from the purse's blow.

"You've got good aim, I'll give you that." The man rubbed the side of his face where she had walloped him.

It was the handsome stranger from the restaurant.

He regained his balance and pointed to Jeff. "Didn't you hear the lady the first time? She said to leave her alone."

Jeff pulled himself onto his knees. "Listen, I don't know who you are. But this is between me and the lady."

"Not anymore." Megan lifted her purse, threatening to smack him. "If you don't leave me alone, I'm going to call the cops."

"Okay, okay." Jeff raised his hands in surrender. "Who is this guy, anyway?"

Megan shrugged as she looked at the stranger.

The man stepped forward. "We don't know each other. But it was obvious that she was saying no."

Jeff sneered. "Well, maybe you should mind your own business next time before . . ."

"Before what?" the stranger asked.

"Before meddling in mine."

Megan stepped around the strange man. "Maybe you should try acting like a gentleman before coming on to a woman. Now beat it."

Jeff stumbled to his feet and fled into the restaurant.

Megan turned to the stranger. "Are you okay? I'm so sorry."

"It wasn't so much the purse that hurt, but that metal clasp." The dim light outlined his face. He rubbed the five o'clock shadow across his jaw where it was still red from the impact. "So what made you say yes to that winner of a date?"

"I didn't pick him. My friend set us up. A blind date gone wrong."

"Next time, maybe your friend should think twice before setting you up with a loser."

What business did he have judging Aspen? All she wanted was for Megan to be happy. Her protective instinct kicked in with the ferocity of a wildfire. "He seemed nice at first."

"Then I'm not sure I'd trust her judgment in men."

So her roommate had set her up on a date with a covert narcissist. It wasn't entirely her fault. Jeff had good manners and had seemed charming until you crossed him.

She kicked a stone with the pointed toe of her high heel. She didn't need a knight in shining armor, especially one this cocky. "You don't really know my roommate, and she meant well. It's not her fault he turned out to be a lousy date."

"It might not be her fault, but why did you stay?"

Like she'd tell him the truth. She was lured by the promise of a cheeseburger. Who was he to judge her for that? She could take care of herself.

Megan took a deep breath, trying to appear calm, but she had the feeling he could see through her. His gaze rattled her. "My friend had good intentions. She believes the best about people before making a judgment. Now that I know how quick you are to make grand statements about her character, I'm not sure I feel bad about hitting you." Megan spun on her heel to leave.

"You're right." His voice softened, but his eyes remained dark and intense. "I'm sorry. Men who behave badly hit a raw nerve. They should know better."

"At least we agree on one thing." Megan didn't know whether to trust his apology. Why did he care about her welfare? In the dark, she could barely make out the sculpted lines of his face. She hardly knew the man, but there was a connection between them. She lifted her purse. "You already got a smackdown by yours truly, so I should be the one apologizing."

She searched for her convertible, and that's when she remembered she had walked to Brewster's. It was a warm, clear July night, and she had assumed Aspen would drive her home. The reality of the situation hit her. She was stuck.

"Is something wrong?" He slid his hands in his pockets.

"Not at all." She dug around in her purse, searching for her cell phone. Maybe her sister could pick her up.

"Let me guess. You don't have a ride home."

Her gaze cut to his smug smile. It was an expression she had seen before, in another face that looked somehow similar, although she couldn't place where. She shifted uncomfortably in her leopard-print heels, her big toes pinched. Oh, why of all nights had she worn her most uncomfortable shoes? Somehow, they hadn't bothered her on the way here. But after the tussle in the parking lot, her feet throbbed.

"It's okay. I can walk." She tried to sound breezy, like it was no big deal that she was walking in shoes that tortured her feet.

"You need a ride?" He pulled out a pair of keys.

"Nope, I'm good, thanks." She didn't need a man's help. She walked toward the street.

He cleared his throat, alerting her. "For your information, your date just left out the side door of Brewster's. If you don't want him to spot you, I'd suggest taking a different route."

Megan stiffened and took a step behind a landscaping bush to keep from being seen. A car engine roared to life. "Is he gone?"

The man put his finger to his mouth to quiet her.

The motor swelled, then drifted down the street, fading.

"Coast is clear. By the way, my name's Finn Avery." He held out his hand.

"Megan Woods." She felt the warmth of his palm against hers. It was electric.

"If you need a ride, I can drop you off. It's really no problem."

As much as this guy rankled her, he seemed to be her best chance of getting home at this point. Not that she usually allowed strangers to take her home. But in this case, she could wait around or take a chance on Mr. Tall, Dark, and Handsome. She looked him over. He didn't appear to be a mass murderer. She scrolled her list of contacts on her phone. But then again, they never do.

"I'll be fine." She shifted her feet, ready to take her heels off and walk home barefoot. "I'll wait inside until one of my friends can swing by."

"Suit yourself." As he turned to go, he rubbed the spot on his jaw where she had hit him.

"Wait . . ." Something in her wanted to reach out and touch the injury on his perfect cheek, but she held back. "Despite what

I said earlier, I really am sorry about—" She pointed to his cheek.

"You've got a good wallop. Maybe we'll run into each other again. Just not so forcefully next time." He gave her a lopsided grin before turning, the kind that made her heart do backflips in her chest.

He had no clue the effect his smile was having on her. Megan exhaled slowly, calming her bucking bronco heartbeat. He was charming, even if he seemed too arrogant for his own good.

She cringed at the thought of hitting such a beautiful face.

Oh well, at least she wouldn't see him again.

CHAPTER TWO

MEGAN

"Are you going to hold it against me forever?" Aspen stood at Megan's bedroom door looking repentant with a doughnut in one hand and a coffee cup in the other.

"Maybe." Megan sat in bed, petting her dog, Ollie, hoping the memory of last night would fade like a bad dream.

"If it helps, you can have my doughnut." Aspen held up her favorite glazed doughnut as a peace offering. She had already apologized at least a half dozen times.

"I don't want your doughnut, and I've already accepted your apology. Just don't set me up again."

"Even if I find a fabulous guy who's perfect for you?"

"Aspen!"

"Okay, okay. No more matchmaking. But what about that guy you clobbered with your purse? Who was he?"

"Some guy trying to be the hero and save the damsel in distress."

"He wasn't from Wild Harbor?"

"I don't think so, but his face seemed familiar to me, like we've met before"

"He didn't offer any other information about himself?"

"No, we didn't exactly hit it off. He had the audacity to blame you for my terrible date."

"As he should. It was entirely my fault."

"You didn't know. Your heart was in the right place." Megan squeezed her friend's hand.

"I appreciate the show of support, but he was only pointing out the obvious. Even if it didn't work out, I want you to be happily dating someone."

"How about happily single? I've got a great job, a loyal dog, and a fabulous roommate. What else could a girl ask for?"

"Just one good date?" Aspen sipped her coffee.

"Not going to happen. At least, not for me." Megan slid on her fuzzy slippers.

She and Aspen rented a ground-floor apartment in a Victorian home, where the wood floors and dark oak trim were etched with age and the floorboards creaked. From their wraparound porch, Megan could make out a tiny sliver of lake between the trees, a reminder of afternoons at the beach. The soft white sand under her toes, the lull of waves, and the warm sun on her back.

When was the last time she'd sat on a beach chair and watched the waves? Months? She couldn't recall. She spent all her time in front of her computer writing articles.

The lake beckoned, but she had to resist its pull. Dale, her boss at *The Wild Harbor Newspaper*, had called an urgent staff meeting first thing this morning.

The lake would have to wait.

After showering and pulling on black jeans with a dressy T-shirt and jacket, she grabbed her laptop bag and piled into her cherry-red Mustang convertible.

Megan checked her watch. Just enough time to stop at the French Press Café on the way.

As she pulled her convertible in front of the coffee shop and turned off the low rumble of her engine, two ladies sitting in the window waved. Everyone in town recognized the vintage Mustang that her father had restored for her before he'd suffered a stroke this year.

Edna Long sipped a black tea, her cheeks faintly highlighted with a pink rouge that matched her floral blouse. Edna reveled in her role as the town matron, passing mint candies to the kids from her enormous purse, which contained an endless supply of goodies. Her short curled hair was teased into a billowing white puff at the beauty salon each week and was so solidly hair sprayed in place that a breezy day on the lake couldn't move it. She was rarely seen without Peaches, her beloved Pekingese, who was yapping outside the coffeehouse's entrance, begging for some attention. Edna sat with the mayor's wife, Harriet Brinks, who was the closest thing Wild Harbor had to a first lady. She regularly rubbed shoulders with the elite of Wild Harbor.

"Good morning, Megan." Edna took a sip of tea as Megan detoured toward their table.

"What a nice Friday morning surprise." Megan stood next to their table, wishing she could stay and chat.

Max called across the room to Megan. "You want your regular order, Megan?"

"Yep. To go."

Edna put her cup down, suddenly interested in the latest gossip. "What's the scoop this morning? When Dale stopped in, he picked up two coffees and didn't stop to talk. Is there a breaking story I don't know about?"

Megan shrugged. "Your guess is as good as mine."

Dale rarely bought coffee for anyone. A self-proclaimed cheapskate, he was always trying to save money for the newspaper, saying that if he hadn't counted every penny for the last two decades, the paper would have folded years ago. Now that the publication was in financial trouble again, Megan wasn't about to let the newspaper fail. She was just as invested as he was.

"Be sure to let us know." Edna added more sugar to her tea and stirred. "I love reading your stories in the paper, but it's even better finding them out ahead of time."

Edna supported the newspaper in return for being privy to the latest town gossip. Well-acquainted with Megan's parents, she was an unofficial auntie of the family.

"By the way, I heard a rumor that you weren't alone at Brewster's last night. I have to admit, I was shocked." Edna's eyebrows lifted. Prying for juicy details was her specialty.

Harriet smiled and patted Edna's arm. "Now, you can't know everything about Megan's love life. Perhaps she wants to keep some things private." Harriet wore a dress the color of banana cream pie, a soft blend of pale yellows and meringue whites.

Edna frowned. "I've known Megan Woods since birth. Even changed her diaper in the church nursery. I have every right to know who she's dating."

As if wiping a baby's bottom gave Edna unlimited access to Megan's personal life.

"You weren't the only one who didn't know about the date. It was a surprise setup by Aspen. She tricked me into meeting him and then left me there."

Edna leaned forward and lowered her voice. "I heard there was a scuffle in the parking lot between two men fighting for you."

Harriet's eyes grew as big as silver dollars.

Megan didn't know where Edna got her information, but as a reporter, she wanted to stop the gossip mill. "Is that the rumor going around? Just to clarify, I hit a random stranger with my purse—by accident—when he tried to save me from my blind date. It all started when I dumped my drink in my date's lap and left."

"Really?" Edna snorted. "I wish I had been there to see his face. That's even better than the version I heard."

Max rushed over and handed Megan her usual hot coffee and blueberry scone.

"Thanks, Max. Sorry to run, but I've got a meeting at eight. Can't be late."

As she crawled into the front seat of her car, she balanced the flaky pastry on top of the hot drink. It might be risky, but after last night, how could this morning get any worse?

When she pulled into the cramped newspaper parking lot, she accidentally dropped her scone in her lap, spraying buttery crumbs across her black pants. Looking down to retrieve it, she bumped the curb and spilled coffee down the front of her white T-shirt.

"Oh, great." She jammed the car into park, then reached into the glove compartment to grab a pile of napkins. She dabbed at the brown stain. So much for looking professional.

She bolted to the second-floor newspaper office just as the cathedral bell chimed the hour.

Please don't let Dale beat me to the conference room.

She bounded up the stairs two at a time, then burst through the doors of the office, hustling toward the conference room. She stopped at the door, taking a deep breath, and covered the coffee stain with her laptop. At least she wanted to appear composed.

Dale crossed his arms, glaring as she stepped in. "Now that Ms. Woods is here, we can begin."

Megan slumped into the closest chair and checked her phone. Eight on the dot. Just in the nick of time.

Her relationship with Wild Harbor's chief editor was a mixed bag. Dale was old school. He hated technology and butted heads with anyone who wanted to upgrade their office's way of doing things.

A few months ago, Megan had suggested they revamp their website because it was archaic and clunky. Subscribers were down. Dale claimed that technology had caused the demise of newspapers nationwide. Never mind that she had raised more in advertising last year than any other staff person. She wanted the newspaper to modernize so they could get out of financial trouble, but Dale pushed back, often citing his success at keeping the paper alive through multiple recessions.

Even though they didn't always see eye to eye, Dale liked her. She consistently delivered her articles on time and never complained when he assigned more work. Stories were her heartbeat. Dale understood the power of sharing them.

But her boss was also getting older, and the pace was wearing on him. He limped from bad knees and frequently sat down during staff meetings. How soon until he retired? Though she'd never admit it, Megan dreamed of taking over Dale's job. She wanted more than anything to save the newspaper because it was important to the town's heritage and bolstered community pride. Who knew this place better than she did? Her résumé checked all the boxes: a graduate from journalism school, born and raised in Wild Harbor. No one could deny that writing was in her blood. Her grandfather had been the editor-in-chief before Dale and had relished the role. He single-handedly saved the paper when the town went through a recession.

The only problem was convincing Dale that she was the right fit. He recognized her writing chops, but did he trust her with the newspaper's future? She wanted to change his mind. Position herself as a prime candidate, even if that meant putting a kibosh on the jokes around the water cooler.

"Big news to share with you." Dale pulled out a folder of notes. "First off, I talked with the mayor yesterday about the upcoming summer events in Wild Harbor. Thousands of tourists will visit, and it's how our local businesses thrive the rest of the year. We discussed how we can highlight Wild Harbor as a summer destination and emphasize our summer events schedule. This year, we're covering summer events in depth, including our hallmark summer event: the sailboat regatta. Our coverage will double compared to previous years. This means an intense season of reporting. With Damien recovering from major surgery, we're short-staffed. Megan, you're going to take the lead with the bulk of our summer events calendar."

Megan nodded and took another swig of her coffee. The coffee stain on her shirt had dried, leaving an ugly brown mark.

"I also want to announce that Larry is stepping down from his position at the newspaper. He was ready for a career change and is going to mortuary school instead."

Larry raised his hand.

Dale frowned. He didn't like to be interrupted. "Do you wish to say something?"

"I do." Larry stood. "I've had fifteen good years at the paper. But it's time for me to pursue my passion."

Rebekah gave a little snort as she sipped her diet soft drink and leaned toward Megan. "I didn't know mortuary school could be a passion," she whispered.

Larry had confided in Megan a few months ago about being burned out. The news wasn't surprising. Larry had long complained about article assignments and disliked attending local events because he was a self-proclaimed hermit. The only thing he seemed to relish was covering the obituaries, spending far too much time on them while neglecting his other assignments. Becoming a mortician was a perfect fit, but his absence would leave a hole in their staff.

Rebekah lifted her hand. "I hope you won't expect us to cover Larry's sections." She only worked part-time, juggling motherhood and reporting so that she could pay the bills. It was no secret that her true love was roller derby, and she took part on Wild Harbor's team. Just like Larry, being a reporter wasn't her first love.

Megan scribbled some notes on her phone. *Cover summer events and recommend someone to replace Larry. Pronto.*

Without Larry, most of the summer stories would fall on her, but this would also make her more valuable to the paper. Maybe this was just what she needed to convince Dale that she could step into a leadership role. Becoming *The Wild Harbor Newspaper*'s first female editor-in-chief would be a dream come true. She'd follow in her grandfather's footsteps and carry on the family legacy.

Dale cleared his throat. "Thanks, Larry. Best of luck. With Larry leaving us soon, we'll have to endure some tremendous changes. It's rare we have the opportunity to hire a journalist with both the experience and qualifications from a big news outlet..."

Wait a minute. Hiring who? Megan's eyes circled the room, searching for an unfamiliar face. Her coworkers stared blankly at Dale.

Dale walked slowly over to the door. "We're a small operation, and when I hire, I can't compete with the offers that the big papers make to talented journalists. So when you find someone who wants to work at our paper, you don't wait. He's fresh from an internship at the *Detroit Free Press* after getting his degree in journalism at the University of Chicago. So would you all welcome our newest reporter..."

Megan's head jerked toward the door at the oddly familiar face entering the room. As her eyes met his, the truth walloped her as hard as a purse to the face.

She'd know that jawline anywhere.

Finn Avery was her new co-reporter.

CHAPTER THREE

MEGAN

F inn looked different in the florescent light of an office.
The shadowed lines of his face were less pronounced. A
small, faded mark on his cheek still showed the impact of his
brief encounter with her purse. But something about those
perfect cheekbones stirred a vague feeling in Megan.

If only she hadn't hit her new coworker.

"Finn, have a seat and introduce yourself." Dale pointed to
the chair next to him. The one that was always empty. Dale had
never invited anyone to sit next to him before.

Finn slid into the chair with a commanding presence. "Like
Dale mentioned, I graduated with a degree in journalism. But
before that, I served in the Coast Guard as a rescue swimmer
for four years of active duty and four years in reserve. I've
completed several internships, first at the *Chicago Tribune* and
then at the *Detroit Free Press*. I learned everything about how a
newspaper runs, and my goal is eventually to become an editor-
in-chief."

Megan sat up in her chair. Not only had she struck the

newest staff member, but he'd blatantly hinted at wanting Dale's job. The same job she'd thought she had all but wrapped up.

"I've known Finn since he was a boy," Dale added. "His dad and I were college frat brothers. Finn's family settled about an hour away, and we've occasionally seen each other. It was only in the last year that Finn's dad called and bragged about how his son had graduated with a degree in journalism and was interning for the *Free Press*, where he raised a lot of money. He asked for a favor as one of my college brothers. Could I find a place for Finn on staff? At the time, I turned him down. Didn't have any openings, but when Larry announced he was leaving, I knew who I'd hire in a second. In fact, it seems like perfect timing, since we need someone who is good with money since I can't work here forever."

Megan crossed her arms, covering the stain on her shirt.

So, Finn was being considered as a future candidate for Dale's job. Megan wasn't about to give up so easily.

This new guy might have experience at the big leagues, but what did he know about Wild Harbor? He didn't know the best people to interview or how to get the inside scoop.

If there was one thing Megan had, it was town connections and history. Five generations of her family had lived here. Her grandfather had been editor-in-chief. Her parents were pillars in the community. That was something you couldn't force. It took trust.

Suddenly, an elbow poked her in the ribs. Rebekah whispered, "Your turn."

Megan cleared her throat. "I'm so sorry. I missed the question."

A heavy pause punctuated Dale's reply. "We're introducing ourselves."

"Oh, yes." She could feel the heat prickling up her spine as she avoided Finn's eyes. Did he recognize her from last night? It had been dark, and they had only talked for a few minutes.

"I'm Megan, a staff reporter. I've been here for four years now, graduated from U of M journalism school, and I'm originally from Wild Harbor."

Her eyes flicked past Finn. Not only was he staring at her, his lips pulled into a smirk.

Of course, he recognized her. Whatever he was thinking, it couldn't be good.

"I think we've met." Finn leaned across the table toward her, still staring hard.

Megan wanted to sink into the floor and disappear.

"You two know each other?" Dale asked.

"No, no," Megan retorted at the same moment as Finn responded, "Yes."

A questioning glare passed between them, followed by an awkward silence.

Megan tapped her pencil on the table, a nervous habit since high school. "I mean, we met briefly. We ran into each other by accident at Brewster's last night. Didn't realize he was working here. Too bad I didn't know that little tidbit beforehand."

"Great! Because you're going to be seeing a lot of each other." Dale folded his hands. "For the rest of the summer, Finn is going to be working with you. You'll help him assimilate into Wild Harbor and connect with its key members. You'll be his mentor, even though, technically, he's your equal. Finn has the chops to become a brilliant reporter, but he doesn't know Wild Harbor the way you do, Megan."

The last person she wanted to help was her competition for the job, especially when he seemed so confident already. Plus, she didn't need a good-looking guy distracting her from work. Couldn't Larry help?

"I'm not sure that's going to work. With Larry's departure, I won't have time with the extra assignments and the increased coverage of summer events." Given their rocky start, she wasn't sure it was the best plan.

"Sure you are. Let's talk about that afterward." He checked his watch. "Everyone is excused from this meeting to get started on their day *except* for Ms. Woods."

Rebekah offered a sympathetic look to Megan before she shuffled out with the rest of the staff.

As the room emptied, Dale leaned over the table. "Ms. Woods, I want to talk with you privately about Mr. Avery. I think you're the perfect person to train him."

"How about Larry? Or even Rebekah?" Anyone but her.

"Larry's moving on, and Rebekah only works part-time. The coverage of Wild Harbor's summer events will be too much for one reporter. I need two people on the ground getting interviews, and Finn needs to be assigned to all stories with you. The first one is the local beach volleyball tournament this weekend. Who's going to cover the tournament and write the human-interest story? You've covered the tournament before, so it's your responsibility to get him up to speed. Oh, and he'll need to share an office with you too until Larry leaves."

"Are you sure this is the best arrangement?"

"With Damien out, we don't have a choice. We're short-staffed already. You can make it work, right?" He gave her a thumbs-up.

She slowly nodded.

She wanted to be the type of employee who never backed down from a challenge, but this partnership might just do her in.

Dale walked to the door to summon Finn as Megan stood to face her new coworker. Yesterday, her job had been the perfect fit. She was at the top of her game. Nobody to distract her from her goal.

But today, everything had shifted. She had competition. Not only was he talented but also incredibly handsome.

Finn walked in, and their eyes met. The heat in the room ratcheted up.

Dale fiddled with his folder, searching for his list of articles. "If you two are going to work together, I need you to start on the right foot. Finn, I was just telling Megan that both of you will cover the volleyball tournament this weekend, winners and losers. That story will headline our sports section. The other story is a human-interest one, featuring one of our local volley-ball players. Barring any other major news, that one will be front page."

"I'll take the human-interest story." Megan wanted to stake her claim before he did. "I have an idea who we should zero in on for the story."

"You and Finn need to cover it together."

"Wouldn't it be best if he covers the overview of the tourna-ment and I do the human-interest piece? It just makes sense. He doesn't know the volleyball players—"

"Which is why I want you to do it as a team. I'll leave you two alone to get the details worked out." Dale leaned toward Megan and whispered, "Be nice to the new guy, okay?"

She was certain Finn could hear every word.

Dale snapped the door shut behind him, leaving them alone.

"I guess you're stuck with me." Megan pulled out her laptop, afraid she'd melt into a puddle if she looked his way.

"Lucky me." Finn shifted his chair to face her. "Dale had all kinds of good things to say about you."

"Really?" He rarely complimented her in person. "He obvi-ously thinks a lot of you."

"We'll see if I can live up to it. I have the feeling we didn't get off on the right foot last night. How about we pretend last night didn't happen? Start over. My name's Finn." He reached his hand out to shake hers.

She glanced at the gesture, then at his face. "Okay. I'm Megan." She shook his hand, and her body warmed to his touch. "I know Dale wants me to be your . . . I don't even know what to call it. Mentor? Trainer?"

"I prefer Jedi Master." He didn't even crack a smile, but a flicker of mischief lit up his face.

Her mouth twitched, trying to keep a straight face. "Well, this Jedi Master is used to holing up in her office alone."

"So, having an office mate might be a little distracting?"

Most definitely. Especially one as handsome as Finn Avery.

"It's possible." Her eyes flicked back to her computer screen as she pretended to concentrate.

Finn leaned toward her, studying her. "How about instead of work, you tell me about yourself?"

What was this guy's game? She didn't know him well, and her defenses were up. After dating a few charmers who'd turned out to be duds, she was like a dog who had been kicked too many times.

She closed her laptop. "What do you want to know?"

"Where you've lived? Anything interesting I should know?" He gave her that same mesmerizing smile, the one she could fall into, like a comfy hammock on a warm day.

"I've lived in Wild Harbor all my life, except for the four years I went to college. I haven't interned at any of the big papers, but my grandfather was the editor once. All my training has been under Dale. Sounds exciting, huh?"

"For a journalist, you're remarkably succinct. What about hobbies? Quirky things I should know about you, like your favorite foods or how you like your coffee, since I'll be fetching it for you." He gave her a boyish grin that softened the tension in her shoulders.

"For the record, I'm only succinct when I'm trying to get things done. Working for the newspaper is both my work and my hobby. I don't have time for anything else. But I do like pizza with everything on it. And I can't stand tomatoes or cats, which annoys my cat-loving sister, Lily. I own a golden retriever, who doesn't know a stranger. And coffee is my only addiction. I like copious amounts of it. Dark roast, one shot of caramel flavoring and a splash of almond milk."

"Copious. Got it." He made a note on his phone, then paused.

She was staring at his eyelashes. They were so perfectly shaped and long-lashed. The kind women would kill for.

"Since you asked about me . . ." He gave her a slow grin.

She blinked, embarrassed he had noticed her gawking. "Oh, yes. Sorry. And you?"

"I grew up an hour away, near Grand Rapids, but I always loved coming to the beach. My family rented a beach cottage on the weekends. That's where I fell in love with boating, the summer festival, and the annual masquerade party. Wild Harbor is the reason I went into the Coast Guard."

"Really?"

"Yeah. My plan was to stay in for as long as possible. Turned out I wasn't cut out for the Coast Guard after all." He waved his hand. "That's a story for another day. Have you ever gone to the masquerade at the Bellevue Mansion?"

Megan tapped her pencil on the table. "Yep, once on summer break in college. A friend got sick, so I took her ticket. The Bellevues haven't held the event in the last five years, but rumor has it they've discussed bringing it back. Did you go?"

"My brother talked me into it one year. He wanted to play a practical joke on his date. We went in the same clothes so we could switch places in the middle of the night. His date never noticed the entire night until after I pulled off my mask."

Megan's stomach clenched. She'd thought he looked familiar, like they had met before last night. "Wait a minute, was that seven years ago?"

"Yeah, how did you know?" His smile fell, searching her face.

"Because I was the girl you played the trick on."

CHAPTER FOUR

FINN

Megan shoved her computer in her bag, turning on her heel, her long black hair flying as she rushed out the door. "I'm sorry. I need to go."

Finn raced to stop her. "Wait. I don't understand. You were the girl we played the joke on?"

She stopped. Faded red blotches inched up her neck. "Yes. I never knew your name, only your brother, Tyler. Since you wore a mask, I had no idea what you looked like. Something in my gut told me we had met before last night. I hope you got a good laugh out of switching places, especially since when I kissed you, I still thought you were Tyler."

The mention of their brief kiss brought back the memory, like a sweet summer day. He hadn't forgotten about that kiss. Not for seven years.

He wanted to show her he wasn't that type of guy anymore. Not the kind who would trick a girl into kissing him. "Listen, this is a terrible coincidence . . . I'm sorry about what happened. We were just being stupid. Tyler talked me into it."

"It doesn't matter now. It was a silly joke, right?"

Of course it was, but did she believe it? Finn stepped forward, wanting to touch her arm, but holding back. "Please don't leave. I said I was sorry. What more do you want?"

She spun around on her heel. "Nothing. It's fine. Really."

But was it?

She headed toward Dale's office.

He wasn't sure she was telling the truth. Finn walked back to the conference room table.

That went well.

He slumped into a chair. Hadn't Dale told him he'd be sharing an office with Megan until Larry left? He pulled a laptop out of his bag as he thought about the practical joke Tyler had talked him into.

Tyler's voice echoed like a standup comedy routine's opening act. "So I met this girl at the beach—"

His brother flopped down on Finn's bed and stared at the ceiling. "She's going to be at the Bellevue Masquerade Party. If we dress the same, wouldn't it be hilarious if we switched dates? She'll never know the difference."

Finn looked up from the magazine he was flipping through. "I don't have a date for the masquerade. Don't really want one." He was home for a short break from the Coast Guard and wasn't interested in finding a date.

"We can still do it. I'll see her at the beginning of the night, and at some point, I'll go to the restroom and we'll do the whole switcheroo. Later, I'll return and we'll both pull off our masks. I bet her face will be priceless."

"What's the point?" Finn set his magazine next to the bed. "She'll probably be too mad to go out with you after that."

"So what? It's not like I know her that well. What do you say?"

It was a bad idea. But Tyler thrived on jokes.

"I don't know, Tyler. It sounds lame. What if she discovers our prank?"

"No way. We look enough alike that she won't suspect. We're even the same height. You've got to do this." Tyler leaned toward Finn, his eyes dancing.

Finn tapped his fingers together. It couldn't be that bad, could it?

He never could have guessed his stupid joke would haunt him years later. Worst of all, Tyler showed up at the most critical moment: when his lips met hers.

What was he thinking? That kiss was not part of the plan. He wasn't even the type of guy to make a move on the first date.

He still wasn't sure what had driven him to do it. They had snaked through the crowd, finding a deserted corner while the music pulsated in the background, the bass line thumping like a heartbeat.

Megan looked exotic and beautiful, her large brown eyes like a dream he could fall into. Her dark hair was pinned up in an elaborate style on her head. He fell hard and fast, until Tyler interrupted and ruined their night.

Megan stepped back, her mouth slightly agape, shaking her head. "What is this? Some kind of joke?" Her voice was strangled. "I thought you were—"

Before she could finish, she bolted away from him, weaving through the crowd, fading into the darkness. He wanted to follow, but Tyler grabbed his shoulder.

"That was hilarious! I can't believe you kissed her. Dude!"

"It wasn't funny." He stomped away.

Finn shook his head to clear out the memory. Now, the joke was on Finn.

Because Megan had been wearing a mask, he hadn't been able to make out her distinct features. He hadn't even remembered her name. But something had seemed vaguely familiar about her last night at the restaurant. What were the odds that the girl at the masquerade would turn out to be his coworker?

Apparently, pretty good.

If only he could tell Tyler. *Thanks, man.* That prank had ruined his first day—and any chance of making a good first impression with Megan.

Finn rested his elbows on the table. Megan was obviously excellent at what she did. Respected in the office. She had every right to be ticked, and it wasn't just because of the masquerade party.

Every newspaper office had reporters vying for front-page articles, scrambling and clawing their way to the top. Megan was clearly the front-runner for the top stories—until he walked into the room.

"Finn. What are you still doing in here?" Dale's voice startled him.

"Megan and I needed an introduction. Although I'm not sure about sharing an office."

"We might as well work this out now." Dale motioned for Finn to follow.

Megan's office was down the hall, the last door on the left.

Dale knocked and leaned around the frame. "Got a moment?"

Megan sat at her desk, intently studying her laptop. "Sure." She turned to Dale, her eyes flicking over to Finn. "What's up?"

"Finn needs a temporary workspace, and you have a sizable office. Are you okay with him moving in?"

Megan considered for a moment. "I can make it work, but Larry is leaving soon."

"Larry has the smallest office, and he's packing. No room right now. It's a short-term arrangement."

"How short-term?"

"Don't know yet. But it won't be long." Dale glanced from Megan to Finn. "What's the worst that could happen?"

Everything. Finn stepped into Megan's office.

"I owe you for this." Dale pointed at Megan. His footsteps faded down the hall.

"You can put your stuff on that side of the office." Megan nodded toward a chair in the corner.

Finn settled in, pulling out his computer. Megan's fingers danced across the keyboard. He cleared his throat. "So, should we get started?"

"On what?" Her shoulder-length black hair hung in loose waves. She had been dazzling at the masquerade. And highly distracting. Which was a problem now, since he was going to be working with her.

He needed space. A chance to prove himself. "Hashing out responsibilities."

"I've got a story to finish in the next hour. Maybe after that?" She avoided his gaze. "But if you want something to do, you can always fetch my coffee." A smile pricked the corners of her lips.

"Coming right up." He stopped at the door. If she was busy, now was the time to ask. "If I'm covering the volleyball tournament, could I ask a favor?"

Megan stopped typing. "Ask away."

"Could I cover both stories at the tournament?"

She rested her chin on her hand. "Why would you want to take both?"

Because he couldn't fall for her. Not after he promised his father he'd work toward securing Dale's job. Love and competition didn't mix.

Plus, he needed to get on Dale's good side. Work hard. Do things his way. Prove himself.

When Finn had picked journalism, his dad had scoffed at his decision, calling it a low-paying career with few rewards.

But when his father had reconnected with Dale at the golf course, Finn had seen hope bubbling over in his father's eyes. It's like a switch had flipped. "Imagine, you could take over

Dale's position. That would be something. So much better than a dime-a-dozen reporter."

It was the first time he had seen a spark in his dad's eyes.

"Megan, I know we started off on the wrong foot. I'm really not trying to make your life harder. I need this job." He wanted her to understand, but he wasn't ready to explain. Not yet.

"You *need* this job?" She narrowed her gaze.

He noticed the intense shades of brown and gold in her eyes. A mesmerizing blend of mocha with a hint of fire.

She shut her laptop. "Just in case you didn't know, I've worked here for the last four years, writing articles on ladies' luncheons, the county fair, and local retirements, just like my grandfather did his entire career. I've done every pathetic job in this place—including cleaning the toilet—because I believed that if I worked hard, I could keep the newspaper from dying. So, don't think you can come in here with your fancy internships and then tell us you need this job. You could have any newspaper job in the area. If you want to move up in this office, you start at the bottom. You do the work because you want this paper to survive. It's important for the town's heritage, but it's more than that. It's a town I love."

She stacked her papers and rose to go.

He'd asked for too much, too soon. He could fix that.

But no matter how he framed the situation, one thing was obvious. Megan would not be an easy assignment.

CHAPTER FIVE

MEGAN

Megan parked her convertible next to the beach volleyball courts and scanned the crowds, trying to single out her new coworker. Children splashed in the waves under a clear blue sky.

As much as she wanted to sink her toes into the sand, only one thing was on her mind. *Finn Avery.*

She wasn't about to let his green eyes sway her, even if Dale's plan was to force them to get along. Sure, he was handsome. But handsome didn't work on her anymore.

She wanted a man who would place her above himself, who wasn't afraid of sacrificing, and who knew how to give more than he takes.

But Finn Avery? Nothing more than eye candy. Even though he was crowned the new favored child, she wasn't about to fall for his charms.

It was the same ploy her parents used when she had a fight with her siblings. Dad's solution? Stay in the same room until they worked things out.

Forced proximity may have worked for her family, but business relationships weren't like sibling rivalries. Finn was her competition. She wouldn't become his stepping-stone to success.

She slammed the door of her Mustang and smoothed her palms down her clothes. She had chosen a summer skirt that showed off her calves and had swept her hair into a tight ponytail.

Not that she wanted him to notice her.

Okay, maybe she hoped he did. Just a tiny bit.

The morning sun reflected across the shiny shoulders of the volleyball players slathering on white sunscreen. Die-hard fans, dressed in Wildcat T-shirts, lugged along coolers of sodas and colorful beach chairs, staking out their territory for the day. Megan slid on her black sunglasses, pulled out her iPad, and stalked the two players she needed to interview before Finn could.

You know what they say about the early bird, Mr. Avery.

As she stepped onto the sand, she immediately regretted her shoe choice. Small heels were terrible in sand, and yet she had chosen a pair of dress mules with a slight rise. They looked great with her outfit but were horrid on the beach. She wobbled across the sand, trying to pretend her balance wasn't affected.

"Hello, Mr. Stinson." She waved at the Wild Harbor coach as he watched his team warm up. She scanned the athletes, making a mental note of who she wanted to interview first. Her brain worked best this way, always thinking of the next thing. She couldn't let Finn distract her.

Bethany would be her initial interview, followed by the team's rising star, Scarlett. With her olive skin and shiny chestnut locks, Scarlett looked like a cover model for *Sports Illustrated*. The woman was blessed with the complete package: toned muscles, long legs, and curves.

No wonder Scarlett had every unmarried man in town wrapped around her pretty finger.

Out of the corner of her eye, a man caught her attention. She spotted Finn Avery chatting with a player from a visiting team, a six-foot blonde beauty with legs as long as a giraffe's, accented by the cut of her tiny volleyball shorts.

Megan nearly dropped her tablet. How'd he beat her here? She'd told him nine, and he was already interviewing the leggy blonde at 8:30.

She hoped the darts in her eyes landed right in the middle of Finn's forehead.

Judging by the blonde player's smile, he had already won her over.

The volleyball player laughed at something Finn said as he pulled out his phone to take notes.

Was he still trying to take her story? She had made it clear. He was only supposed to cover the tournament, not conduct personal interviews.

She beelined toward him, ankles wobbling as she kicked up sand.

Halting behind him, she noticed the outline of his muscles through his T-shirt. His clothing choice showed off his physique —the perfect way to draw the attention of elite volleyball players. He was no dummy.

She cleared her throat. "Good morning, Mr. Avery."

He spun around, his mirrored sunglasses flashing in the sunshine. "Oh, hello, Ms. Woods."

"You've met some players." Her gaze drifted to the blonde athlete.

He nodded toward the Amazon woman. "This is Zoe from the Lansing team. Zoe, meet Megan Woods, my coworker from *The Wild Harbor Newspaper*."

"Nice to meet you." Megan gave her a tight smile. "Sorry for the interruption, but I need to talk to Mr. Avery alone. Would you excuse us?"

Zoe showed off her perfect white teeth. "Sure. Finn, if you need anything else for the article, don't forget to call."

Zoe offered a flirty grin before running to join her teammates on the court. A small, crooked smile played across Finn's lips as he watched her retreat.

He obviously enjoyed getting to know the players. Too much.

"Don't forget to call?" she echoed Zoe's response.

"It's not how it appears."

"Oh, really?" Megan raised her eyebrows. "She gave you her number and an invitation. It's pretty clear how it appears."

"The coach asked me how much longer the interview would take. She offered her number in case we ran out of time."

How convenient.

He pulled his sunglasses off, and his green eyes disarmed her. "I'm happy to have you follow up with her if you think my intentions were anything less than professional."

"Oh, no. I'm sure I don't need to remind you why we're here." She shifted her aching feet. Stupid heels. "I'll take the interviews while you'll cover the tournament. It's best if we divide and conquer."

"Yeah, I got the message, loud and clear."

"Good. Then my job here is done." She tried to step forward in the sand, but her heel had sunk so low that her ankle turned and she tripped forward. Finn grabbed her elbow instinctively to catch her before she fell.

His touch was electrifying, even if their mental jousting was exhausting.

Keep it together.

"Are you okay?" At least he showed concern for her.

"I'm fine. Just clumsy." She stepped away from him. "But, thank you."

"Next time, consider wearing different shoes." He glanced at her feet, trying to hide his amusement.

"Thank you, Captain Obvious." She slid her feet out of the mules and picked them up, guilt pricking her conscience. She'd come down hard on him even though he'd rescued her twice—first, from her blind date, and now, from falling on her face. The least she could do was be cordial.

She backed away from him. "By the way, I'm setting up camp by the Wild Harbor team if you need anything."

"I'll stay here. Perfect view from this vantage point. But thanks."

"No problem."

He tipped his face toward the sun and crossed his arms, showing off the outline of his biceps.

From her seat, Finn would be directly in her sight line. There was no way to avoid him now.

THE CROWDS FILLED the beach as the tournament stretched into the afternoon, culminating in the championship game between the Wild Harbor Wildcats and the Lansing Cougars. The volleyball players glistened with sweat, applying more sunblock to their pink-tinged faces between sets.

Megan crossed her legs as she watched Finn approach the players. The girls circled around him like animals on the hunt, their bronzed legs shining in the sun. Scarlett casually stretched her hamstrings next to Finn.

Megan cut across the court, tired of Finn stealing the show. She cleared her throat. "Ahem." She pointed at the muscular athlete. "I was wondering if I might ask Scarlett some questions."

The other players drifted off to snag more drinks as Scarlett held the volleyball.

"Oh, sure. Be my guest." Finn stepped aside but didn't leave. Instead, he just watched her.

Sweat broke out between her shoulder blades.

"So, tell me how you're feeling going into this final matchup." She pulled out her iPad to take notes and noticed Finn doing the same.

Scarlett tossed the ball from one hand to another. "We're a strong team going into the final match against the Cougars. My injury is still healing, so my ankle isn't feeling great, but as long as I can get through this game, I think we'll be good."

"I didn't even realize you had an injury." Finn focused on her ankle. "You've been in top form today."

"Oh, thank you." Even though sweat gleamed on Scarlett's face and her hair was slicked into a simple ponytail, she was gorgeous—one of those naturally pretty girls whom other women loved to hate.

Scarlett spun the ball in her hands. "You mentioned you love beach volleyball. Maybe we could hit the ball around sometime?"

Finn nodded. "Yeah, maybe."

Megan narrowed her gaze at Scarlett. *The nerve of some people.*

The Wildcats' coach tapped Scarlett on the shoulder. "Ready to get started?"

"Yeah. Gotta run. Sorry I couldn't finish the interview." She gave Finn an apologetic look, then jogged toward her teammates.

Finn held up a hand. "Before you say anything . . ."

"Why do you think I'm going to say anything?"

"It's your vibe." He took a swig of his water, then smirked. "You don't approve."

"Whether or not I approve isn't important."

"For your information, I'm not interested in dating right now."

"Oh, really? I wouldn't have guessed that."

"Did you assume that since I'm single, I'm always looking for a date?"

"Everyone seemed so eager to meet you. I just thought—"

"Well, perhaps, Ms. Woods, you'll figure out that I'm full of surprises." His boyish grin gave her a shot of adrenaline.

"Megan!" Her sister's voice cut through the crowd as Cassidy frantically waved from across the court. "Am I too late for the final match?"

"It's just starting. Perfect timing. I'm on the opposite side." Megan rushed around the court to help her sister.

"Really, you're going to make me lug this stuff even further?" Cassidy peeked around Megan. "Who is that?" She elbowed her sister.

Megan ignored her request. "Why did you bring so many books with you?" Megan took the heavy bag, stumbling under the load.

"I don't know. I thought I might get bored. You didn't answer my question. Who's that guy?" She nodded toward Finn.

"Our new reporter, Finn. He's replacing Larry and covering the tournament while Damien is on leave," Megan whispered under her breath.

"You're working with him?"

"Could you stop staring?" She grabbed her sister's elbow to spin her away from Finn. "It seems like every woman here is trying to get a date with him."

Megan lugged the bag toward her chair.

Cassidy followed, trying to keep up. "And you're surprised about that? He's not bad to look at."

"Regardless, it's inappropriate. He's my coworker."

"It's not his fault if women ask him out." Cassidy pulled out a bag of dried wasabi peas. "Want some?" She shoved the bag near her sister's nose.

"Ugh." She waved the bag away. "I don't want to kill people with my breath."

"Suit yourself, but I only brought this and kale chips."

"I should have asked Lily to join us. At least she brings chocolate."

"So what's wrong with him?" Cassidy's eyes followed Finn as the game continued.

"Besides the fact that Dale assigned me to train him, he wants to be editor-in-chief."

"How do you know?"

"He pretty much declared his intentions."

"You think Dale would consider him?" Cassidy popped another pea in her mouth. "Especially after all you've done for the newspaper?"

"Dale hired him. Since he's the new guy, he can do no wrong."

"That might be the case right now, but give him time."

The one thing she didn't have. *Time.*

Megan sat in silence as the Wildcats took an early lead winning the first set while the Cougars took the second. During the final set, Scarlett spiked the ball, earning them another point as the crowd exploded in cheers.

If the Wildcats won the tournament, Dale would request a front-page article covering their win in addition to the sports section coverage and human-interest piece. Megan wanted to make sure she got that third story, even if it meant keeping it from Finn.

The Cougars scored another point, tying up the game. Whoever won the last point would win the tournament.

Megan leaned forward, her eyes tracking a car in the parking lot. "It looks like the mayor just arrived. I need to snag an interview with him afterward."

Scarlett stepped up to serve, and the crowd hushed. She tossed the ball in the air and pummeled it with a powerful spike across the net. One of the Cougars returned the serve and the teams bumped it back and forth several times before Bethany passed it to Scarlett. She jumped in the air and spiked it from the back of the court. The ball sped across the net and landed in a corner just as a Cougar player dove into the sand. She missed the ball, securing the Wildcats' win. The Wild Harbor fans burst into cheers.

Megan rose to her feet, clapping. "I couldn't have planned a better ending. The fact that she scored the winning point will cap the article perfectly."

Fans gathered around Scarlett as Megan raced to the Wildcat bench to get reactions from the team.

But a figure next to the mayor caught her attention. Finn was talking to the mayor.

Megan made a split-second decision. She made a quick turn toward Mayor Brinks, ignoring her wobbly heels.

Megan squeezed through the crowd, apologizing as she bumped into people. "Mayor Brinks, I'm so happy you're here to celebrate our town's win."

"Good to see you, Megan." The mayor's voice was flat. He never seemed pleased to see her. "I gave Finn my reaction to today's win. He'll share it with you."

"I'm sure he will. But in case he doesn't—"

Mayor Brinks ignored Megan and turned his attention to Finn. "Let me know if you want to ride on the boat tomorrow with Dale and me. I'll show you the town from a different point of view. Just text me in the morning. If you'll both excuse me, I need to talk with one of the town council members."

"Thanks for your reaction to today's tournament." Finn waved. "It was great to meet you, Mayor Brinks."

The mayor strode away. The day had turned sweltering hot, but somehow Megan hadn't noticed until now. "A five-minute conversation and you're in the boys' club now?"

"Just helping. I wasn't trying to get an invitation."

"Seems like that's happened a lot today."

"And it seems like you have a problem with that. Do you want to talk about it?" He lowered his sunglasses and his green eyes glittered.

She wobbled on her heels. "We might write for the same paper, but that doesn't mean you can take over my responsibilities."

"Then give me a chance to prove myself." His mouth held a determination Megan hadn't seen before.

She lifted her chin, ready to draw a line in the sand. "On one condition. Let me do my job. Got it?"

"If that's what you want." He crossed his arms. "As long as you let me do mine."

"Fine." She could already see what a disaster this arrangement was turning out to be.

As she strode away, she had the sense someone was watching her. Glancing over her shoulder, her gut feeling was right. Finn's eyes were on her. And he wasn't at all pleased.

CHAPTER SIX

FINN

Finn didn't know why he'd agreed to a morning ride on the mayor's yacht. Something about the guy seemed a little too polished and full of himself. Hanging around people with money and power wasn't really Finn's jam.

But being on a boat? That was his weakness, no matter who his company was. Ever since he'd arrived in town, he'd been searching online for a used sailboat, wanting to recapture the familiar smell of wind and water. His love for sailing lured him back to Wild Harbor. Boating would take his mind off things, especially his beautiful dark-haired coworker with the striking eyes.

Finn met Dale and Steve at the marina, and before long, they were zipping along the shore in the mayor's boat, the wind whipping through Finn's hair.

As Steve slowed his engine and drifted along the coastline, Dale pointed to two houses. "See those two white cottages? The Woods family owns those. Megan's sister, Lily, lives in one, and her parents moved in next door. Their homes were renovated by Alex Briggs, the TV star from *The Property Bachelor*. Ever heard of him?"

"Who hasn't?" Finn shaded his eyes to get a better view.

"The scuttlebutt in town is that Alex and Lily are pretty serious. I'm betting a proposal is coming soon."

Finn nodded. "Interesting. So, Megan could be the sister-in-law to a big TV star? Wonder how she would feel about doing a story on her own family member?"

Dale chuckled. "She won't do anything Lily doesn't want. Their family is fiercely loyal. You mess with one of the Woods family, you mess with all of them. But they're also the most welcoming bunch. Bill and Becky don't know a stranger. I'm sure you'll get an invitation to dinner some night."

So that was the key to Megan's family. If you wanted in, you had to do things on their terms. Their way.

"How did Alex meet Lily?"

"Alex is a hometown boy. He returned to do an episode in Wild Harbor, and that's when they reconnected." Dale looked out at the water. "Everybody speaks highly of the family, but Megan is a spitfire, like her grandfather. I like her, but you want to stay on her good side."

Oh, great. Get on her good side. Like that's easy.

The mayor pointed at a gigantic grey stone mansion that resembled a castle. "That grand place is the Bellevue Mansion. The family is talking about reinstating their masquerade party this year. They halted it five years ago because of Agnes's health, but now that she's made a full recovery, they want to celebrate. It will be the event of the summer."

"Finn, that's the perfect event for you." Dale took a sip of water. "You'll meet all the business executives and their spouses. People with influence. But you'll need to figure out a way to convince Megan to attend. You can do that, right?" Dale slapped him on the back.

"I can try." If only he could explain to Dale that it might be impossible.

"Talk to Alex Briggs." Dale leaned toward Finn. "See if he can give you some advice on the Woods family."

Finn leaned back in the seat and watched as the boat cut through the waves, the engine tuning out the world around him. As he rested his head on the seat and closed his eyes, the sunshine and hum of the motor eased his mind.

He'd figure out a way to get on Megan's good side. He just needed a little luck and a second chance.

FINN PULLED up to a stoplight and impatiently tapped his fingers on the steering wheel. Normally he'd take his time, enjoy a scone and coffee at the French Press Café or scarf down a bacon and egg platter at Hank's Diner. But this morning, he'd skipped breakfast. Beating Megan to the office took priority over his empty stomach, and that meant talking to Dale first. His best chance for a front-page article on the tournament win could only happen if he secured the spot before she did.

There was only one catch. He suspected Megan had written the same tournament recap as he had, alongside her human-interest story. In other words, she had staked her territory for two front-page articles.

Finn spent hours on the tournament coverage, hoping his article wouldn't be relegated to the sports section alone. Even though he hadn't asked her yet, he suspected their stories overlapped, which meant Dale could only choose one to include in the paper. It was a shot in the dark, but it was only fair to let the editor-in-chief decide whose article would take the front page.

As he pulled into the cramped parking lot behind their hundred-year-old brick building, he noted that Megan's cherry-red Mustang was missing.

He skipped up the steps to the second-floor office, whistling to himself.

Cheri Marks, the newspaper's administrative assistant, greeted him with a full smile as he walked into the office.

"Good morning, Mr. Avery." She fiddled with her glossy pink fingernails which looked unnaturally long and spiky. "Dale would like to see you in his office this morning when you're ready."

"Thank you, Mrs. Marks. Did he say what it was about?"

She shook her head. "By the way, you can call me Cheri. No one around here says Mrs. Marks, unless they're referring to my mother-in-law." She laughed and tapped her artificial nails on the desk.

"Thanks, Cheri. Anything else I need to know for today?"

"You know where the bathroom is?" She picked up a pencil to point toward a hall at the back of the room.

"Got it covered."

"Just checking. Kind of embarrassing to be the new kid on the block and not be able to find the little boy's room. Not that you're a little boy, but—how old are you?"

"Twenty-eight."

"Oh my, you're a baby! My oldest just turned twenty-two. You could almost be my son." She let out a shrill laugh that made Larry poke his head out the door in disapproval. "By the way, there's more coffee in the carafe if you need some." She nodded toward the coffee station.

Judging by the huge container of bargain coffee, he was sure the brew was unbearable.

"Don't be shy if you need any help." She tapped her pink fingernails again.

"Thanks, Cheri."

He walked past Cheri's desk toward Megan's office. He would settle into the corner chair and take a few minutes to read through his article before sending it to Dale.

As he stepped into Megan's office, he jolted. She was sitting at her desk, staring intensely at her computer screen.

"You're here." He halted in the doorway. "I wasn't expecting that."

Her eyes remained glued to the screen. "I work here, in case you've forgotten."

He walked in and set his bag down next to the lone chair. "Didn't see your car in the lot, so I assumed you were . . ."

"Late? No, I'm not always late. Personally, I like to arrive in the nick of time, and I don't always park in the lot. It's too crowded, and I worry someone will back into me or mar the paint on my Mustang. I parked on a side street." She hit the return button with a big flourish of her hand and stopped to look at him. "Just hit *send* on my articles. Do you have yours in? Dale hates it when he has to ask for them."

"Uh, no. I was going to do that now." He pulled out his laptop, hoping Dale wouldn't be mad at him. Suddenly, the tension in his shoulders was making his neck hurt.

"How was your weekend?" He was trying to lighten the mood, but this turn of events distracted him. He should have brought up the article with Dale when he'd had the chance.

Her eyes flicked over her laptop to him. "Fine. How was yachting with the mayor?"

"Interesting. He gave me a tour of the coastline. Pointed out your family's homes." There was an awkward silence.

"Sounds like you two are chummy now."

"Not really. If anything, he told me you're the person to know around here."

"Really? I doubt it. I'm just a lowly reporter." She waved away his suggestion while scribbling on a sticky note.

"Should we talk over the articles on the Wild Harbor tournament win?"

Her eyebrows furrowed. "What do you mean? I covered it."

"Yes, but Dale didn't know that Wild Harbor was going to

win. I was told to cover the sports section article, and you took Scarlett's story. Who takes the article on their win?"

"Since a win guarantees front-page coverage, he won't want someone new writing the article. No offense or anything." She offered him a sympathetic smile.

Finn thought it was cute, but he wasn't about to play her game. "No offense taken. Since Dale is the boss, why don't we let him decide?" He folded his hands. It was competition time.

"What do you mean?" She crossed her arms and leaned back in her chair.

"I just sent him my story." He mirrored her body position.

Suddenly, Dale's voice erupted in the hallway. "Ms. Woods and Mr. Avery, in my office now."

"Are we in trouble?" Finn stood, frozen in place.

"Probably." She grabbed her laptop and headed down the hall.

When they entered Dale's office, he was sitting behind a heavy wood desk, his forehead deeply lined with creases. He pointed at them.

"You two, sit down." Dale sounded irritated.

Megan looked like a schoolgirl called to the principal's office. He almost felt sorry for her.

Dale gave an audible sigh. "Why did you each send me an article about Wild Harbor's victory?"

Finn nodded at Megan to begin. "Ladies first."

"I knew you'd run their tournament victory as a front-page story, and Finn is brand new, so I thought . . ."

Dale shook his head. "Doesn't matter what you thought. You both sent me essentially the same article. I'm not paying you to write identical stories. This isn't acceptable."

"I'm sorry, sir." Finn was on the defense. "I should have clarified this with Megan. It's just that . . ."

He stopped, afraid to admit the truth in front of her. Dale leaned forward, eyeing Finn. It was now or never.

"I'm not sure this arrangement is going to work."

Dale folded his hands together and placed his elbows on the desk. "Listen, you either learn to work together, or I'll find two people who will."

"But . . ." Megan leaned forward.

"No excuses. For the rest of the summer, we're covering a full lineup of events, and you need to be working as a team. It's too much for one person. The parade, the food alley, the summer festival, the sailboat regatta, and perhaps one more big event."

Finn's muscles tensed when Dale hinted at the masquerade. He didn't dare reveal the Bellevues' potential plans yet.

Finn shifted in his seat. "Is there a way to split these events so we can cover them separately?"

"Nope. I need two reporters on the ground covering multiple stories. Plus, it will be great preparation for the sailboat regatta coverage, which is going to be bigger than ever. I want us to be right in the middle of the race, representing our team."

Megan held her pencil in the air and waved it around. "What do you mean by *our* team?"

"We're going to be forming a sailing team this year. To be in the race."

"*We?*" Megan scrunched her nose.

"You and Finn."

Megan's mouth dropped open. "I'm sorry to tell you this, but I don't sail. I don't even know the first thing about boats."

"That's why you're being paired with Finn."

Finn cleared his throat. "Excuse me?"

Dale leaned back in his chair, his mind already made up. "You were in the Coast Guard. You know your way around the water."

Dale didn't seem to understand that Finn wasn't a sailboat expert. His skills were rusty at best.

"I haven't sailed in ages." Finn wasn't about to admit he had been shopping for a used boat. "My time in the Coast Guard was not spent on sailboats. I was a rescue swimmer."

"But you know the water, right? You can relearn this." Dale motioned toward Finn. "This is what you both need to learn to work together. You'll start training together—pronto." He slapped the desk with his palm.

"Wait a minute." Megan shook her head. "What does sailing in the regatta have to do with the newspaper? I can cover the race without competing."

"You could. But we'll garner more attention if we put you right in the middle of the experience. Most of Wild Harbor watches the race, but they don't know what it's like to be in it. You're going to cover the race, from start to finish. Plus, it will give us some great marketing. Seeing two locals document the experience will help generate the town's interest in the paper, and hopefully, more subscribers and advertisers." He folded his hands and placed them on his belly. "Even the mayor agrees."

Megan tapped her pencil on her palm. "I'm the wrong person for this assignment. Finn can take the articles. I'm happy to do something else."

She was searching for a way out. Anything to get away from sailing with him.

Dale shuffled through a stack of papers on his desk. "Megan, I need you on this article."

"Finn seems more than qualified to handle it." She faced Finn. "Right?" Her wide eyes locked on to his. Something had subtly shifted. Her pupils nearly swallowed her brown irises, the same look an animal has when it senses danger.

"Sure. If that's what you want—"

Dale shook his head. "I want both perspectives. Male and female. Experienced and inexperienced. You're not going to give up an award-winning story, are you?"

Megan moved to the edge of her seat. Dale had finally

captured her attention. "Are you submitting the regatta article for the Michigan regional newspaper awards?"

"Might be worth a shot, depending on how the stories unfold. It's beyond what we'd normally cover, but it could be our golden story for the year."

"What about Scarlett's story?" Megan asked.

"Human-interest stories on athletes are a dime a dozen. But a reporter learning to sail so she can compete in a race? That's something different. Something special." He shifted his attention to Finn. "If you're willing to take the story, it would help folks in town to get to know you better, regardless of whether it wins an award. What do you say, Finn?"

If he was looking for a chance to prove himself, now was the time.

Megan paused, her body tense. "If you think this will help the newspaper, I'll try a few sailing lessons. But I'm not making any promises."

Dale smiled. "I thought you might come around. I'll send you both the schedule of events to cover for summer. Just don't bother writing duplicates of the same story. You need to figure out how to work together. Got it?"

Megan stood. "Loud and clear." Then she turned on her heel, her black hair flying, leaving the scent of something delicate and floral hanging in the air, a smell Finn couldn't resist. He wanted to bottle her scent and bury his nose in it.

"Any questions?" Dale interrupted Finn's thoughts.

"Any advice on how to win over my coworker?"

Dale gave a soft chuckle, then pointed at him. "Just don't mess up."

CHAPTER SEVEN

MEGAN

Megan leaned her head back on the porch swing at her parents' house and set the newspaper aside. Her gaze drifted to the water, where the grey-blue waves lapped the shore under puffy white clouds.

"It's one article." Lily picked up the newspaper and examined the front page. "So what if Finn's article about Wild Harbor's win was picked over yours? Your piece on Scarlett is right next to it." She slapped the paper down on the swing between them.

"It's not just that." Megan's sisters were far different from her, always seeing things from a rose-colored viewpoint. Cass was like a baby bunny, soft and effusive, while Lily's people-pleasing personality made her a friend-magnet. No wonder they got along with everyone in town.

"Dale pushed me into agreeing to compete in the Wild Harbor Regatta. Besides the fact that I can't sail, you know how I feel about the water."

She wanted her sisters to agree with her. Instead, Lily sipped her iced tea and remained silent, pushing the swing with her foot. "Did you tell Dale?"

"No. What would Dale say about a silly childhood accident?"

He'd probably laugh in her face. After all, she hadn't drowned.

Cassidy crossed her legs and leaned back in her white wicker chair, the dappled sunlight reflecting off her rosy cheeks. "But your accident didn't happen on a boat. It happened while swimming off the beach. Isn't that different?"

Megan shrugged. "Not enough. The riptide pulled me out. Deep water makes me panic. It's my trigger button—the way my brain has processed the trauma." She expected her sisters to understand, even sympathize. Instead, they seemed to side with her boss.

Hazy images of swimming in the lake when she was seven drifted into Megan's mind. The whitecaps breaking across the water. The wind blowing sand into her eyes. She had been mad at her parents for some childish thing—she couldn't even remember what now—but her anger had fueled her to plow into the water, away from the rest of the family as they played on the beach. She kicked out from shore on a small inflatable ring, the flimsy kind from the dollar store, designed for a pool.

"Don't go too far," her mother called as she paddled away. Her mom and dad had never been helicopter parents.

She didn't turn to acknowledge the instruction. Her emotions drove her forward, as distant as possible from her family. She hadn't realized how far she had drifted until she turned to look over her shoulder. Her family appeared minia-ture-sized, as if magic had shrunk them. Her mom waved at Megan, then turned to help the other two girls build a sandcastle.

Megan tried to kick toward shore, but the float seemed resistant to the water's pull. She attempted again, and still floated further out. Her parents had mentioned the dangers of the lake and how a riptide could exhaust even the strongest of swimmers. Was she caught in a riptide now? Just then, a speedboat zipped by, creating a flurry of waves. One lifted her too quickly, toppling the ring, knocking her off the float into the water.

Instinctively, she paddled toward shore, but the sudden pull of the undertow dragged her down as if her body was weighted. Her head bobbed on the surface of the water.

"Daddy!" she screamed as another wave hit her face. Panic gripped her as she fought against the pull of the riptide. Head tilted back toward the sun, she gasped for air, her arms and legs burning as she struggled toward shore. How much longer could she swim? Was anyone coming for her? Bleary-eyed from the pummeling waves, she strained to see her parents on the beach.

A man's voice called from somewhere in the distance. "Meg!" *Daddy?*

She clung to the familiar voice, but the darkness rose, causing her to slip beneath another wave, where there was nothing but murky water and the hollow sound of emptiness echoing in her ears . . .

Becky Woods stepped out onto the back porch. "That was the realtor on the phone."

Megan blinked back to reality. Why was this near-accident such a sore spot? Everything had turned out okay. Yet, the thought of being on the water made her chest tighten.

Her mom moved to the other wicker chair and sat down. "Someone wants to look at our old house. She said they're really interested in buying it."

"That's great." Lily set down her tea and put her hand on her mom's. "How does Dad feel about it?"

"Remarkably positive. We love the peacefulness of our new home on the lake." She tilted her head toward the house. "Your father and I love to sit here in the mornings. I think it's been good for his recovery."

Megan's eyes flicked toward her sister, Lily. Their father's stroke had changed everything. Dad was the rock in their family, the voice of reason, a man who had provided constant stability throughout their upbringing. Dad still couldn't walk since his stroke, which had made their childhood home unmanageable. Their new lake home was the perfect downsizing solution, but the change was still difficult. The burden of Dad's care fell mostly on Mom and Lily. Although the new arrangement was a huge blessing, it had also come with a cost, and Megan felt guilty about not being around more to help.

Cassidy waved her hands in the air to gain Megan's attention. "Earth to Megan. I told Mom about the handsome guy at work. What's the scoop on him?"

"Finn?" Megan wanted to dodge any conversation involving her new coworker.

"Yes, who else would I be talking about?"

A timer from inside the house beeped. Saved by the bell.

"The casserole!" Mom hurried inside.

"I'll get the plates and utensils." Lily followed, leaving Megan and Cass alone.

"There is no scoop. They hired Finn because Dale knows his dad. A favor for a friend." Megan shifted on the porch swing. "The problem is, I have the feeling that Dale has Finn pegged for the editor-in-chief position."

"You don't know that for sure."

"Know what for sure?" Lily returned with a stack of plates and some utensils.

"That Finn was hired to be the next editor-in-chief." Cassidy took the plates from Lily and set them on the outdoor table.

Megan pointed to Finn's article. "It just seems like he's giving him preferential treatment from day one. When I started at the newspaper, I covered the articles buried deep in the paper, like student of the week and the Lutheran church's rummage sale. He gave Finn a front-page story."

"But you're short-staffed since Damien broke his leg, right? He's desperate." Lily straightened the knives and spoons. "Besides, if he thought you weren't qualified, he wouldn't have assigned you as Finn's mentor."

"Maybe. But more than likely, it was out of convenience."

Lily rolled her eyes. "Maybe there's no plot to steal your job, and Finn is just a nice guy. Ever think of that?"

"And incredibly good-looking," Cassidy added, giving her sister a sly smile. "You'd be blind not to notice."

Her sisters weren't siding with her, no matter how hard she tried.

"Well, he certainly has charmed everyone in the office." Megan avoided her sisters' glares, hoping they couldn't see that her walls were crumbling at the mention of his name.

She had two choices. She needed to put him out of her mind or face him head-on.

Megan climbed off the porch swing. "I know one thing. I'm not about to let Finn steal the show. I'm going to the sailing lesson on Saturday."

~

WHEN MEGAN ROSE ON SATURDAY, a sense of dread loomed in front of her. She didn't want to learn how to sail any more than she wanted to volunteer for a painful surgery. Both ideas seemed equally bad. Right now, surgery sounded like a good excuse not to get on a boat. A vague pain throbbed in her stomach.

Maybe she was sick. Coming down with the flu. She should cancel.

She picked up her phone, ready to send Finn a text backing out. But a message and picture had already popped up on her screen.

Finn: Meet me at the dock by ten. I found a boat for us. She's a beauty! Meet Bertha.

Megan examined the picture of a boat that was marked by a faded sail, a dingy exterior, and peeling varnish on the wood deck. The vessel looked more likely bound for a junkyard than a race.

Megan bristled at the thought of learning on this decrepit boat. She didn't even want to ride in it. Just a few days ago, she had felt confident of her decision to go through the training, but now all her resolve had disappeared.

Why had she agreed to this? She flopped back on her bed.

"Hey, are you up?" Aspen peeked in her room.

"I'm up, but I'm not going today." Megan pulled her elbow over her eyes.

"You made me promise I wouldn't let you back out of this." She could hear the door squeak as Aspen entered her room and sat on her bed.

"I'm regretting I made you promise anything. Besides, you still owe me for the terrible blind date. How about we call it even?"

Aspen yanked Megan's elbow off her face. "If I do that, you'll regret it later."

"Ugh. Why did I choose to be a reporter?" Megan threw the covers over her head.

"Because you're a good one, and you're not going to let anything stop you." Aspen pulled the blankets off of Megan's body.

"Maybe I should quit my job and become a barista. Coffee makes everyone happy."

"But it wouldn't make you happy. Not the way writing does. Your grandfather would be proud. Think of it this way. It can't be all bad spending the day on a boat with a handsome guy. For once in your life, forget about the fact that he's your coworker.

Just enjoy yourself." Aspen smiled. "Who knows? He could be a nice guy."

~

MEGAN SHOWED up at the dock wearing a hoodie, carrying a small tote bag that contained a notebook, a water bottle, a cell phone, and a large bottle of antacids. From all appearances, she looked ready for a day of sailing. But inside, a voice was screaming for her to run. *Fast.* She folded her hands and pasted on a placid smile, willing the voice in her head to shut up. She prayed her motion sickness pills worked today.

Finn stood on the deck of the vintage sailboat, coiling a rope. "You came." His sunglasses glinted in the sun. Dressed in a light jacket with a pair of shorts, he appeared ready to pose for a sailing magazine. Relaxed and unstressed. Everything Megan was not.

If he weren't her job-stealing enemy, she might have considered him a potential date. Not that he'd even consider her now that she'd given him the cold shoulder.

"I almost turned around at least a dozen times." She put her hands on her hips. This was going to be a disaster.

"Once you're on the water, you'll love it." He smiled, and her stomach did a tiny, nervous somersault. She skimmed over the old boat, which only looked more dilapidated in person.

"Where did you find this interesting boat?"

"I found Bertha online, about two hours away. Drove up last night to pick her up, like a proud papa. She's one of a kind."

"That's one way to put it." Megan tried to hide her smile. "Bertha doesn't exactly look like a fierce competitor, though."

"The owner named her after his wife when he bought her fifty years ago. He's retired now, and his wife has cancer, so he thought it was time to let go of the boat. He doesn't have energy for sailing now that he's taking care of his wife."

The man was giving up something he loved in order to take care of his wife. Megan knew that scenario well. Her parents were living it.

"I told him I'd take good care of his boat and fix her up." He brushed his hand over the deck. "This is even the original wood. Isn't she a beauty?"

Megan squinted in the morning sun. "I'm sure she once was." She scanned the boat's interior, which needed a good cleaning and a fresh coat of varnish. Compared to the gleaming boats that lined up for the regatta every year, Bertha would stand out as an eyesore. "I'm assuming you've checked that she's safe?"

"Sure. But you should probably wear this just in case." Finn grabbed a life vest from one of the seat compartments and tossed it to her.

"You're not inspiring my confidence." She slipped the life vest on. "How long has it been since you've sailed?"

"Uh, I'm not really sure." He glanced at her. "Don't worry. Sailing is like riding a bicycle. It all comes back." He searched the boat for something as Megan's confidence waned. He looked like a kid mesmerized by a new toy.

"Maybe I should come back when you've had a chance to get comfortable with this craft." She took a step back, ready to abandon ship.

"You're not leaving, are you?"

"No offense, but you just bought an old boat from a stranger." She crossed her arms. "Not to mention you don't even remember the last time you sailed. It doesn't exactly allay my fears."

"I can tell by your body language that you're uncomfortable."

"I'm fine."

"You haven't even stepped foot in the boat. I'm not a novice. I've spent more than a few days on the water. Why don't we start with the basics? Some boating terminology. We'll go through that first, then we'll head out for a quick trip on the water. If you want to stay on shore, you're more than welcome to. But I won't be the one explaining your reasons to Dale."

The thought of quitting made her sick. She couldn't fail now. "If we're learning about the boat, I guess I can do that."

He put his hand out. "Hop in. You can't learn from the dock. You need to develop some sea legs first."

His fingers nearly enveloped her hand as he guided her into the craft. "First, the basics. The bow"—he pointed to the front—"is the front of the boat. The stern is the back. Anything near the front of the boat is forward, and anything toward the back is astern. Port is anything to the left and starboard is right. The tiller here"—he grabbed a long wooden rod—"is how we steer, and it's used to control the rudder."

She touched the tiller. "I did know that already."

"For the sake of our lesson, I'm going to assume you know nothing." He pulled on a rope. "These are what we call sheets. This is the mainsail, the largest and most important sail, with the boom that rotates here. You need to be careful when you change the sail's position to not get hit by this." He touched the sail's boom and moved on to the next sail. "We also have a head sail that we'll put up when we get out on the water."

He crawled over the boat easily, scrambling around like he'd been doing this for years. His time in the Coast Guard made it seem like the boat was a second home, and he glided around it like a pro.

"Okay, got all that?"

Megan squinted her eyes. "Yep."

"So, I think the best thing to do now is take her out for a quick trip. I can explain how things work better when I'm actually doing them."

Megan shifted her feet and checked Finn, who was coiling lines. She couldn't help but stare. He seemed so sure-footed. So confident. Something about him made her want to run away, but she couldn't bail now. He'd think she was a chicken if she stayed on shore.

His gaze flitted to hers before she could look away. The heat rose in her body as her eyes darted to the water.

A voice from the marina parking lot broke her attention.

"Finn? You here?" Megan shielded her eyes from the blinding sun to see a beautiful tan brunette prancing down the dock.

"Oops. I forgot something. Be right there!" The brunette stopped and turned back to her car.

Scarlett. What was she doing here?

Megan cocked her head to the side. "You invited Scarlett?"

"She invited herself. Scarlett loves sailing. Growing up, she took junior sailing classes. Thought she'd be a good first mate today, if you didn't show."

"You thought I'd bail on you?"

"That's why I was surprised when you showed up." He moved his bag off the seat to make room for another guest. "I may have mentioned to Scarlett that I was taking Bertha out on her first trip. She said she might stop by, but I never dreamed you'd both be here."

Megan sat down on the boat, jealousy threading through her body. She wasn't about to be bested by the towering volleyball player with the endless legs. Like it or not, she had to prove that she could get through her first sailing lesson.

Scarlett hauled a large canvas bag on her shoulder alongside an insulated lunch cooler.

"Thought I'd bring some snacks and drinks for the trip." She held up her oversized bag which bulged at the seams.

Had she planned for an all-day event? What in the world did she have in there?

"Oh, hello." Scarlett's eyes skimmed over Megan, then swung to Finn. She flashed a million-dollar smile. "Nice boat, Finn. So retro." She slid one long finger along the boom, delicately tracing the line, then took that same finger and touched the curve of his shoulder. "You are one lucky guy."

Finn didn't react. His face was steel. "We'll see how lucky I am after I take her out."

Megan was a silent observer. A third wheel. She shouldn't be here. Let Scarlett work her charms on Finn. She didn't care, did she?

"I didn't expect to see you here today." Megan pressed her lips together.

"Yeah, I couldn't miss the opportunity." Scarlett tossed her hair over her shoulder.

"Let's take this out for a spin before Megan changes her mind." Finn winked at Megan. She gripped the bench.

"You're not comfortable on the water?" Scarlett pulled off her shades to get a better view of Megan. With her glossy pink lips and long hair, Scarlett was a perfect match for Finn. Everything about the girl was effortless.

Megan tucked her hands in the pockets of her hoodie. She was a lump of sweatshirt while Scarlett was all curves and shimmer.

Megan waved her hand in the air. "I'm fine. Just not my favorite thing in the world."

Not her favorite? How about she would rather do anything but this? Megan sat awkwardly, folding and unfolding her hands, like she was under interrogation.

"Where do you want me to help?" Scarlett dropped her bags and glanced around the boat.

Finn started the engine, and it roared to life.

"You might want to warn us before you do that again." Megan placed her hand on her chest to slow her pounding heart.

As Finn steered the boat away from the dock, water gurgled, stirred by the motor. Megan glanced over her shoulder and wondered if she should make a jump for the dock. *Last chance.*

"Don't even think about it." Finn glanced from her to the water ahead, a smile playing on his lips.

"What do you mean?"

"Staying back on shore. Just sit there and relax. Scarlett and I will man the ship, and I'll explain things as we go. You feeling okay?" He seemed concerned.

"I'll be fine." Megan fidgeted with her fingers, then pulled her phone out. Truthfully, she was anything but fine. Her stomach lurched uncomfortably, whether from nerves or seasickness, she wasn't sure.

Finn frowned. "You're as white as a sheet."

Megan pulled her cap down over her face, hoping he couldn't see how sick she was. Her stomach churned as she swallowed hard. She'd get through this. All she needed was to keep breathing and not get sick. She popped two antacids and leaned her head back.

What notes could she scribble down for her first article? Her mind blanked as she watched Finn's muscles pull taut in his arms. Writer's block was never a problem for her normally, but now, all she could think about was how good Finn looked. Yeah, write about him. Good idea.

They reached the channel and puttered past the park where tourists meandered along the path. A few bystanders waved to Finn.

Finn waved back. "It's a great day to be on the water, don't you think?"

"Sure." She didn't dare look at him. If she did, she was sure her face would betray her.

Even though the water was relatively calm, Megan could feel every jolt and swell. Her body tensed when the boat rocked. Her stomach protested with every movement.

"It's gorgeous," Scarlett yelled from the bow. She stretched out, sunning her legs. She lounged on her elbows, lengthening her lean body, while Megan stiffened at every buckle.

"Are you okay?" Finn took off his sunglasses to examine Megan. "Your knuckles are white from gripping the seat."

Megan froze. Until now, she hadn't noticed she was clutching the bench or that her head had dropped, her eyes focused on the wooden floor. All she knew was that she was *not* okay. She was about to throw up, and there was no holding back now.

"Megan?" Finn reached out and touched her shoulder. Any other time, she would have been flattered at the attention. But now, all she wanted was to run away.

The heat of embarrassment swelled inside her chest.

Don't get sick now. Not in front of Finn.

But it was too late. Her stomach was overcome by seasickness.

She quickly pivoted and bent over the side of the boat to release the nausea that had built up inside her. If she'd thought she was embarrassed before, that was nothing compared to now.

CHAPTER EIGHT

FINN

Finn poured sugar and cream into his coffee and stirred it with a spoon so that the black liquid turned a milky shade of brown. Almost the color of Megan's eyes. Most days, he drank his coffee black. But the brew at the French Press Café was potent, and he needed to take the edge off. Now, as he stared at the coffee, he was reminded of her.

Why'd he come here? Did he think a change of venue might take his mind off her?

An older gentleman with weathered hands approached, carrying a cup of the same hot brew.

Finn stepped back to allow the stranger to doctor his coffee. The man gave him a grateful smile. "You new here?"

"Yes, I'm Finn Avery." He held his hand out.

The stranger shook it, then poured cream into his coffee and stirred it. "I'm Joshua. You look a bit lost."

"Oh, well, I'm fine." Finn rubbed the back of his neck.

"That's what most people say. Even when they're not."

"Being new to town, I'm still adjusting. Haven't unpacked my boxes yet. Probably should get a table since I've been eating on a TV tray. You know of any good places I could get used furniture?"

"Depends on what you're looking for. If you're willing to fix it up, I've got used furniture at my salvage shop." Joshua picked up a napkin and pulled a pen out of his pocket. He scribbled something onto the napkin. "There's my address. Stop in when you have a chance. I can tell you everything you need to know about Wild Harbor." He gave Finn one more nod and handed him the napkin.

Finn tucked it into his pocket without reading it. "Thanks. I'll remember that."

Joshua meandered toward the door, lifting his hand in a half-wave. Even though his appearance was a mixture of country boy meets thrift-store find, Finn sensed the old man probably knew the history and people of Wild Harbor like the back of his wrinkled hand. It was just a hunch, but his intuition was more often right than wrong.

Finn stirred one more time and then clinked the spoon against his cup. His transition into Wild Harbor had not gone like he hoped. No matter how awkward it would be, Finn needed to face Megan after Saturday's disastrous sailing lesson. If he had known about her motion sickness, he would never have pressured her to accompany him. His goal had been to work together as a team in a non-competitive way. Instead, the plan had backfired.

At that point, there had been no way to remedy the situation —or to mitigate the embarrassment she'd felt. Not that he wasn't used to dealing with seasickness. Training in the Coast Guard meant he was ready to assist in all situations—whether people were sick, injured, or even unconscious. Seasickness was nothing compared to pulling someone out of the water during a rescue. But nothing had helped Megan that day. She hadn't even looked him in the eye as he'd taken her back to the dock. He'd offered to drive her home, but she had adamantly refused.

"I think you've done enough today," she'd blurted out, her face still white as a sheet as she'd hid her embarrassment behind her sunglasses. "Have fun with Scarlett."

His eyes had lingered on her as she'd made her way down the dock toward the parking lot. For a moment, he'd almost forgotten he wasn't alone.

"Do you want to head out again?" Scarlett had moved to sit next to Finn and pulled a drink out of the cooler. "Thirsty?"

"Sure," he'd said, taking a can of flavored water and cracking it open. "Let's go."

Being on the water was one of the best ways to relax. But as he looked at the water, he wished it was Megan, and not Scarlett, who was with him on the boat. That's what he couldn't make sense of. He'd had fun with Scarlett on the water, but she was definitely no Megan.

Why couldn't he stop thinking about his coworker?

He needed to get his feelings sorted out before he faced Megan at work again. Not only would his attraction to her impede their working relationship, but it would ruin any shot he had of advancing in the office. He couldn't throw away his shot at a promotion. He had to prove it not only to himself, but to his dad, once and for all.

The barista interrupted his thoughts as he wiped a table with a rag. "Just holler when you need more coffee. I'm making a fresh brew now. By the way, I'm Max."

"I'm Finn."

"New in town?"

"Is it that obvious?" He sipped his coffee to see if it had cooled. The copper liquid was perfect. "You're the second person to ask me."

"Only in Wild Harbor, where everyone knows your name."

"There's no hiding in this town, huh?"

"Pretty much. But it's not so bad. I'm new here too. Opening the town's coffee shop has been a good way for me to get to know everyone."

"I'm glad I'm not the only new guy around here. Maybe you can show me the ropes? I'm working at *The Wild Harbor Newspaper*."

"A journalist, huh? If you need the latest scoop, talk to the book club ladies who meet here. They know things long before the paper announces them. I swear that's where Megan Woods gets her leads."

Finn nodded. "I work with her. What can you tell me about her family?"

"Good people. Matt's a friend of mine."

"Let's just say someone was already on the wrong side of one sister."

"Already?"

"What can I say? I've got talent."

Another man walked into the coffee shop.

Max lifted his hand. "Morning, Alex." Then he turned to Finn. "This is the guy you need to talk to. He might have some tips for you."

"Can I get my usual?" Alex took his phone out of his pocket.

Max grabbed a cup. "I wanted to introduce you to Finn. He's the new reporter in town."

"Hey, Finn, good to meet you." Alex held out his hand.

Finn shook it, then pointed at him. "You're from that home renovation show."

"Not anymore. I just started a renovation business in Wild Harbor, and I'm launching a new show."

"Oh, really. Why did you leave?"

Max interrupted before Alex could respond. "A girlfriend. Why else?"

Alex's face lit up. "Lily Woods and I reconnected when I returned to town. One thing led to another."

Max frothed milk into a creamy cloud of white. "Which is why I thought you should talk to Alex about your coworker situation."

"I'm sorry. I'm not following." Alex frowned.

Max jumped in to explain. "Finn's working with Megan Woods, and he's wondering how to get on her good side."

Finn appreciated Max's help. He was sure that Alex wouldn't open up to him otherwise.

Alex chuckled. "Megan might just be more stubborn than Lily. My advice? Don't make her mad."

Too late for that. He'd already made all the rookie mistakes.

"What if I already have?"

"Good luck, man." Alex shook his head. "Megan is driven. Goal-oriented. Doesn't want to lose. So, let her win."

"At what?"

Alex shrugged. "That's for you to decide."

What was he supposed to do with that advice? He had no idea.

Max handed Alex his coffee and turned to Finn. "Oh, if you want to meet up sometime, a bunch of us guys come here early Saturday mornings. Megan's brother included." Max handed Finn another coffee. "Give this to Megan. It can't hurt."

"Thanks." Finn held up the coffee cup as he swung the door open. He didn't know if the coffee would work. But a jolt of caffeine would be a small win. Right now, he needed all the help he could get.

THE NEWSPAPER OFFICE was only a few blocks from the coffee shop, which gave Finn enough time to think about his approach after the awkward boat situation.

"Good morning, Cheri." Finn slid through the door. As he

passed Larry's office, he noticed stacks of boxes that appeared untouched since the last time he had walked by.

"Hey, Larry, how's it going? It seems like your office move has stalled."

Larry rested his chin on his fist. "Uh, yeah. Haven't had time to work on things since I started mortuary school. Looks like I won't be leaving for a few months." Larry flipped through a giant stack of papers on the floor. He had worked at the paper for the last fifteen years, and it appeared he hadn't cleaned out his office once. Maybe never.

"So, I won't be moving into an office anytime soon. Not that I want you to leave, but I get the feeling my current office situation—"

"Get the feeling of what?" a voice echoed.

Finn spun around. Megan stood behind him, coffee tumbler in her hand. She still wore her sunglasses from outside, and her hair was slightly tousled from her convertible. "Did I interrupt a highly confidential meeting?"

Finn cleared his throat. His mouth was bone dry. "Uh, no . . . Larry's transition to his next job has been delayed, which means I can't move into his office. I guess we're stuck together a little longer. Maybe coffee will help?" He held up the white cup from the French Press Café.

She peeled off her shades and took the coffee. "Thank you. As long as you bring me coffee or chocolate, I'll deal with it." She gave him a small smile and crossed around him.

Larry shook his head at Finn. "Good luck, man."

Why did everyone keep wishing him good luck? It was annoying him, like he had already failed. What he needed was a plan. Something to change Megan's opinion of him. Letting her win, like Alex had recommended, was good—in theory. But how could he do that while proving himself to his boss?

Dale tapped him on the shoulder. "My office. Now." Then he turned and hollered for Megan.

Dale wasn't the type to plan his meetings. He worked off the cuff, ready to assign stories at a moment's notice, which worked in the newspaper business where the latest developments needed to hit papers before word spread through town. But it also meant that Finn never knew what to expect when he walked into work.

Megan seemed unfazed by the last-minute request. She leaned against the doorframe, keeping her distance from Finn. "So, what's the story?"

"Join us." Dale pointed at the chair next to Finn. Megan slid into it, her legs inches from Finn's. Now he couldn't escape the scent of her perfume or the fact that her legs were in full view.

Dale pulled out a yellow legal pad covered with scribbled notes. "The summer festival is one of Wild Harbor's biggest draws for families. It opens this weekend, and I've decided we're ramping up our float in the parade on Saturday. I want you both to take part."

"But, Dale, the parade is your thing." Megan frowned. "You always ride on the float in costume. Everyone loves it."

"They do, but I can't this year. The mayor asked me to be the grand marshal of the parade. Because I have to ride in a special car, I need someone to be the official representative on the newspaper float. You two would be perfect. Finn, I normally dress up like Ben Franklin, one of the best journalists in colonial America. I thought you could take over the role."

Finn looked from Dale to Megan, his mouth stuck. That was the last thing he wanted to do. "Um, wow. Never thought I'd be dressing up as Ben."

"Am I dressing up too?" Megan's voice cracked slightly, a hint of desperation coloring the edges.

"How would you feel about going as Mrs. Franklin?"

Megan waved her hand. "I'm not really the colonial type."

"I've already had Cheri order the costumes. They're being overnighted. It'll be fun."

Meg rubbed her forehead. "Fun for who?"

"The community, of course." Dale opened his arms. "What do you say?" He seemed way too excited about this.

"Is there any way out of this? Another event I could cover?" Finn wasn't joking. He needed an escape plan.

"Nope." Dale's mouth spread into a mischievous smile. He suspected Dale got some secret pleasure from forcing them to work the parade together. "Since the parade opens the two-week summer festival, you'll also cover the food tour. It's new this year. All the local restaurants will have a booth in the alley off Market Street. Questions?"

"Not right now." Megan crossed to the door and leaned out, like an animal ready to escape. Finn didn't blame her. The longer they stayed, the more humiliation they suffered.

"One more thing." Dale's voice stopped her before she could make it to the hall. "How'd your first sailing lesson go?"

Megan froze. "As expected."

Whenever she was cornered, her answers got more succinct. Her way of ending the conversation.

"Good, huh?" Dale eyed Finn, with his eyebrows raised. He expected more details.

Finn rubbed his hands together. "It was great to be back on the water."

"And?"

Megan's and Finn's eyes locked. Would she confess Saturday's debacle or just pretend it didn't happen?

Megan backed up against the doorframe for extra support. She appeared smaller, less sure of herself. Finn wanted to shield her from more embarrassment.

"What Finn's not telling you is that I was sick, which is why I'm not sure I can continue with the assignment. I'm sure Finn can oversee the articles on the regatta."

"Meg, I'd really like you to try again," Dale pleaded. "We

want the dual perspective on these stories to pull in our female readership."

"I'm sorry to disappoint you, but you assigned me to someone from the Coast Guard. How can I even compete?" She threw her arms in the air and fled down the hall.

Dale rubbed his forehead.

Finn slowly rose from his chair. "Maybe I should talk to her about this." He followed Megan to her office, where she had already closed the door. He knocked softly.

"I'm busy." Her voice was muffled.

"Can we talk?"

"No. Please don't come in."

Finn opened the door anyway.

Megan swiveled in her chair. Her face was red and blotchy as she wiped her eyes with a tissue. "Didn't you hear me?"

"I did, but I didn't listen. If you're avoiding me because of what happened on Saturday, I want to talk about it. Dozens of guys in the Coast Guard got sick because of rough waters, stress, or motion sickness. It doesn't faze me."

"I'm not embarrassed." A defensive edge colored her tone. "I'm sorry. It's not fair to take this out on you." Her face softened.

"Then what is it? Because we're supposed to be a team. So far, I get the feeling you don't trust me."

"It's not you. I failed. All because of something that happened long ago."

Finn glanced down at the faded tile floor, history etched into every square. So they both struggled with the past.

"If you're not comfortable on the water, I won't twist your arm. But if you change your mind, I'm happy to teach you."

"I'm not like Scarlett."

"If you want to know the truth, Scarlett was more interested in getting a tan than sailing." He offered a small grin, a peace treaty between them.

Something shifted in her expression, and the corner of her mouth twitched. "At least she didn't get sick all over your boat. That counts for something."

Finally. She was loosening up.

"Like I said, it doesn't bother me. If you want to try again, you know where to find me." He nodded toward his lone chair.

She didn't answer. Maybe that was progress?

He grabbed his folding chair from the corner and tucked it under his arm.

"Where are you going?"

"To find a quiet spot in the hall. It's not right that Dale forced you to have an office mate."

"You don't have to leave." Her voice barely rose above a whisper. "You can stay." She didn't force the words. Instead, it was an invitation, proof that she trusted him a little, even if it was only one percent.

"I shouldn't." As he retreated backward out the door, his elbows bumped into everything. He placed his chair outside her office, like a guard on duty. Her request tumbled around in his mind. *You can stay.*

If she offered it once, would she offer it again?

He set himself an impossible little target. A goal of sorts. He thought it would be nice to learn to work together amicably, but that wasn't enough.

He wanted to prove he wasn't her competitor, but something more. Maybe even someone she could trust. If he earned one percent of her trust, then he could shoot for two. Then ten. That's the way trust worked. It was earned, not demanded, and it compounded over time.

If she trusted him ten percent, then there was hope he could earn fifty percent. Maybe even all of it.

Because one percent didn't satisfy him anymore.

CHAPTER NINE

MEGAN

The sun peeked over the horizon, casting a warm glow as Megan walked downtown for the parade.

So what if she had to dress up in a silly costume? It's not like she cared what Finn thought.

Except she did care. Quite a lot, actually.

Over the last few days, she had quelled the butterflies in her stomach by pretending that the parade didn't exist. But as she watched people lining the streets this morning, setting up their lawn chairs to snag a front-row view, she could no longer ignore reality.

She was about to ride on a float with the handsome new guy in town. People would inevitably make predictions about whether there was something between them. She'd be elbowed and teased. How many exclamations of *you're so lucky* could she stand in one day?

She had pulled her hair back in a plain bun so that she could play Mrs. Franklin, but one tendril kept slipping out, and she tucked it behind her ear for the tenth time.

All she had to do was get through today. Easy, right?

Finn stood on the corner and smiled when he saw her, holding up a hanger covered by a plastic bag. He'd look dashing as Ben. She'd be a plain Jane next to him. Seeing Finn waiting made her want to give up. She wasn't ready for this kind of humiliation.

"Good morning. Ready for a parade?" Finn beamed as she approached.

"As ready as I'll ever be. I'm not sure anything in my life has prepared me for dressing up as Mrs. Franklin. To make it slightly better, I brought this." She held up a shopping bag filled with a huge stash of colorful hard candies and suckers.

"Mrs. Franklin, are you addicted to sugar?" He gave her a sly smile.

"Not for me, but the kids watching the parade."

"Genius idea." Then he shook his head. "I'm going to be a terrible Ben. I only wish I had thought of the candy."

"Nonsense. What are you going to do about your hair? Wasn't Ben bald?"

Finn had thick brown hair, and she resisted the urge to touch it. She hadn't liked working separately from him this week. Occasionally she'd tilted her office chair just right so she could peek into the hallway to check on him.

Finn ran his fingers through his hair. "My costume is supposed to include a bald man's wig. Which Dale never needed. I wonder if people will mistake me for him?"

"Not a chance." She cracked a smile. Their boss was liver-spotted, bald, and rotund. Finn's body looked chiseled out of stone. Someone would have to be blind to mistake the two.

"By the way, here is your costume." Finn handed her the hanger covered in dark plastic. "I haven't actually looked at them yet. Cheri left them in the office."

She pulled up the plastic cover and noticed a leaf-green skirt hanging out.

"Wait a minute, I think you picked up the wrong costume. This must be someone else's." She pulled the cover off to reveal a fairy dress with wings attached. "What in the world? This is not my costume."

Finn grabbed his cover and ripped it off to reveal a crimson pirate's waistcoat and breeches made of velvet. A leather sash crossed diagonally down the front of his coat and a sash hung around the waist. A large brown hat held an exotic white feather. They were costumes from the book *Peter Pan.*

"Uh-oh." Finn glanced at her. "There must have been a mix-up. These were the only costumes in the office."

Megan's eyes widened. "You don't think—"

"They sent us the wrong costumes?" Finn looked from his costume to hers. "I can check, but they were the only things hanging on your office door this morning. Cheri labeled them with our names."

Megan checked her watch. "We don't have time. The rental place must have made a mistake."

"This is going from bad to worse." Finn pulled out his phone. "I'll text Dale and see what we should do."

"I'm sure there is a simple fix." Megan scanned the crowd and found a parade organizer with a clipboard. Her glasses slid down the bridge of her nose. The sweltering humidity made everything feel unusually sticky.

"Mrs. Mahoney." Megan ran to her, carrying the fairy getup. "There's been a mistake. They sent us the wrong costumes."

Mrs. Mahoney pushed up her glasses, then burst out laughing. "It'll be perfect. So much more kid-friendly."

"No, no, no. I don't think you understand. Ben Franklin is our mascot. That's who Dale has been playing for years."

"But Dale isn't on your float this year, and honestly, a storybook character is a lot more fun than Dale's Ben Franklin. You'll be swamped with pictures today."

Finn tapped Megan on the shoulder. "Dale says to go with it. It was an error, but right now, there's no way to fix it."

"Same answer I got from Mrs. Mahoney." Megan covered her eyes and shook her head. "I can't believe I'm going to be dressed like this."

"If you want to know the truth, I'm not exactly excited about this wig." He held up the curly, longhaired wig included with his pirate costume. "But if we're going to get through this, then we might as well have fun." He rushed toward the men's dressing room tent, calling over his shoulder, "See you soon, Tink."

"Thanks, Captain," Megan shot back.

The things she did for this job.

When Megan came out of the dressing room, the awkwardness of her fairy costume made her sweat. She tugged at the seams around her waist, hoping the bodice would magically stretch. It hugged her curves too well.

Finn stood outside the tent, dressed in full pirate regalia. His eyes swept over her costume. "You make a pretty decent fairy, for the record."

"Thanks. I feel ridiculous. I'm not really fairy-tale material." Growing up, Cass had always loved princess stories, prancing about the house in elaborate costumes. Megan had strayed from the typical girl costumes and instead embraced rodeo cowgirls and ninjas. Fairies were definitely not her style.

Megan's mouth twitched as she looked at Finn's shapely legs dressed in red breeches. "Nice socks, by the way."

"It brings back terrible memories of my first high school musical, *The Pirates of Penzance*." He pulled at his tights and grimaced. "I don't envy you at all in those tights. I could never make it as a theme park actor."

Megan adjusted her wings, which shifted crookedly on her shoulders. "This would have been perfect for my sister, Cass. I always played the wicked stepmother or some other villain."

"Really? I wouldn't have guessed that about you."

"You think I'm the princess type?"

"Not at all. You just continue to surprise me, Tink."

"Ugh. Are you going to call me that all day?"

"Pretty much."

"Okay, Captain. Get ready to be overwhelmed by children."

Mrs. Mahoney picked up a bullhorn from the sidewalk and turned it on with a piercing squeal. "Parade volunteers, please join your floats. The parade starts in five minutes."

Megan pulled at her skirt. "I guess this is it. Time to royally embarrass myself." She attempted to step onto the float and realized her costume made it impossible to lift her leg more than a few inches. "Oh, this is awkward. I can't even make this step."

"You need help?"

She shook her head and lifted her leg again. If she hitched it any higher, she was going to rip out the seam on her costume. "Stupid costume. How does any real woman wear this? If you don't mind, could you give me a little help up?"

Finn wrapped his hands around her waist and lifted her up. His grip felt secure around her, and her body tightened in response.

"The costume looks good on you." Finn's eyes swept over her. Then he hopped onto the float behind her. "Ready for this?"

"Only if you are." Their float jerked forward, and Megan grabbed Finn's arm for support for a second. He glanced down at her touch, and she pulled away.

"Sorry. For a minute, I thought I was going to be tossed to the sidewalk."

"No apologies necessary."

"How about we make an agreement? You and I promise this little secret doesn't leave Wild Harbor, okay?"

"After people in town plaster your picture all over social media?" He gave her a quick wink. "Your secret's safe with me."

He'd accepted this change of plans far better than she had. If she could just follow his lead and enjoy the moment, she'd have more fun.

As soon as the first group of kids approached the float, Finn dove into his role, throwing candy, waving for pictures, and even stopping the float to offer photo opportunities.

When the parade turned onto Main Street and the number of spectators swelled, Finn worked the crowd better than anyone. He jumped off the float in character and even took some selfies with the older ladies in town, including Edna and Thelma, who were most delighted at the attention.

When Megan saw her family, Lily frowned and mouthed, "Where's Mrs. Franklin?"

Megan shrugged and threw some candy their way.

Cassidy caught a piece and hollered, "Oh. Your costume!"

Megan frowned and shook her head.

"Is that your family?" Finn leaned in close.

"Yes, Mom is taking a million pictures, and Dad is next to her in the wheelchair."

Finn swung off the float and headed to her sisters. He was fully embracing his role today, high-fiving children and winning over the silver-haired ladies. Finn was holding up the parade, but he didn't care. He wanted to meet her family. How could she not like the guy?

"Let me take a picture of you both." Mom motioned to Megan.

She shook her head, embarrassed.

Finn rushed over and put his hands out to help her down. "Come on. I'll help you."

Her sisters started chanting, "Megan, Megan—" Soon, the crowd joined in.

"Do it for your mom and dad." He waved her forward. "Jump. I'll catch you."

"There's no way—"

"Are you scared I'll drop you?"

"After the warm welcome I've given you at the office, I don't know."

"I promise not to let you fall." His eyes grew suddenly serious. A warmth tingled inside her. She couldn't pull away from that gaze.

Megan jumped as Finn caught her around the waist and placed her on the ground.

She smoothed her costume, trying to regain her composure. "Thanks for not dropping me." She needed to stop giving him reasons to touch her. It was more than she could handle.

"Thanks for trusting me." He gave her a boyish smile that made the warmth in her body grow into a full-blown heat wave.

If only he wasn't her coworker.

Megan's heart raced as the crowd gathered, holding up their phones, capturing the moment.

She passed it off as adrenaline from the jump. But as he wrapped his arm around her waist and posed for the photo, she couldn't help but notice how much she enjoyed being close to him.

AT THE END of the parade route, the floats slowed to a stop as volunteers gathered in groups to celebrate what everyone said was the best parade ever.

Megan couldn't wait to change out of her Tinkerbell getup. The costume itched, and a layer of sweat coated her skin. Despite the discomfort, her mind buzzed with anticipation, mostly because of Finn's exuberance at embracing the moment.

A line of children followed their float as it parked. Finn teased a young girl, tossing candy in the air as she giggled with glee.

"Hey, Pirate Man, betcha can't catch me," a girl taunted from the sidewalk.

Finn jumped off the float and chased her in a circle, then scooped her up in his arms and swung her around, her laughter dancing in the air.

As Megan watched from above, a tiny heaviness pushed against her rib cage, the weight of a secret grief hidden deep.

For months, she had been suffering from unexplainable pain in her lower abdomen. When her sickness had led her from one doctor's office to the next, she'd finally discovered the truth. She would not have children.

The doctor's words had slid through her skin like a scalpel. "Your endometriosis is extensive. The chance of you ever getting pregnant . . ." He shook his head. "It's unlikely."

His face had been emotionless, his tone clinical. "Maybe you will be one of the lucky ones. But from the results of your tests, it looks impossible."

Impossible. She hated that word. It grated against her belief that she could change things if she tried hard enough. She was an overachiever, but this wasn't something she could fix.

Since hearing her doctor's words a year ago, she had allowed the diagnosis to settle on her like a jail sentence. *Impossible.* A done deal. Biological children would not be in her future.

Even though she'd accepted that she would likely never carry a baby, it hurt her to see someone like Finn, who was obviously stellar with children.

He was a natural around kids, and a girl didn't have to be a genius to guess he would make a great dad someday.

When Aspen harped about the challenges of finding a man who had all the desired qualities, including the makings of an incredible dad, Megan passed it off with a joke. "I'm not looking for someone who is good with kids. I'm looking for someone who is good with me."

It was true. *Partially.*

But how could she be a mother now that her body had betrayed her? She knew there were other ways, like adoption or fostering, but both people had to be on board with it. Those alternative paths were fraught with complications—endless paperwork, failed adoptions, and foster placements that didn't work out. She couldn't heap any more hurt onto her grief.

She had always imagined motherhood would come easily. But like most things that seemed easy, the truth was rarely so simple.

She could not marry someone who wanted a van full of little faces who looked like miniature versions of them. She wouldn't hold on to hope for a baby bump, like some magical object just out of reach. If that meant she had to reject a man who wanted that dream, then so be it. But admiring a man who was good with kids pricked her wound just enough to hurt.

That's why she couldn't let Finn get too close. She couldn't hurt him. Nor could she face his rejection. She needed to focus on her career, the perfect fit for her child-free life. The editor-in-chief position could fill her time, and she'd be able to carry on something that was important to the town's heritage.

But now, even that seemed in jeopardy.

As she tried to step down from the float, she climbed awkwardly in her costume. She was anything but graceful in this crazy getup.

"Need a hand?" Finn offered, just as she was dangling her foot in the air, trying to find a step.

"I'm good." She attempted to lower herself by grabbing hold of a piece of tulle like a climbing rope, hoping that the delicate fabric would hold until her feet hit the pavement. As she clung to the netted cloth, the fabric tore from the float, sending her spiraling backwards.

Finn raced to get her, but was too late. She landed flat on her back, staring up into his worried face.

"Are you okay?" He bent down next to her, concern etched between his furrowed eyebrows.

"I will be." She couldn't stop herself from making a fool of herself in front of Finn. It seemed to be her punishment for treating him so rotten.

He glanced down at her disheveled costume. "Let me help you out." He straightened her fairy wings and then pulled her to standing. "Please don't be afraid to ask for help a little sooner next time." His eyes flitted down to her skirt before he looked away. "Oh, your skirt is . . . um . . ." He cleared his throat.

Megan glanced down to see her costume had inched up when she fell. Although she was fully covered, the skirt had taken on a decidedly adult look, showing off a small portion of her thighs. She yanked it down.

"Ugh." Megan straightened her rumpled costume. "As if I needed to embarrass myself any more today. I'm sorry."

"Believe me"—he gave her a boyish grin—"I'm not." He was obviously enjoying this way too much.

His smile only made her heart flutter more. She needed to get out of here. *Pronto.*

"Yoo-hoo! Meg, dear!" Edna Long rushed over with Peaches yapping under her arm. In a brightly colored floral blouse you could see a block away, Edna had a flair for drama, shown in the sparkly outfit she stuffed Peaches into. Edna set her Pekingese on the ground and opened her arms for a wide embrace.

"You look so pretty," Edna gushed, pulling her into a bear hug. "What book is that character from?"

"*Peter Pan,*" Megan squeaked as Edna squeezed her too tight.

"Ah, yes. I didn't know you were going to be in costume."

"I was supposed to be dressed as Ben Franklin's wife."

"What? To Dale?" Edna laughed. "He's too old and stodgy for you, don't you think?"

"Finn was going to play Ben this year." She pointed to her coworker, who stood a few feet away.

Edna held out her hand. "I finally get to meet the new journalist."

"Finn, this is Edna." Finn shook her hand. "She's your key to knowing everyone in town." Megan scratched Peaches behind the ears.

"Well, I don't know everybody." Edna touched her white hair, which was stiff with hair spray. "But if there's a stranger, I usually meet them during the summer festival. I'm headed over to the food alley now. You two coming?"

"I'm going to change out of my costume first." Megan tugged at her skirt again, which was clinging uncomfortably to her legs. Drops of sweat formed under her costume.

Finn took off his pirate coat while loosening the collar of his white shirt.

Megan glimpsed the outline of his collarbone.

"We need to cover the food article for the paper sometime. I'm game for grabbing lunch if you are."

Edna lifted her eyebrows and leaned toward Megan. "I have some juicy gossip about the mayor."

Edna had a reputation as a good lead. The invite was enough to entice Megan. "See you in the food alley?" She gave Megan a wink before picking up Peaches.

"Give me ten minutes." Megan lowered her voice to Finn. "She knows how to bait a journalist."

"Do you think she has a lead?"

"It wouldn't be the first time. Although I was hoping to spend the afternoon recovering from the parade."

"If you're tired, don't let Edna pressure you. I can talk to her."

Suspicion circled in her mind. She didn't know if she could trust Finn fully. Would he steal a lead from her?

"I can't let you have all the fun with Edna. Let me change first."

"Okay, Tink. The magic is over." He pulled off his pirate hat and placed it on her head.

She started toward the dressing room, turning one last time

and tossing him the hat. "Hey, thanks for making this disastrous costume mix-up bearable."

"Just bearable?" He lifted his eyebrows, questioning her choice of words.

"More than bearable," she corrected herself. "You made it fun, and I didn't think that was possible."

"If you'll give me a chance, you'll see a lot of things are possible."

As she stepped into the tent to change, she glimpsed herself in a mirror. She hadn't noticed before, but her cheeks were flushed and she was smiling.

For the first time, she wondered if he might be right.

CHAPTER TEN

FINN

Brightly colored flags flapped in the warm breeze as food vendors lined the alley, the scent of sweet and spicy food permeating the air.

As Finn made his way through the crowd, he salivated over the decadent turtle fudge and pink tandoori chicken with fresh garlic naan.

Megan matched her step with Finn's as they snaked through the crowd. "In the past, the festival only sold the typical greasy carnival fare. Hot dogs, french fries, funnel cakes. But this year, the town council attempted to showcase a wider cuisine by inviting restaurants from all over the state to join the food alley. Apparently, it's a hit." She squeezed past a long line of people.

This year's festival boasted an array of flavors—from flavorful street tacos to gooey cinnamon rolls. Finn was hungry enough to eat all of it.

Vivid murals by local artists decorated the walls as lights twinkled above them. The smells of slow-roasted meat and decadent apple dumplings made Finn's stomach ache with hunger pangs. Spicy chorizo with sautéed red peppers and onions, homemade doughnuts laden with a sticky sugar glaze, and barbecue chicken drenched in a sweet, tangy sauce —every booth offered a delicious lineup of finger-licking foods.

"Where do you want to start?" Megan dodged a family with a stroller and cut through a long line. "There's no way I can sample these now."

"I'm so hungry I probably could eat a horse. Just might regret it later."

"Do you like tacos? Ricardo's has the best in town."

They stopped at the brightly colored booth, where meat sizzled on a grill. The smell of rich chipotle peppers wafted through the air as they ordered two plates of tacos and found a table with an extra seat for Edna.

Even though the older lady had beaten them to the alley, she was too busy talking to indulge in any treats. As she saw them, she wiggled her fingers in a little wave and then went back to stroking Peaches.

"Ricardo's tacos are my favorite." She sat down on a chair as they dug into their food. "Too bad my heartburn keeps me from eating them. I might have to settle for some barbecue chicken and loaded potato salad." She sighed as if this sacrifice was a burden.

"I'm not sure that's settling," Finn teased. "That chicken smells amazing."

"My kind of man." Edna patted Finn's hand.

He liked this woman. She looked like a grandmother but with a little more sass.

"What's the story? It sounded urgent." Megan tilted her head. It was one of her endearing traits whenever she interviewed someone. Getting the scoop was all that mattered now.

Edna leaned forward, secrets dancing in her eyes. "Well, you didn't hear it from me."

Megan fought back a smile. "My lips are sealed." It was no secret who had her finger on the pulse of Wild Harbor.

"Honey, this one's bigger than the next ladies' aid society president."

Edna had been elected president of the ladies' aid society for the last five years and didn't have any plans to step down. Her win made the news every year, a gift from Dale that kept her on the paper's good side.

"What now? Did someone in your bridge club forget to put out their recycling? Or did your neighbor's chihuahua get loose again?" Megan teased between bites of tacos.

"If I find the Mitchells' dog in my flower bed one more time—"

Megan wiped her hands. "Forget I brought it up. You were saying you had news about the mayor."

"Ah, yes. Concerning the new contracting company that's considering relocating to Wild Harbor. They're in the preliminary stages of exploring options so they can build a new headquarters. It's only a fact-finding mission, but they're looking at land that's largely been undeveloped on the east side, within town limits. Have you heard of Sutterfeld Contracting Incorporated or SCI?"

Megan squinted her eyes. "Dale reported something about it from the town council meeting. The council discussed whether they want SCI to move in town limits. The mayor said it could be a positive asset for the community."

"That's the way it was presented. Painted as a golden opportunity. But there's more to it." Edna lifted her eyebrows. "The council reported that by locating their new building in this undeveloped part of town, it would provide economic advantages without upsetting our established neighborhoods. Portrayed as a win for all."

"Then how is it a problem?" Finn was trying to find the hook for the story and coming up short.

Edna stroked Peaches's head as he sat on her lap. "They left information out from the town council meeting. News that might have been useful for the public to know. Apparently, they've been meeting with the mayor privately, and he's all gung ho to have them move here. He even suggested that when the council is ready to renovate Williams Park field house and grounds, SCI should be given a no-bid contract."

Megan stopped eating. "So he's favoring them?"

Edna paused. "Here's where it gets interesting. When they first started their fact-finding mission, looking for property, the mayor wasn't interested in them moving here. He wanted that vacant land to become a housing development or condominiums. Then, he suddenly changed his mind."

"How is that a problem?" Finn asked.

"It's not. Unless they used an underhanded method to get the mayor on their side." That was the bomb Edna had been waiting to drop.

"What do you mean?" Megan put down her taco.

"The mayor apparently received some compensation for agreeing to promote their relocation in exchange for giving them future city contracts."

"That's a serious accusation, Edna. You're accusing Mayor Briggs of accepting a bribe."

She shrugged. "I know, which is why I'm passing along this information to you. I don't want to figure out whether or not it's true. But as the lead reporter, you can." She pointed at Megan.

Megan shifted uncomfortably on the bench. "Edna, who is your source for this information? I can't go on hearsay."

"You won't believe it." Edna leaned forward and whispered. "The mayor's son."

"Harrison?" Megan's eyes widened as she threw a napkin on her empty plate. "Edna, I can't out the mayor's son against his father."

"But this is important." Edna raised her eyebrows. "It needs to be you."

"Thanks for the tip, but—" Megan tapped her fingers on the table. "I'm not sure I can make such a grandiose charge against the mayor unless Harrison agrees to talk to me. It could cost me my job."

"But not reporting it could be costly to the town. Because once SCI is located here, it will be next to impossible to force them out."

"Edna!" Thelma's high-pitched voice cut through the noise from the crowd. "The line for the barbecue chicken is getting longer by the minute." Thelma scurried to her friend. "Meg, you were fabulous in the parade. Every guy in town is going to be lining up at your door!"

Megan groaned. "Thanks, but no, thanks."

"You just wait and see." Thelma's eyes twinkled, while Finn clenched his jaw.

"Have you met Wild Harbor's newest reporter?" Edna squeezed Finn's arm.

Thelma put her hand out grandly, like she was royalty. "No, but I'd like to."

Finn hesitated. He wasn't sure if he was supposed to shake her hand or kiss it. "It's good to meet you." He did an awkward shake.

Thelma smiled, squeezing Edna's pink, fleshy arm. "Excuse me for stealing Edna, but I'm starving, and I don't want the chicken to sell out."

"Enjoy your date." Edna winked before leaving.

Megan's mouth fell open. "The nerve of those ladies. They're always trying to fix me up."

"They want to see you happy."

"No, they want to embarrass me. I've told them I'm not interested." Megan lowered her cup, her eyes darting around.

Finn glanced over his shoulder. "So what do you think of Edna's information?"

"If it's true, this could cause a huge shake-up in our community. I need to go to the source."

"The mayor?"

"I doubt I can get the mayor to talk. I need the story from Harrison."

"But how?"

"I don't know yet, but I'll figure out a way."

People stared at Megan and Finn, recognizing them from the parade. The last thing he wanted was to be on display.

Megan turned her face away. "I don't know about you, but I need to get away from the crowd. How about we order our food and take it somewhere?"

"Great idea. Then we can hash out story details before tomorrow. Any idea where? The beach is going to be packed today. We could take my new boat."

"And get sick again?" Her answer was obvious.

"Okay, so that's a no. You have a better idea?"

Megan nodded. "I know the perfect spot, as long as no one else is there. We can take my convertible. I go there all the time to work on my stories."

"A secret hideaway?"

"Just don't get any ideas about stealing it from me." She narrowed her eyes in mock seriousness.

"I won't tell a soul." He held up his right hand. "Promise."

MEGAN TOOK a back road past the last beach house and turned onto a wooded gravel path.

"Where are we?" Finn asked.

"It looks like a place where a criminal would hide his

hostage, but I promise I'm not going to kill you." She grinned. "You'll understand when you see this place."

As the path curved around a grove of trees, she slowed to a stop. A gate blocked the entrance. Megan hopped out of the car, unlocked the chain, and swung the gate open.

"Are we there?"

"Almost." She jumped back into the driver's seat. "He keeps it locked to deter trespassers."

"Who?"

"Joshua. He owns this land and the cabin on it. He's given my family full permission to use it. I come here to write or escape from life." The car ascended a small hill, where the gravel mixed with sand. Her car tires spun as she tried to gain traction. "Come on, Nellie. You can make this little incline."

"Your car is Nellie?"

"You don't name your cars?"

Finn shook his head. "Just boats."

Meg laughed. "It's one of those family things. We've had a Brown Betty, Rumbling Ruby and Geezer Gary—that's the clunker our parents gave us in high school. He could barely make it above fifty-five without sounding like he was going to fall apart."

"So is she Noxious Nellie? Or Noisy Nellie?"

"Nope. Just plain Nellie, the red Mustang convertible."

Megan followed the gravel path as they crested the hill and headed down a steep descent. As the forest suddenly ended, the hill provided a privacy barrier to the other side: a cabin overlooking the lake with an astounding view of the horizon.

"Welcome to my happy place," Megan exhaled.

"Wow, this is the best-kept secret in Wild Harbor." Finn opened his car door and stepped out, shielding his eyes from the sun. "I'm in awe of the view. I've noticed this hill from the road, but I never knew who owned this enormous property or why it was vacant. Who knows about this place?"

"Oh, it's belonged to Joshua as long as anyone can remember. Since it's private property, and the town has great respect for Joshua, people stay off his land most of the time. He's caught a few trespassers over the years, sneaking over the hill. With a view like this, how could they stay away?" She stepped out of the vehicle and leaned against the hood. "These days, he gets requests from developers who'd love to buy the land. We're talking big offers."

"To be honest, I don't blame them. Imagine a house on this beach. Waking up every day to your own private paradise." Finn put both his arms out wide, trying to capture the view in his arms.

"Exactly why Joshua doesn't want to sell it. He doesn't want it to become another place where a gargantuan beach house is built."

"But does he use it? I thought that man never left his shop."

"Sometimes. He has more than one place. One in town above the salvage shop and one here on the outskirts where he can get away. He likes to keep the natural beauty of the beach. A place to think." Megan slid down to the bumper. "It's just extraordinary."

With the sunlight glinting off her hair, Megan was radiant, more captivating than the view. The sudden whoosh of wind whipped her hair, and for a second, he caught the smell of her perfume. The scent was enough to make his head spin.

He peeled his eyes away from Megan to keep from lingering too long. She was his coworker, and that meant he had to keep their relationship professional.

"Here. We've got a second lunch to eat, and you're hungry." She thrust several take-out boxes into his hands. "Let's sit on the porch." She nodded toward a wooden swing on the porch facing the lake.

"You come here alone?" Finn set them on the hood of the car.

"Yep. Mostly to think, pray, and figure out how to deal with my problematic coworkers . . ." Her mouth turned up at the corners, but he wondered if there was a hint of truth underneath.

He took his shoes off and tossed them to the side, sinking his toes into the sand. Then he balanced the stack of take-out boxes, like a game of tumbling tower blocks. "I know I haven't made life easier for you. Dale thrust me into your work life without warning."

"I'm still working through it. Sit." She patted the swing as he handed her the boxes. As he settled next to her, she set a Styrofoam container of chicken in his lap and slid a container of pie his way. "Don't worry. Barbecue chicken and Ada's apple pie can solve all your problems."

"Let's test your theory." He bit into the pie first.

"You're not supposed to eat dessert first. Seriously, that's against the rules."

"Who said there are rules to the order? I can start with dessert. In fact, I'm going to eat that funnel cake while it's still warm." He reached for the box containing the fried, powdered sugar–laden concoction.

She tried to hide her smile. "You're so bad. We need to do this right. We're food reviewers."

"Confession time: I'm not a food reviewer. I'm a journalist. So I'm going to report that this pie is amazing. Honestly, everyone should eat dessert first." He licked the last of the gooey sauce off his fingers.

Megan laughed and leaned one arm on the back of the swing. "While you cover dessert, I'm going to start with the chicken." She pulled a barbecue chicken drumstick out of the container and took a bite, then wiped the sauce off her fingers with a napkin. "So, I know we're supposed to be working on a food article. But since we're stuck together, tell me what led you into journalism."

Finn studied the horizon where a sailboat was drifting north. The wind had died down, and the lake was calm as glass. "I'm not exactly sure. After I quit the Coast Guard, my dad encouraged me to pursue journalism because I'd always had a love for words. It's my need to find out the truth." He pulled off another piece of funnel cake. "I loved serving in the Coast Guard, but I couldn't get over what happened."

"Like what?"

"My brother's death, mainly."

"Finn, why didn't you tell me?"

"It's awkward to bring up, especially after the debacle between you and Tyler."

"Now I feel like a total jerk. I had no idea. What happened?"

"It was a seizure. It happened six years ago, about a year after the masquerade where I met you. The doctor diagnosed him with epilepsy when he was four, but it was under control with medication. He hadn't had a seizure in years. Then one day when he was home alone, an uncontrollable seizure came on. I was the one who found him."

Megan put down her plate of food. "Finn, I'm so sorry." She touched his shoulder.

"It affected my ability to serve in the Guard. I was in the reserves, and my job was to save people in the water. After Tyler's death, any accident would trigger my PTSD. I started experiencing panic attacks. You can't have someone freaking out on the job because of past trauma. So I left the Guard." He picked at the funnel cake, realizing the weight of this conversation had suddenly turned heavy. "Sorry if that was too much information."

She shook her head. "Not at all. I wish I had known sooner. How can you be so brave on the water after everything that has happened?"

"Being in a boat isn't a trigger for me. It's rescuing someone that brings it back. I was too late for Tyler."

Even now, the weight of regret almost sickened him. If only he had found Tyler sooner, he could have administered the emergency seizure medication. But he couldn't go back, and he didn't want to fail anyone else.

To make matters worse, his father hadn't understood why Finn needed to quit the reserves.

"Why are you giving up?" his father had asked when he'd turned in his resignation. "Tyler never would have quit over this."

Finn had tried to explain, but he couldn't get past his father's unfair expectations. It was like competing with someone larger than life. The memory of his brother would always overshadow him.

"I wish there was a way I could fix us both." Megan opened another container containing tandoori chicken. She pulled out a few meaty bones and handed them to Finn.

"What do you mean?"

"Compared to your story, I sound like a sissy."

"That's not true. Trauma never makes us weak. Only stronger."

"Or it teaches us to flee. I nearly drowned as a child, and my natural instinct is to run from anything that scares me."

"Like the water?"

"Like everything."

Finn looked at her, and their eyes locked, an understanding between them.

He wanted to brush his fingers across her face, but he held back. She'd pull away, or worse, it would create an awkwardness between them. If he did anything to cross the line, she could have him fired. He had to stay in control and hide his feelings, no matter how Megan stirred his emotions.

"We probably should try these." Megan opened the last two containers. "I'm getting full, and we haven't even touched the homemade pretzels or the three-layer cake." She took a bite of the pretzel, then handed the cake to Finn.

He put a hand up to stop her. "I can't. No more food."

"You're a reporter. You have to."

"I ate too much dessert. I'll be sick." He rubbed his stomach.

"You wouldn't be the first."

He leaned away from her, waving his hands. "I'm not taking it, unless you force me to eat it."

"Is that a challenge?" Her eyes narrowed. She wasn't letting him off easy.

He lowered his voice. "You wouldn't dare."

"Oh, I would." She slowly picked up the cake, ready to shove it in his mouth.

He tried to stand before she could grab his arm, but he was too late.

Her hands gripped his forearm, pulling him off-balance as she tackled him. They fell together off the porch into the sand.

He was flat on his back as she pinned his arms. "I won!" she teased, hovering over him. "You're stuck now. That means you have to eat it."

"But you smashed the cake in your hands while tackling me." He could have overpowered her, but he delighted in letting her win. Wasn't that what Alex had recommended?

"Excuses." She laughed, then popped a piece of smashed cake into his mouth. His lips brushed her fingers as her eyes drifted down to his mouth. He saw the sunlight spill across the high planes of her cheek, and the desire to kiss her almost overwhelmed him.

The wind stirred her hair before she looked away. *Moment gone.*

"I'm sorry. I don't know what came over me." She brushed the sand off her clothes as she stood up, her cheeks flushed pink.

A tumble in the sand may have crossed the line, but Finn

didn't want it to end. His walls were crumbling as quickly as she was resurrecting her own.

"Don't apologize. Someday I hope to wrestle around in the sand with my kids."

She shifted to the side, her face guarded. She was keeping him at a distance again, pushing him away. Why had she closed him off?

He needed to solve the puzzle that was Megan Woods. If only he could put the pieces back. Touch the curve of her neck. Trace his finger across the length of her collarbone. Figure her out, one piece at a time.

"Maybe we should head back." She glanced at her watch. "It's been a long day."

As he watched her leave, he wondered if she felt it too. The magic of something between them. The spark of a flame burning into an uncontrollable wildfire.

This time, he couldn't stop it.

CHAPTER ELEVEN

MEGAN

Megan sprawled across the couch in her apartment, trying to figure out what had come over her yesterday. One minute she was eating with Finn, and the next, she was feeding him cake in some ridiculous display of affection. Why had she let her guard down? She could only imagine what Finn thought of her now.

The slow twinge of regret soured her stomach. He was her coworker, not her boyfriend.

But what if he could be both?

Her mind wandered back to the moment she'd tackled him with the cake. A fleeting feeling of happiness had swept over her. When their eyes had met, she'd seen him differently.

Like he was someone she could fall for.

If she was going to be his boss someday, they couldn't be acting like flirty teenagers. Even the memory of it made her skin prickle, like she'd walked through a thorny patch.

Aspen burst into the apartment, interrupting Megan's thoughts, her arms overflowing with grocery bags.

"Are you still on the couch?" Aspen's eyes swept over Megan as she kicked the door shut with her heel.

"I'm taking an official day off. Yesterday was exhausting. Remind me not to do that again."

"You and Finn were a fabulous hit at the parade." Aspen dropped the bags on the counter. "Everybody's talking about what a cute couple you were."

Megan pulled a pillow over her face. "Don't bring it up. I've already embarrassed myself enough for one day."

"Do you want to head out tonight?" Aspen pulled the canned goods out of the bag and stacked them in the pantry.

"I don't know. I'm tired."

"But don't you have to do more stories on the festival?"

"I don't have to attend every second." Megan rose from the couch to help Aspen unload food from the bags.

"But what if I told you that the mayor is coming tonight? It might be the perfect opportunity to corner him."

She had mentioned her need to run into the mayor for a future story, leaving the details vague.

"How do you know the mayor is attending?"

"That's what happens when you get a tip from a grocery store clerk who heard the mayor's wife mention it." Aspen winked. "I'm good."

"A future Edna Long."

"At your service." Aspen gave her a curtsey, like she belonged on some British TV show. "Now, will you tell me what's going on?"

"Can't. Top secret. Honestly, I don't know that it's true either. If I talked to him, maybe he could set the record straight."

"Then come with me," Aspen pleaded. "I'm meeting Matt at the carnival."

"My brother? Doesn't he have some fires to fight or a triathlon to run or something?" Megan put a bag of chips on top of the fridge. She spun around. "Wait, is this a date?"

Aspen tilted her head. "No, of course not. I would tell you if I was dating your brother. He wants to play that target shooting game at the carnival. You wanna come?"

"Be a third wheel?"

"No, keep the town gossips from spreading rumors about Matt and me."

Megan narrowed her eyes. "So, I'm just a decoy to throw people off the scent of a date?"

"Something like that. Plus, you need an excuse to work less. Do something fun for once. Who knows, maybe you'll meet someone?"

"Ugh. Don't even say that after the blind date you arranged with Mr. Football." Megan wanted to squeegee the memory from her mind. Wipe it away for good. "If you dare set me up again . . ." Megan poked her in the ribs.

"Ow." Aspen held her side. "Got it. No matchmaking. No romance. Just fun."

WHEN THEY ARRIVED at the festival, the carnival was beginning to swell with sunburned teenagers and families weary from a day at the beach. Teenagers, still dressed in wet swimsuits, cooled off on carnival rides while overtired kids slurped slushies.

Aspen and Megan stood behind Matt as he practiced his aim. He zeroed in on a small rubber duck and took a shot. *Missed.*

"I'm pretty sure they rigged this game." Aspen munched on a bag of caramel corn as carnival music blared in the background. "Either the guns are trash or the ducks are glued on those shelves so it's next to impossible to shoot them."

Megan rested one hand on her hip as she eyed the game. "I don't know. I'm a pretty good shot. I used to beat Matt when we were young."

"Ha, yeah, right." Matt took aim again. "Your memory is fading. Don't you remember who won the stuffed bear in middle school?"

"Me," Megan said.

Matt shook his head. "No way. It was me."

"I didn't know middle school boys liked stuffed bears," Aspen teased, tossing more caramel corn in her mouth.

Matt fired and missed, then rolled his shoulders back. "I won it for Cass."

"Let me try a game." Megan pulled a bill out of her pocket and slid it to the carnival worker. The lights from the carnival rides were twinkling in the darkening sky, and the music from the carousel drifted over the noisy crowds.

Megan pointed her gun at the duck and exhaled. The gun cracked as she pulled the trigger. She struck the duck, knocking it off the shelf.

"Beginner's luck." Matt watched her take aim again.

The gun cracked as she struck a second duck.

"Wow, Meg." Aspen stopped eating. "I didn't know you were a sharpshooter."

"Don't ruin my concentration." Megan held up the gun one last time. If she made this shot, she'd score a prize. Not that she cared about the cheap carnival toys. It was about outperforming her brother now.

"Don't choke." Matt lifted his gun and took aim at his duck.

"Stop." Meg squinted, trying to focus.

"On the count of three." Matt adjusted his aim. "One, two, three . . ." The crack of guns pierced the air as both Megan and Matt missed.

"Nice. I didn't know you liked to shoot." A familiar voice surprised her.

Finn stood behind her, arms crossed, watching her intensely.

"How long have you been there?" she asked, suddenly embarrassed.

A smile played across his lips. "Long enough to see you make two and miss the third. Not bad, if I do say so myself, Annie Oakley."

Matt stepped forward. "Are you the new reporter? I'm Matt. Heard about you from Megan."

"All good, I hope? I'm not sure I want to know what Megan said."

"Me, too." Aspen stood by Matt, her tiny five-foot frame dwarfed by Matt's six-foot-two body. "I'm Megan's roommate, Aspen."

"Ah, yes. The one who set her up on the blind date."

"You know about that?" Aspen glanced from Finn to Megan.

"I was the one who rescued her from that guy." Darkness flashed across Finn's face.

"I didn't need rescuing, thank you very much." Megan turned away, practicing her aim.

Finn motioned toward the gun. "A hidden talent of yours, Annie?"

"Some say I have many hidden talents, but I'm no Annie Oakley." She closed one eye and focused her gun on the duck.

"We're just showing some healthy sibling rivalry." Matt held up his gun. "Wanna try? I could go another round."

"Sure." Finn drew close to Megan's side and her heart leapfrogged in her chest.

"I'll take a break." Megan offered her gun to Finn.

Matt threw some money down for another round. "You're not afraid of competing against the boys?"

As her older brother, he always knew how to rub her the wrong way, like sandpaper on skin.

She lifted her chin. "I don't want to make you look bad."

"Oh, Matt." Aspen took a step back. "You just got burned."

"You can talk smack all you want. We'll see who the winner is." Matt motioned to Finn. "You in?"

Finn threw a bill across the counter.

Megan felt her pockets for more money. *Empty.*

"I've got it." Finn pulled another bill out of his pocket.

"You don't have to bother. I can run to the ATM—"

"It'll take too long. I'll cover you until you pick up some cash. In fact, we'll leave it this way. If you beat me, you don't have to pay me back."

"And if you win?"

He pivoted toward the Ferris wheel. "You take me for a ride on that." He pointed to the spinning circle of rainbow lights.

Matt clapped his hand on Megan's back. "No pressure, Meg." Then he leaned toward Finn. "She hates Ferris wheels."

Megan cleared her throat. "I can handle it." But deep down, her stomach somersaulted. He'd already seen her sick once. She didn't need more embarrassment heaped on her.

An urgency rose in her gut, but Meg pushed it aside. She had a weakness for competition, a need to prove herself. She wanted to show up the boys.

Her competitive nature had started in high school, fueled by her brother's taunts. Whether it was grades, sports, or music, she constantly worked to improve. Sometimes she secured the number one spot, but other times, she failed, and her sense of worth tottered on the brink of collapse. This need to achieve drove her, but it also had a dark side. The pressure to perform came at a cost. If her accomplishments didn't make her happy, then what would? Failure was part of the deal in this life.

"You ready?" Matt glanced at them both.

"Yep." Finn clenched his jaw.

Megan aimed her gun. Matt's gun cracked first, followed by Finn and Megan.

Megan struck the duck, causing it to fall off the shelf with a thud. Matt and Finn had both missed. She took a deep breath.

One down, two to go.

All three aimed their guns again. Megan's shot echoed behind the pop of their guns.

Missed.

She glanced at the men's targets and saw the ducks tumble to the ground.

They were tied, one shot each. Their last shots would determine the winner, unless they all lost in a three-way tie.

She exhaled slowly, steadying her nerves while Matt and Finn readied their shots.

It was just a game. But it had become more than that for her.

Guns popped. Out of the corner of her eye, she caught Finn's duck falling to the ground.

Her hands trembled as she pulled the trigger. The shot nicked the duck's head. It tottered briefly, but refused to tip over.

Megan pointed to the rubber toy. "That should count. I hit the duck."

"Nope. Read the rules." The carnival worker nodded toward the sign hanging above his head: *Duck must fall off the shelf for a prize.*

Matt smiled. "Rules are rules, sis."

She narrowed her eyes. "I feel cheated. That should have counted. I can't believe you guys aren't standing up for me."

Finn smiled triumphantly, his eyes twinkling. "Looks like you're taking me on a Ferris wheel ride."

CHAPTER TWELVE

MEGAN

As she climbed onto the Ferris wheel, Matt and Aspen stood below, eating ice cream, giving her a final wave.

"Have fun, and don't throw up this time, okay?" her brother taunted. Ever since she was a child, she'd struggled with motion sickness, and Matt offered no sympathy.

Typical. Why did she play that stupid game, anyway?

She'd known better than to agree to it, but she'd gotten sucked into the game. She couldn't let the boys show her up.

Except that they had, and now she was paying for it.

Finn seemed only too happy to ride the Ferris wheel, rubbing in her loss.

Something about him made her jumpy. He kept staring at her, like he knew something she didn't. Did she have food in her teeth? Or did he just enjoy seeing her lose? Ever since the cake incident, she couldn't stop thinking about him.

"I can't believe I agreed to this." She waited for the carnival worker to open the next car as the wheel spun to a stop.

"I can't believe I won." Finn moved aside to let her go first.

Megan stepped into the car and slid down the metal seat, grasping the safety bar. Spinning rides always triggered her motion sickness.

Just focus on something else. That was always what her dad had told her when she'd had stage fright. But how could she focus when her emotions were all topsy-turvy?

She squinted at the setting sun, which washed everything in a pinkish-orange glow.

Finn scooted closer to her. "I felt a little bad after the boating incident. So I brought this." He held up a small paper bag. "I snagged it from the caramel corn stand. Quite useful as a barf bag."

She plucked the bag from him. "Thanks, I guess?" It was thoughtful in a weird way.

The Ferris wheel jerked to a start and Megan instinctively gripped the bar.

Wimp.

Finn put his hand on her shoulder. "It won't buck you off. Once it gets going, it's like sailing through the air."

The Ferris wheel rose to the sky, pulling her body like a balloon on a string. Her stomach soured at the lifting sensation. She closed her eyes. *Breathe.*

"You're hating every second. I can tell." Finn was staring at her. She didn't have to open her eyes to know. She could feel his breath on her cheek.

"Not hating it. Just enduring it." She screwed her eyes shut even tighter.

"Try looking around, it's an amazing view."

She opened one eye, then closed it. "No, thank you."

"Suit yourself. But Main Street is incredible."

It was enough to entice her to peek. As her gaze adjusted to the steep height, everything shrunk to toy proportions. Main Street's brick buildings. The historic houses on Poplar Street, surrounded by lush maples and oaks. The wide expanse of the lake in the distance opened before her, a deep blanket of blue illuminated by the dazzling brilliance of the bleeding sun's last show.

"This is amazing." She released her grip as the lake captured her attention, stretching like an endless basin until sky and water came together as one. "I've never seen our town this way before."

"You've never been on a Ferris wheel before?"

She pulled her gaze back to Finn. "I tried the flying swings when I was six, and that's when I discovered I had the curse of motion sickness. I can't even manage the carousel."

As the wheel descended, her stomach tumbled with it, and she instinctively closed her eyes again.

"Whoa, let your body relax into the ride." Finn angled his body toward hers. "Don't fight the feeling. You're white-knuckling again." He placed his hand on hers, prying her fingers from the bar. His grip lingered on her hands. "Hanging on won't help. I promise I won't let you fall." She cracked open her eyes and glanced down.

Yep, still holding her hand.

At least his touch took her mind off the movement of the wheel. She liked his hand covering hers. Maybe too much.

Their car reached the summit, then plummeted again. As her stomach dropped, her body felt weightless. Alive. Floating.

The wheel suddenly slowed to a stop as their car lifted higher, leaving them dangling from the top.

"Check out the people down there." Finn let go of her hand and leaned over the edge of their car, tipping it slightly.

She grabbed his arm, yanking him toward her. "One fall, and I'll be writing tomorrow's front-page article on how you plunged to your death."

"This thing is safe." He banged on the safety bar. "I used to rock these seats all the time in high school." He started showing off, swaying the car back and forth, which was enough to set off alarm bells in her head.

Megan gripped the rail again. "Don't be an idiot."

He stopped rocking. "Just wanted you to loosen up a bit. You seem tense, except for that moment earlier—"

When he'd grasped her hand? She hoped he hadn't noticed.

He rested his arm on the back of the seat, just behind her shoulders, the way couples sat. If she leaned back just a little, his hand would touch her arm.

He angled toward her. "When we were at Joshua's, I saw a different side of you. One I really liked."

She memorized the color of his eyes. More green than brown. Almost the shade of a jade stone.

What was she supposed to say now? *It was a mistake?*

Humidity thickened the air as heat crawled up her spine. She felt a raindrop hit her arm. Then another.

She shifted toward the lake, which had turned navy blue as the last of the light slipped away and dark clouds approached from the west.

He tapped her shoulder. "Don't look now, but the couple in the car behind us are having a moment."

"What?" Megan swiveled around to eavesdrop on a man and woman locked in an embrace. "Oh, that kind of moment. They're certainly not worried about anyone spying on them."

The Ferris wheel rotated as they sat in silence, the rain sprinkling their faces. His arm was still on the back of the seat, his wrist lightly touching her back. Megan thought she'd be relieved to exit the ride, but now that it was almost done, she wished it would continue. Like so much in her life, just about the time she finally figured things out, the ride was over.

As they stepped off, Finn smiled. "You know, I'm proud of you." A raindrop fell on her nose. Finn wiped it with his index finger.

"For what?"

"As much as you hate Ferris wheels, I think you enjoyed the ride. Am I right?"

Megan stepped ahead of Finn so he couldn't see her face in the carnival lights. "It wasn't as terrible as I expected."

"If you can conquer Ferris wheels, then maybe sailing is next."

"Nice try, but no. I'll leave that to you. Knock yourself out in the regatta."

"I want you on my team."

"Oh, it's *your* team now? I thought it was Dale's idea."

"It's my team because it's me and nobody else. Unless I can convince you to join me. What if I bribe you with ice cream?"

"I don't take bribes." She stood on her toes, searching for Matt and Aspen, who were nowhere in sight. The rain made Megan's head swim. She waved her hand like a fan, stirring the thick air.

In the distance, thunder rumbled, and raindrops poured steadily.

"I didn't know it was supposed to rain." She peered at the sky. A line of dark clouds had swallowed the moon. A storm was moving in. Drops pelted them as the thunder echoed in the distance. Lightning bolted over the lake as the crowd scrambled for cover.

"We'd better get inside." Finn pulled out his phone. "The only problem is that we're at the far end of the park and most places are closed."

"Could we make it to the newspaper office before the storm hits? It's only a few blocks away."

He opened his weather app and showed her the radar. "We don't have much time."

A huge blob of red and orange was ready to swallow them. A bolt of lightning illuminated the sky as the thunder rumbled louder.

People ran for cover in all directions. Rides shut down as passengers scurried toward the streets and piled into their cars.

"Good thing we aren't on that Ferris wheel." Finn ran ahead as thunder rattled around them. The rain drenched their clothes as Megan lagged behind Finn.

"Come on, let's go." He sprinted ahead of her.

Thunder cracked as people scattered, bolting in between them as they rushed down a row of carnival rides. Megan slipped on a mud puddle, nearly falling. Finn reached out and pulled her forward. "Hang on to me. It will be easier to stay together."

They ran through the crowd, hands locked, and turned toward food alley, where tables sat empty, illuminated by the flashes of lightning. They raced through the alley and halted at the intersection. Cars clogged the road, their wipers pumping.

"We won't make it to the newspaper office," Megan shouted. Her shirt was nearly soaked now, and it clung uncomfortably to her body. "We need to find somewhere else." Her car was parked blocks away, and all the shops had closed.

The rain blanketed the streets now, while thunder shook the windows of the buildings.

"This way," Finn yelled and yanked her hand. They ran toward the only place that would keep them somewhat dry— one of the abandoned carnival games. The lights were still flashing in the rain, but it had a roof and would shelter them from the storm. A carnival worker had locked the gate and lowered a tarp across the opening. The only way in was to climb over the counter and loosen the tarp so they could slide under it.

"Get in there!" Finn yelled. "I'll help you climb over."

"We can't." She'd rather be in a building than a rickety carnival game, but she didn't have a choice now. They needed to ride out the storm. The thunder boomed in sync with the lightning. She could barely see as she blinked back the rain.

Drops splattered across Finn's face as he lifted her over the counter. She unhooked the tarp and slid under it. Finn's body was behind her as he swung himself into the tiny carnival game booth. They both fell to the ground, wet and breathless.

It wasn't much of a shelter, but at least they were out of the rain. While Megan found two step stools, Finn secured the tarp, leaving them trapped in darkness, except for the occasional flash of lightning that seeped through the edges.

Megan perched on the stool and wiped her eyes. "I feel like a drowned rat." Her dripping hair cascaded down her shoulders, sticking to her arms. "I never dreamed I'd be stuck here with you."

"A dream come true, right?" he mused. "Alone in a carnival game . . ."

"Almost getting struck by lightning, dodging puddles, trespassing on carnival property." She laughed.

He wiped his face. "You look nice as a drowned rat."

"Oh, thanks. Is that a compliment?"

"Sort of."

She hit him on the arm.

"It's easier to tease you than tell you the truth."

"That I look worse than a rat?" she shot back.

"That's not what I meant. You're beautiful right now."

His words made her heart beat out of control. She didn't feel beautiful. The weight of her soaked clothes, dripping down her legs, stuck to every curve of her body.

"Let me fix this," he whispered, pulling a tendril of wet hair stuck to her forehead out of the way. "That should help." Then he moved closer and brushed his hand across her wet cheek.

She was alone with Finn Avery, and he stared at her in a way she hadn't seen before. Next to her, he was tall and strong, but when he touched her, it was gentle, like he was afraid of hurting her.

This wasn't the man she knew at work. But she wasn't the

same person either. In the office, she had been so focused on why she couldn't fall for him, she had smothered her emotions, living by these imaginary rules she had created for herself.

But now, she had nowhere to hide. Finn wasn't someone she could let into her heart. Or could she?

Everything was up for grabs now.

Their eyes met, and he paused for a moment, studying her face. Then he ran a thumb over her cheek and leaned in, closing the distance between them. His lips slowly met hers in a tender, warm kiss. She let out a small gasp as he coaxed her mouth to move with his. It had been so long since Megan had let anyone get close to her. She angled into him and wrapped her arms around his neck, letting the rain drown out her doubts.

This was reckless and crazy, but she didn't care right now. Her arguments floated away with the storm. She let herself fall into his arms, her lips drinking his, his hands in her wet hair.

She wouldn't think about facing him tomorrow or what she would say then. All she wanted was this moment, right now.

CHAPTER THIRTEEN

FINN

He didn't want it to end. The feel of her lips on his. Her hair in his hands. *All of it.* But his brain spiraled toward desire, and he needed to get it under control. *Now.*

It took everything to pull away from her. No doubt this kiss was going to complicate their relationship, especially since he was trying to earn her trust. Logic told him that dating a coworker, especially someone he was competing with for a promotion, was a risky move.

He pulled away, looking into her eyes, which seemed to glow golden brown in the dim light. He tunneled his fingers through his wet hair and exhaled. The rain was subsiding, and he suddenly felt her silence like a weight on his chest. He searched her face, waiting for an explanation.

As much as he wanted to tell her how he felt, there was no way he could admit his intense attraction. He didn't even know how she felt. What if she thought this was a big mistake?

He needed to get some space before he kissed her again and

lost his mind. "I'm sorry . . ." He shifted away from her and checked the sky. The storm had passed, but he could still hear the low rumble as it moved east, a hypnotic lightning show in the distance.

She stood, her forehead furrowed, her eyes narrowed. "For what?" Her body was rigid with tension.

"I hope this doesn't make things awkward between us." If Dale found out, he'd probably be fired in a heartbeat. What was he thinking? He already knew the answer. He wasn't.

She cocked her head, her eyes laced with questions he didn't have answers for. "So, now what?"

He wanted to know the same thing, but he could barely think, let alone give a coherent answer. Did she want him as much as he wanted her?

Instead of revealing his feelings, he chose the safe route. *Escape.* "I probably should head home. It's late, and I have an article due in the morning."

"Oh . . . okay," she whispered. Then she pulled away, avoiding his eyes. A pained expression flitted across her face before she covered it with a vacant look, like a blind unfurling across a window.

He wanted to sweep her up in his arms and tell her she drove him crazy, but something inside battled for control. It was madness to think this could ever work. The best thing he could do was protect his heart.

He grabbed her arm to help her over the edge of the carnival booth.

She recoiled from his touch, swiftly swinging her legs over the counter, enlarging the distance between them. "You've done enough tonight."

"You can't just leave. At least let me walk you to your car."

"I'd rather be by myself."

Finn jumped over the counter, matching her step. "Megan." He grabbed her arm, and she spun around to face him. Her eyes held anger and sadness in balance. Then she blinked, and they were gone. *Blind pulled.*

"Just leave me alone." Her voice quivered the slightest bit. "Tonight was a mistake."

The words pinched and twisted inside him. "I'm not letting you walk alone in the dark."

"I don't want your help." Then she spun on her heel and left, the damage already done.

∼

WHEN FINN WALKED into the newspaper, he didn't know what he was going to say to Megan. He'd been working to earn her trust, but after last night, he wondered if he'd lost any gains he'd made.

The best course of action? Apologize and pretend that kiss didn't happen, even though his entire body was electric when she was near.

He walked by Larry's office, still stacked with boxes. How long did it take to pack an office? Larry worked like a sloth, slow and methodical. His exit would solve Finn's problem.

Larry was kneeling next to a box, looking through a manilla folder, piles of papers circling him like a ring. "Hello, Finn. Or should I say 'ahoy, matey'?"

"Excuse me?" Finn gripped his coffee, his mind working out a solution for how to get into this office sooner.

"Your character in the parade?" He held up his finger in the shape of a hook. "The pirate?"

"Oh, yeah. I'm a little tired." More like exhausted from tossing and turning all night long. The last thing he wanted to be reminded of was the parade with Megan. And that kiss.

"Everything okay?" Larry peered down his nose at him through large bifocals. Finn wasn't about to pour his heart out to the future mortician. His goal was simple. Get Larry moving.

"Uh, yeah. I was just wondering how packing is going?"

"Slow. I'm trying to make headway on this office, but it's not going so well." Larry scanned the room and scratched his bald head. From the looks of the mess, he hadn't made any progress.

"Let me help." Finn bent over to grab some papers.

"I'd rather you not." Larry took the papers from Finn's hands. "I have a system."

"Oh. Do you know when you'll be moving?" Finn put his hands in his pockets. He was trying to drop hints without pressuring Larry. "It's been hard to share an office with Megan. You know, the office is *her* turf."

"She kicked you out?"

"Uh, no—"

Larry pressed on. "Because rumor has it she booted you from her office."

"No—who told you that? Never mind. I don't want to know. But for the record, I volunteered to move. But working in the hallway is not exactly ideal."

"You're saying you want me to leave sooner?" Larry paused, his lips stretching into a thin, tight line.

Finn hadn't realized how callous his words had come across. "No, Larry. It's not that. I was wondering if you have a timeline, so I can be ready."

He couldn't explain to Larry the awkwardness of his working relationship with Megan now that they had shared a kiss.

"Sorry, mate. I don't have a clue how long this is going to take me. I haven't cleaned anything out of this office since I started this job. I'm meticulous about keeping things, in case I need to reference it later."

An office hoarder. *Great.*

"No worries, Larry. Just keep me posted." Finn headed toward his hard metal chair in the hall. He needed a plan B.

Some way of avoiding Megan until he could control these feelings for her.

Before passing her office, he stopped to listen. He could hear the machine gun keystrokes on her laptop. The squeak of her chair. A brief pause, then the *tap, tap, tap* of more typing.

Dale's voice boomed through the office intercom: "Staff meeting in the conference room, immediately."

Finn let out a long hiss. Saved by an office meeting. At least he wouldn't have to face Megan alone. He couldn't avoid her forever, but this delayed their embarrassing encounter after the kiss.

Megan bolted around the corner, nearly slamming into Finn.

"Oh. I didn't know you were there." Although she never touched him, the proximity of their personal space created an immediate tension.

Finn stumbled backward, avoiding a collision. "I was heading to my chair." He nodded to his seat. "I didn't mean—"

"You don't have to explain anything—"

"I'm sorry about what happened. I didn't want you to think—"

She put her hands up. "There's no need to say anything more."

Dale interrupted their exchange. "Finn, Megan. How are the festival stories coming? Can you give an update in our staff meeting?"

Finn wanted to hug Dale, relieved for his conversation with Megan to be over.

"Yes," he said in unison with her.

"I can do it." Megan avoided looking at Finn.

"Good. Finn, do you have time to cover the barbecue rib competition today? The locals always love to hear who won, and I thought—"

"I can cover it." Megan stepped in front of Finn.

"Finish your weekend stories first. Finn can take today's article."

Dale crossed to Finn. "The mayor is planning on being there. Ask him about the SCI relocation."

Finn could feel Megan's eyes burning into his skull.

"About SCI . . ." Megan placed herself between the two men. "I received a tip about that story this weekend. I need to confirm whether the information is correct. Perhaps I should approach the mayor today?"

"What's the tip?"

"I'd rather not say yet." Megan shifted. "Until I find out more, I can't confirm it's true. But if what I heard is accurate, this could be a major story."

If there was one thing about Megan, she understood how to get what she wanted out of people. Even Dale. It was time to step up his game. His success at the newspaper was counting on it.

"I was there when Megan received the tip." Finn moved next to her. "I could approach the mayor."

Megan glared at him. He was trying to get a piece of the action and claim one of the most important stories of the year. If her eyes held darts, he'd be a dead man.

Dale rubbed his chin. "Megan should go with you. She knows the situation and the people in this town. We'll talk more about it later."

Dale rushed off, leaving them alone.

Megan faced him, frowning. "What was that about?"

"What do you mean?" He tilted his head like he didn't know what she was referring to.

Megan lowered her voice so Cheri wouldn't hear. "You just tried to stop me from getting more information for the SCI story. Edna gave *me* that tip."

"Dale asked me to go. I thought I'd save you a trip."

She gave him a look. "You want the story, don't you?"

"I'll do whatever Dale says. You know the rules."

He could tell the words burned, but he needed to draw boundary lines in the office. If she figured out how he really felt, she could use it against him.

After lobbing callous words at her like a grenade, he was ready for a verbal battle. Instead, she shook her head with a look that nearly broke his resolve. He had rejected her, and now she despised him.

Her eyes narrowed, nailing him with the label he dreaded most: biggest jerk ever.

She turned on her heel, saying nothing more.

He could handle her words, but not her silence. For that, he'd never forgive himself.

CHAPTER FOURTEEN

FINN

The rich smell of slow-roasted barbecue meat permeated the air when Finn stepped out of his car. He slid on his sunglasses. The sky was a cloudless ink-stain blue with temperatures soaring to a sweltering ninety-five degrees. It was the end of the afternoon, and the festival was crowded with people watching the two-man tug-of-war and the barbecue competition.

The Ferris wheel spun in the air, haunting him with memories of the night before. The feel of her hand in his. How his lips had brushed hers. The intoxicating scent of her hair, soft in his palms.

She was like a drug. No matter how many ways he tried to blot her out, the memory of their kiss circled back again. He couldn't get enough.

His phone buzzed in his pocket, and his dad's name appeared on the screen.

"Hey, Pops. What's up?"

"How are things going?"

"Great. Busy working on articles." He snaked around a crowd lined up for slushies.

"Dale says you're an excellent addition to the team."

Finn wished his dad wouldn't meddle in his personal affairs. "That's good. But I can handle this on my own."

"I know. Dale mentioned there's another reporter you're working with. She hasn't been too keen on your arrival. Hope you can win her over."

He was working on it. "One way or another."

Finn strolled past a street performer with a guitar and then dodged two kids carrying balloon animals. "So, what's up? I'm on my way to cover a story."

"Dale brought up his retirement. He wouldn't give me a firm date, but mentioned it's coming. I told him you'd be perfect for the job."

"Thanks for the vote of confidence." Finn approached the barbecue competition, the smoke from the grills curling into the air.

His dad's voice lowered. "Just between you and me, Dale said it's going to come down between you and that girl."

Finn kicked a stone. He didn't need his dad's pressure, especially now. "Megan is good at what she does. She's been at the paper for a long time."

"Is there any way to one-up her? You know, prove to Dale that you're the right choice?"

"I will not play that game. I want her on my side if I move up at the paper."

He certainly hadn't done himself any favors this morning.

His dad's laugh felt like a slap. "That's wishful thinking. If you take the position, she'll never be on your side. That's the way business works."

A small bead of sweat trickled down the back of his neck as he stood at the edge of the barbecue competition. He scanned the crowd for Megan, suddenly wishing she was here.

Dad's voice filled the silence. "I know you won't mess this up."

"I'll try." Finn's shoulders tensed as he ended the call. He wanted to make his dad proud, but he also couldn't see a way to make both of them happy.

Finn stood back and watched the chefs turn their meat on the grill, the savory juices dripping off, while tongues of flame licked the grates.

This wasn't the first time his father had pressured him. When he'd competed on the high school swim team, Dad had stood on the edge of the pool, shaking his head when he didn't swim fast enough.

"You messed up," he'd tell Finn after losing a race.

Those words looped like a song on repeat.

It's your fault. You blew it, idiot.

When he'd lost a race by three-hundredths of a second, he hadn't even needed to look at his father. He had botched the race. *Failed.*

Never mind that he had gotten his best time ever in the one-hundred-meter freestyle. It was never good enough to please his father.

After Tyler's death six years ago, his dad's disappointment had snowballed into something more, a mixture of resentment and unrealistic expectations.

His dad had scoffed at his reasons for exiting the Coast Guard, calling him soft. "What kind of man quits because of panic?"

Finn shoved the reports into his dad's hands explaining his condition. "It's not like a onetime thing," Finn explained. "I have PTSD."

His father threw them aside. "Nobody had PTSD back in my day. We were tough. We pulled up our bootstraps and dealt with it. Didn't cave under pressure. We weren't quitters."

Like you.

He lived with those words every time he didn't meet his father's expectations. As the only son left, he had to make his dad proud.

The sizzle of barbecue snapped Finn back to reality.

He needed this job. Another shot to make his dad say, *I'm proud of you.*

Finn saw a young man snaking through the crowd, his sandy-brown hair strangely reminiscent of his brother's. If he squinted his eyes, he could imagine Tyler. To see his brother in the face of a stranger was disorienting, a reminder of what life would be like if Tyler had never died.

Finn moved away from the crowded festival, down a vacant sidewalk, away from the loud music and shrill laughter. He needed air. Distance from his brother's memory that dogged him everywhere.

As he turned a corner, he almost collided with a man in an old straw hat. His face was wrinkled like worn leather.

"I'm sorry. Didn't see you there." Finn took a step back, recognizing the man from the coffee shop. "Joshua?"

"In a hurry today?" Joshua wore old work boots and a pair of overalls. It was too hot for denim, but Joshua didn't seem to mind the heat.

"Needed to catch my breath," Finn said, noticing the grease stains on Joshua's hands.

"You haven't been by my shop yet." Joshua smiled.

Finn had totally forgotten the invitation. "I haven't finished setting up my apartment."

Joshua cocked his head. "If you need any odds and ends, you know where to find me. Megan could tell you."

Finn perked up. "I'm working with her. Supposed to teach her to sail too."

"Ah. Let me guess, she's not interested."

"Nope. Hey, you don't have any boat parts in that shop of yours, do you?"

"Don't fix up boats, but I love to fish. Got an old fishing boat I take out every morning in the summer. Maybe I'll see you at the dock one of these days?" He strode away, talking over his shoulder before he turned a corner and disappeared from view. "Or better yet, let's go together."

Finn didn't ask him where the shop was located or what his hours were. He only knew that Joshua didn't seem like anyone else in Wild Harbor, and he liked that.

As he made his way back to the barbecue competition, he spied the mayor, cornered by Megan and another man.

He cleared his throat as he approached.

Megan turned, hiding her frustration from earlier that day. "Oh, Finn. I wondered where you were. Thought you'd bailed on me." She was gorgeously dressed in a form-fitting summer dress with her hair curled into waves cascading around her shoulders. It was obvious she wanted to make an impression on the mayor. Little did she know, it was having an effect on him.

"Finn. Good to see you again." The mayor greeted him with a stiff smile. "This is my son, Harrison."

Harrison put his hand out to shake Finn's. "My friends call me Harry."

Harrison was dressed as if he had just stepped off the golf course. He wore an expensive blue polo and khakis, drenched with enough cologne to kill a cat.

"Megan was kind enough to give us an update on the sailing regatta and said the newspaper might be entering. I hear you're the lone sailor, unless there's still hope left for Ms. Woods." Harrison's eyes swept over Megan.

Finn bristled at the interchange. He didn't like the way Harrison looked at Megan, like she was a fresh piece of meat.

Finn moved closer to Megan, brushing her arm. "Yes, unless I can talk Megan into joining me."

Megan tagged along behind the mayor as he moved away to

mingle with other residents. She didn't want to lose her opportunity to talk with him alone.

"Let me give her a lesson." Harrison's eyes were dark.

Finn had met guys like Harrison before. The kind who enjoyed jokes about the boys' club.

"Wish you luck," Finn said flatly. "Megan's not easily convinced."

A man in an official festival T-shirt approached them, clipboard in hand. "You both look young and strong."

"Excuse me?" Finn's eyes dropped to the sheet on the clipboard.

"We had some folks drop out of the tug-of-war competition. It's one-on-one. You two want to compete?"

Megan returned and peeked over Finn's shoulder. "You should do it. We have some time before the judging begins here."

Harrison jutted his chin out. "I don't want to make Finn look bad, but I'm willing to try."

The festival official turned to Finn. "How about you?"

"I'm not really interested—"

Harrison slapped Finn on the back. "You're not scared of competing against me, are you?"

"I don't enjoy being a spectacle."

"This is a crowd favorite. A friendly competition." Harrison smiled, his white teeth gleaming.

Finn glanced at Megan, looking for support. She took a sip of her water bottle. "Do it for the newspaper."

Harrison moved a step closer to Megan. "You don't want to take me on, do you? Promise I'll play nice."

Megan almost snorted water out her nose. She coughed, covering her mouth. "Uh, no. Especially not in this dress."

Finn couldn't stand Harrison's behavior any longer. "I've reconsidered. I'll compete against you on one condition."

"What is that?"

"The winner gets to eat dinner with the lady."

Megan quickly turned toward Finn. "What?"

"Done." Harrison smiled. "See you at the tug-of-war."

Harrison sauntered away as Megan glared at Finn. "What was that all about? You're forcing me to go out with one of you clowns? What is this? Some kind of testosterone battle?"

"The guy needs to be taken down a few notches. He looks at you like you're his next catch."

"Harrison's always been like that. He's got a big ego and a lot of money. Don't take it personally." She leaned toward him. Even though the air was heavy with the smell of barbecue, he caught the scent of her perfume. Floral and sweet. Just like their kiss.

She lowered her voice, oblivious to the effect she was having on him. "Harrison's also the key to getting more info for the article. When I mentioned the SCI relocation to the mayor, he said he couldn't comment yet because it's just a fact-finding mission at this point. I was hoping to corner him, but it's nearly impossible here. I thought Harrison might divulge some juicy details." Her eyes brightened. "Wait a minute. I have an idea. What if you lost the tug-of-war contest?"

"And let that sleazeball hang out with you?"

"If I have to eat with him, then chances are, I'll have the opportunity to question him." He could tell she wanted him to agree. "It's just for an hour. Please?"

Everything in Finn wanted to say no. He wasn't even going to take part in the tug-of-war initially, but Harrison had poked the hornet's nest.

"Sorry. Can't do it. I'm not going to lose intentionally." Finn walked away.

She tagged along beside him. "You're not losing anything. You'd be giving me direct access to a private interview. It's just a stupid game, anyway."

"If it's just a stupid game, why did he seem so eager?"

"Harrison's always been the type who loves an audience. It gives the town a boost when any of the mayor's family shows up for an event. Just think about it, okay?" She placed her hand on his arm, weakening his resolve.

Why did he have to lose to make her happy?

"I'm not making any promises," he said.

She squealed and grabbed his arm, her smile hitting him like another shot of dopamine.

He said nothing in return. He wanted to please her, but he also wanted to keep Harrison away from her.

He'd backed himself in a corner. There was no way to have both.

CHAPTER FIFTEEN

FINN

The crowd was already gathered around the tug-of-war area when Finn arrived. Harrison was working the crowd, ever the showman, mingling with families just like his father. He couldn't throw away the competition because of Megan's request. Finn wanted nothing more than to wipe Harrison's sleazy smile from his face.

Finn wiped his hands on his pants while the announcer's voice came over the microphone with a crackle and pop of the loudspeaker.

"Our next competitor is Harrison Brinks and Finn—" The announcer stopped and whispered something to the man next to him.

The man with the clipboard rushed over. "We forgot to get your last name."

"Avery." This wasn't boding well for him.

The man with the clipboard wrote it down and hurried to the announcer.

Another festival volunteer approached with a rope and announced the rules.

"The red marker on the rope is the center line. We'll start with that mark above the line spray-painted on the ground. The white marks on either end of the rope determine the winner. Your white marker is on the opposite end of the rope, closest to your opponent. When you pull the white marker over the line marked on the ground, you win. You may not start until I blow the whistle. Understand, boys?"

Finn scanned the crowd looking for Megan, but she had disappeared before the event. She wouldn't ask him to lose and then miss the competition, would she?

"Here is the rope, gentlemen." The official handed Finn the rope. He wrapped his fingers around the rough exterior. This might be painful, but it would be worth it to see Harrison's look of defeat.

He anchored his feet on the ground and readied his body in position for the screech of the whistle.

Wheeeeee. The whistle pierced the air as Finn lunged into position.

He hadn't seen Harrison put on gloves before he began, but he instantly regretted that he didn't have a pair. The rope burned against his hands as he threw his weight into pulling it.

Harrison grimaced as he leaned back, digging his heels into the ground. Despite looking like a prep school boy, Harrison was remarkably strong under his polo. Finn wondered if he'd made a mistake competing against him.

Initially, Harrison gained some traction, causing Finn's marker to slip toward the line between them.

Finn leaned into his rope more and put his back and shoulders into it. Years of swimming had developed those muscles, and Harrison lost some ground as he took a step back.

Harrison shifted his legs to stop Finn's progress. For what

seemed like an eternity of straining, the two men were locked in battle. The rope didn't budge.

Being the new guy in town wasn't helping Finn's cheering squad. He thought he heard Edna's voice and a few of her friends who probably felt sorry for him.

As his hands burned and his legs ached, Finn strained at the rope, which moved a few inches in favor of his opponent. He had allowed Harrison's arrogant attitude to irritate him, and now he was paying the price.

His palms were on fire, and his back and arms hurt from exertion. The sweat on his forehead stung his eyes. He needed to wipe his brow, but if he let go for a second, he'd lose too much ground.

Both men pulled at the rope, their muscles taut, as Megan and her sisters made their way through the small crowd.

Finn focused on one thing: not losing ground to Harrison. The battle between them was an even match, locking them in a standstill. Whoever lost their focus first would forfeit the competition. But he also sensed Megan's plea to lose the match, so she'd have a shot at getting some answers.

Do this for her.

He released some pressure on the rope.

You don't have to beat Harrison.

He'd put up a fair fight. He could call it quits now and let his competitor win.

Finn let the rope slip and his body slid forward.

He was tired, and his muscles ached. If he lost now, no one would question it. Finn's rope moved closer to defeat.

Harrison pulled harder. "You're losing, paper boy."

Finn brushed off the taunt. He didn't have to prove himself to anybody, much less the mayor's son. As his marker slipped closer to a loss, Finn had a decision to make. He could pull harder, but he was doing this for Megan. A few steps more and Harrison would win.

"You're going to lose," Harrison taunted. Then he glanced over at Megan with a dark expression.

Finn clenched his jaw. His eyes flitted to Harrison's smug smile.

A surge of energy plowed through Finn's body as he pulled harder. It was an unexpected move that caused Harrison to slip and lose his footing. Finn took advantage of his stumble and yanked harder, pulling Harrison forward in a fumble as he sacrificed significant ground.

Finn moved his white marker toward the middle while Harrison scrambled to regain his footing. The dirt slipped under Harrison's feet as he struggled to find his position. Finn took advantage of his lead and yanked harder. Taking a deep breath, he focused all his strength on the rope.

Something in him wanted to prove a point. Show he wasn't willing to lose to Harrison. Finn lunged on the rope again. Harrison winced in pain as his leg twisted awkwardly.

"I think I just did something to my knee," Harrison choked out, but he refused to give up the match now. He was just as hungry for this win as Finn. Even an injury wouldn't make him give up.

The sweat on Finn's back trickled down his spine as the muscles bulged in his legs. He tried to ignore the screaming pain in his palms, but it was shooting up his arms now. He couldn't think about losing now, no matter what. His adrenaline surged as Harrison fought against crossing the line. Harrison's feet pedaled in the dirt, slipping beneath him. He tried to adjust his grip on the rope, but Finn took advantage of the brief second and charged backwards even harder, causing Harrison to fall one last time. He dropped the rope and Finn pulled the white marker across the line. The crowd erupted.

He had won. But as he looked over to see Megan's reaction, she had already slipped away.

Harrison lay on the ground, holding his knee.

"You put up a good fight," Finn said, standing over Harrison. "I'm sorry you lost."

But not that sorry.

Harrison pasted on a strained smile, his mouth twitching at the corner, as if the act was difficult. "If my knee hadn't twisted at the end, I would have been able to take you."

You wish. Finn offered him help standing. "Can I give you a hand?"

"Not yet. I'm getting some ice from the slushie cart for my knee."

Finn's eyes scanned the crowd again. No Megan. Was she mad at him for winning?

The festival official approached Finn and held up his microphone: "And now, I present to you our winner, Finn Avalon!"

"Avery." Finn corrected him. "My last name's Avery." Hadn't this guy heard him the first time?

"Oh." The man held up the megaphone again. "Sorry. The winner is Finn Avery!"

The crowd responded with a few lukewarm claps. Most people had already moved on to something else.

The official handed him a medal and shook his hand. "Too bad about Harrison's knee. An ambulance should arrive soon."

"An ambulance? Is that really needed?"

"Festival protocol for anyone who gets hurt during an event."

A few young women huddled around Harrison, offering sympathy. He didn't even seem in pain anymore.

Leave it to Harrison to milk this injury for all it's worth.

A stretcher was carried in by the volunteer EMTs, who loaded Harrison onto it.

"Don't worry!" he exclaimed as he was being carried out. "I'm okay. It's just protocol. I'll be good as new when I return." He waved to the crowd before being carried to the ambulance.

A few people frowned at Finn as he walked by as if he'd done it on purpose.

Remarkably, Harrison had turned his loss into a sympathy vote from the crowd. He was a politician in the making, if Finn ever saw one.

"Finn!" Cassidy waved Finn over to her family. "Great job today."

"Thanks. Did you see where Megan went? We're supposed to cover a story together."

Lily pointed to the barbecue area. "She was trying to catch the mayor before he left."

The competition. He'd almost forgotten. They'd started a few minutes ago. If he hurried, he could still make it.

"Sorry to run, but I'm supposed to be there."

Becky grabbed his sleeve. "Before you go, we're having some homemade ice cream tomorrow night at seven. We'd love for you to stop by. Alex and Matt are both coming."

"I'd love that. Truly."

Finn ran over to the barbecue area just in time to see a row of judges standing by a table, sampling a half dozen platters of meat. They moved around the table, each judge taking a bite and then filling out a paper on a clipboard.

He threaded through the mass of people to reach Megan's side. He touched her elbow, and she turned quickly, appearing as stunning as ever. "Finn, where have you been? The judging started ten minutes ago."

"In case you didn't notice, I got roped into a competition. No pun intended." He was trying to lighten her mood, but it was obvious she wasn't in the mood for jokes.

"Did you stay for the end?" He hoped she'd at least acknowledge his win.

"Yes," she said curtly.

"So you know . . ."

"You won." She tried to suppress a smile. "I can't believe you injured the mayor's son."

"It wasn't on purpose. He was the one who wanted to compete against me."

She lowered her voice to a whisper. "I asked you to lose."

"Against that jerk?"

"Shhh." Megan glanced around to see if anyone had heard him. "You need to be careful about what you say when it comes to the Brinks family. Seriously. Their family has a lot of influence, and I'm trying to help you."

"With what?"

She cocked her head. "Not getting on the wrong side of certain people."

"You think they'll hold a grudge because of a tug-of-war match?"

"I don't know what they'll do. I just don't want to see you get hurt."

Finn didn't know exactly what she meant, but he didn't care what Harrison Brinks thought of him. If the mayor had a problem with that, he could confront him personally.

"Did you have time to talk with the mayor yet?" he asked.

"No. I tried to catch him but couldn't. I have a feeling he's trying to avoid me. He knows I'm onto something."

"What are you going to do?"

"The usual." She turned to face Finn, her dark eyes sparkling. "Wear him down."

Finn shook his head. "You're incorrigible."

"It's called persistence."

"Does it work equally well on you?"

She smiled. "Don't even try."

"By the way, I met your mom. She invited me over tomorrow night."

Megan tucked her hair behind one ear, something he had wanted to do ever since he had his hands threaded through her hair during their kiss. "She's been bugging me about introducing you. Guess she took matters into her own hands."

"Like someone I know."

"At least I get it honestly." She smiled, then paused. "But if Matt asks what happened the other night during the thunderstorm, I'd appreciate him not knowing about . . ."

Her eyes were glued to the judges, avoiding eye contact.

"Your secret's safe with me."

"We can pretend it never happened if you like."

Finn studied her for a moment as she fixed her gaze on the fire.

He could play along at her little game. "I'm not even sure I remember what you're talking about."

Sure, he wouldn't bring it up again. But forget it? *Not a chance.*

CHAPTER SIXTEEN

MEGAN

"Why didn't you tell us about the new guy?" Lily cornered Megan as soon as she entered her parents' house.

"What's there to tell?"

Lily smirked, stacking red plastic bowls to carry to the deck. "You were hanging out with your new coworker on the Ferris wheel. Matt said you were positively glowing."

"More like ready to get sick." Megan evaded her sister's questions. It was like facing a panel of inquisitors.

"Why am I the last to know about this?" Cassidy grabbed spoons from the drawer.

Lily grabbed a few beach blankets, tossing one to each sister.

"There's nothing to say. He's my coworker. I can't think about him like that."

"Why not?" Cassidy grabbed a sweatshirt to throw over her sleeveless shirt. "Office relationships happen all the time."

"I don't need to give Cheri, or the rest of the office, anything more to gossip about. He's in the running for the editor-in-chief position. Dating your boss is not cool."

"You're not marrying him," Lily said, as they headed to the bonfire Matt and Alex had set up. "We're talking about one date here. You're overthinking this."

"I overthink everything. What's new?"

"Ever since the doctor gave you a diagnosis, you've avoided any man who glances at you twice."

"That's not true. I just have high standards." Megan lifted her chin.

Lily shook her head. "It doesn't mean you can't find someone and be happy together. And there are other options for growing your family."

"I know." Megan stopped on the beach. "But I also can't fall for someone who wants to have biological children. I can't take that dream from him."

Lily touched her sister's arm. "Did it ever occur to you that a man who loves you might take the risk? That he might love you whether or not that includes kids?"

Megan shook her head. "And dash his hopes? No, thank you."

"Meg." Lily tried to reach for her sister, but Megan was too fast. She walked away, fighting off tears. Lily didn't understand what it was like to feel broken.

Cassidy caught up to her. "You don't know that the diagnosis is one hundred percent accurate. The doctor could be wrong."

"It doesn't matter. It's not just the diagnosis. If he gets the editor-in-chief position, I may end up working for one of you." She unfolded the blanket, letting the wind whip it like a kite as it settled on the sand. "I can't work for him. We're too much alike. We'd be at each other's throats, second-guessing decisions and driving each other crazy."

"Driving who crazy?" Finn stood behind Megan, hands in his pockets, a smile playing on his lips.

How much had he heard? His face didn't reveal any secrets.

"Finn, when did you arrive?" Cassidy tossed him a blanket. She was apparently wondering the same thing.

"Just a minute ago. I came around the house when I smelled the campfire. Gorgeous place, by the way." His eyes scanned the two houses that Lily and her parents owned.

Lily beamed. "You can thank Alex and his team for that. This house used to be a dump. They did a double house renovation project for his home show."

Alex approached, carrying a few logs for the fire. "Did they mention I fell for Lily while fixing up her home?"

"I'd heard something about that," Finn said.

"That's why I'm here now. Left my life in LA to start over. Can't say I regret it. In fact, it's probably the best decision of my life." He gave Lily a kiss on her head before he dropped the logs on the fire.

"Probably?" Lily raised her eyebrows at Alex.

"Sorry. It was *definitely* the best decision."

"Uh, none of this romantic stuff here on the beach." Matt had just returned from taking a walk along the shore. He turned to Finn. "See what I have to put up with now?"

"You know they're going to give you grief when it's your turn."

"Matt doesn't have time to date . . . so he says," Megan added. "He's always at the fire station." She turned to her brother. "Just wait until you find the right girl."

"Don't worry, it won't happen. Eternal bachelor. Right here."

Becky called from the deck. "Anyone ready for ice cream?"

Matt, Alex, Cass, and Lily strolled toward the house as Finn waited for Megan. She wasn't in a hurry to go. Even though it was a warm July day, the wind had picked up, cooling down the beach. The bonfire smoked and crackled, its flames dancing in the breeze.

"You don't have to wait for me." Megan stuck her toes in the sand. "I love sitting out here. I'm jealous that Lily and my parents can watch the waves whenever they want."

"Do you want ice cream? I could bring you a bowl."

"I was hoping to talk with you tonight."

Finn sat down next to her. "About the date you owe me after winning the tug-of-war?"

"No." Megan ran her fingers over the sand. She still wasn't sure what to do about the date. Her heart was tangled in her emotions enough as it is. Being alone with him was too tempting. "Remember the sailing article Dale wants us to do? Today, Harrison offered to show me the ropes . . . and I told him yes."

"Oh." He squinted his eyes. "Can I ask why?"

"An opportunity to find out more about the SCI story. You know, connections."

"So you wouldn't sail with me, but you're willing to go with him because of a story?"

The way he said it made her feel like a criminal.

"You make it sound like I'm in it only for the scoop. It's my responsibility as a reporter." Couldn't he understand that seeking the truth trumped her personal feelings? She hoped to get to the bottom of the story. Why did Finn seem so defensive?

Finn stared at the water. "So, you're going to compete against the newspaper's sailing team? That'll go over well."

"Your boat is not the newspaper's team. It's only *you*."

"Because you abandoned the team."

"There is no team. I'm not doing the regatta. This is a lesson. Nothing more."

"Not a date?"

"Of course not."

"I guarantee the guy's goal is to get you on his team. And I'm not just talking about sailing. Either way, it would be convenient for the mayor's family to have a connection at the newspaper."

"People's intentions don't always have an underlying motivation."

He shook his head like she'd learned nothing. "Unless they're in politics."

"Just let it go."

He walked away from her as she scrambled to follow him.

"I'm not sure what the big deal is." She didn't want to argue with him. "I don't want to compete in the regatta. I don't even want to ride on Harrison's boat. But regardless of how you feel—"

He turned to her. "Then don't let me stop you. You want to hang out with the jerk? Be my guest."

Megan could see the muscle in his jaw clenching as he turned to go.

"Oh, and by the way," he stopped. "You don't owe me a date for winning."

He strode away, bypassing the house and heading toward his car.

Megan slowly released the breath she had been holding. Maybe there was a part of her that was trying to get back at him since he hadn't lost the competition. If he had, she wouldn't have to find another way to talk with Harrison. No matter what Finn thought about her motivations, she needed to uncover the truth behind the SCI story.

Megan rushed after Finn. "Hey, don't leave just yet." She wanted to explain, to keep him from leaving mad.

"I need to finish an article. Please give your family my apologies." He didn't stop walking to even look at her.

"Which article are you working on?" she asked breathlessly.

"You should know. Don't you have a personal connection with the mayor's son?" It was a jab. An unfair one.

"Don't tell me Dale assigned you to cover his injury at the tug-of-war?"

"Everybody wants to know what happened."

"You shouldn't have to take that story. Let Larry cover it."

"Larry wasn't there."

"Then I'll do it," she offered.

He shook his head. "I'll take care of it. If I need a quote, I know who to call, since you're hanging out with him."

"That's not even fair. You're making this a way bigger deal than it is. He asked me for a boat ride. So what? The mayor took you on one."

"That was totally different."

"How?"

"First, I'm not a beautiful woman."

"You think I'm . . ." Megan's face grew warm.

"Yes, I do. And I'd like to be with you. But apparently, the feeling isn't mutual. Every time I try to get close to you, you push me away. I don't understand. If you want Harrison, that's fine. But stop making me feel like I have a chance with you."

"I don't want Harrison." She shook her head. "Not like that."

He opened his car door and climbed in. "You could've fooled me."

FOR THE NEXT few days at work, they both avoided talking about Harrison. Their interactions were cordial, but she hated the unspoken tension whenever the mayor's name came up.

Finn was brushing her off. Pushing her away. She tried to fill the awkward silence with article discussions and failed attempts at humor.

Every night that week when he left at five, she watched him walk down the street, away from the direction where he lived. She wanted to know if he was making evening treks to his boat, but she always stopped herself from following him. It wasn't her business to know how he spent his free time or whether he was meeting someone.

She should stay away.

But her heart? That was complicated.

Her emotions were the one thing she couldn't control with logic. She knew better than to let her heart get tangled up in Finn Avery. But it was too late. She had already fallen.

No matter how hard she tried to convince herself that Finn didn't affect her, his kiss had shaken her. It's like she'd taken a drink of Finn Avery's affection, and now she wanted a fire hose.

As she finished work, a knock at her door made her jolt.

"Come in," she said, without looking up. Her fingers pounded out the last sentence in an email.

"Do you ever stop working?" Harrison stepped into her office. "You know what they say about all work and no play?"

"I didn't realize it was you." She pushed her chair back and scanned her office, which was littered with papers, old coffee cups, and her signature unicorn file folders. She grabbed a few folders scattered across her desk and slid them into a desk drawer. "If I had known you were coming, I would have cleaned up." Organization wasn't her strong suit, but she could hide things like a pro.

"Please don't clean up for me." He picked up a file folder and smirked at the tiny, glittery unicorns. "Interesting."

"You can borrow one if you like."

"How generous, but I'll have to pass." He handed back her folder. "I stopped by on a whim to see if you were available tonight."

"Oh?" Papers slipped off her desk as she tried to catch them. It was too late to clean up, and he'd already seen her mess.

"It's a beautiful evening on the water. I thought I'd go out for a boat ride, if you're game."

Megan's stomach lurched. "Tonight? Wow, I don't know. I have so much work."

How long could she put him off? She had already promised him one ride.

"It would give us a chance to talk." Harrison gave his *I'm a handsome stud* smile.

Megan wasn't blind. Harrison checked all the boxes. Sandy-blond waves. Blue eyes. Tanned skin. A ridiculous amount of money. Too bad he did nothing for her. Not one fluttery feeling. Still, the chance to get information for her article was enough of a lure.

"Only if you'll answer my questions." She lifted her eyebrows.

"Sure. I'll even treat you to dinner on the boat. What's your favorite restaurant?"

Just then, Finn walked in the door, his head buried in a paper he was reading. "Hey, Megan, did you see . . ." His expression changed as soon as he saw Harrison. "Oh, sorry. I didn't realize someone was in your office." He took a step backward, eyeing Harrison.

"Oh, no. Come on in." Harrison waved Finn in like they were best buddies, even though the tension in the room had ratcheted up. "I was trying to convince Meg to join me for a boat ride. Any advice on how to persuade her?"

Finn's jaw clenched. He forced a tight smile. "I don't know. Why don't you let *Meg* here decide?"

He'd intentionally emphasized *Meg*. The name reserved only for those closest to her. Finn couldn't hide his irritation.

"That's a good point." Megan decided, finally settling the matter. "I'll go." She shut her laptop with a neat snap and popped it into her bag. "I'm ready when you are."

She needed to get answers for the SCI article before it was too late. She glanced at Finn. His expression looked nuclear.

A smile spread across Harrison's face. "Well, that was easy. Let me pick up some food and meet you at the marina." Harrison turned and looked at Finn. "I thought this would be difficult. Turns out, I was wrong." He brushed by Finn before turning back to Megan at the door. "Is twenty minutes okay?"

"I can do twenty minutes." She sounded like someone in a job interview, eager to prove herself. Perfectly submissive. Everything she had never been. She didn't really like this version of herself, but with every passing second, she couldn't wait for Harrison to leave.

"Well, then. See you over there." Harrison gave a wave before leaving her and Finn alone.

A spark of tension hovered in the room. Finn's eyes narrowed, then he smiled and shook his head. Based on the way the muscle in his jaw kept clenching, he was not pleased with her decision.

She cleared her throat. "Sorry to keep you waiting." Her voice sounded unusually saccharine. *Sorry to keep you waiting?* She didn't know what else to say.

"Funny how you suddenly don't seem to mind boating when he asks you to go."

"I'm not looking forward to this, if that's what you mean."

"You put on quite the act for Harrison Brinks." The way he said it felt like a stab in the gut. She had always promised herself she wouldn't compromise her values as a journalist. His accusation stung because there was a sliver of truth in it.

"Who said I was pretending?" She stood and circled her desk. If she was going to defend herself, she needed to be on equal territory with him.

She closed the gap between them, her heart beating faster, the musky scent of his skin snapping her back to their last kiss.

He laughed. "I've never seen you act like that, so don't even pretend that was real."

She lifted her chin to look at him. "Are you jealous?"

It was time he got a taste of his own medicine.

A hint of fire flashed in his eyes. "No, of course not."

She didn't believe him.

He inched closer and her breath quickened. His body was less than a foot from hers, moving in on her with every second.

Why did he have this dizzying effect on her? The same reason his kiss had made every nerve tingle in her body.

"Don't go." His voice was low, almost demanding.

"Give me one good reason not to."

His eyes locked on hers as he opened his mouth, then closed it.

Just say it. Say anything. Talk her out of going. She wanted him to.

Instead, he only stared at her, his green eyes turned to jade stone.

She stepped away from him and swallowed. She needed to regain control. "Then I guess this conversation is over. How I spend my time really isn't your business, anyway."

"You're right. It's none of my business." He threw his hands in the air in surrender as he backed out of the room. His face walled up, his jade eyes cold. "It's your life, *Meg.*"

The way he said her name twisted her heart. She hated that he could destroy her with a word.

Finn didn't look back as he grabbed his bag and exited the office.

If her goal was to drive him away, she had succeeded. She didn't care what Finn Avery thought about her.

She wanted to believe it. But if it was true, why did it hurt so badly to watch him leave?

CHAPTER SEVENTEEN

FINN

Finn sped down the road, ready to escape to the water. He had clashed before with Megan, but today was different. His fingers clenched the wheel as his nails bit into his palms. When he'd seen her with Harrison, all his insecurities had bubbled to the surface, turning to hot anger. It was the same feeling when his father compared him to Tyler. He could never measure up.

As he drove to the marina, an old building caught his eye. Propelled by an unknown force, he swerved into the gravel lot at the last second. The metal salvage sign glinted in the sun.

He knocked at the door, then waited. A hawk turned lazy circles in the sky. The door creaked open, and a weathered face peeked out.

Joshua's eyes widened. "Finn. Hello, son. Come in."

The salvage shop smelled like a mixture of old wood and musty antiques, faded library books and forgotten memories tucked away in attics. The ash of yesterday permeated the air.

"What can I help you with?" Joshua led him back to a workshop where he was refinishing a table. "People rarely stop unless they want to poke around in the shop." Joshua rested on a stool, his eyes sparkling.

"I saw the shop on my way to the marina. I've got time to burn." Finn stood in the awkward silence. "Truthfully, I don't even know what I'm doing here. I should refinish the wood on my boat. Needs a fresh coat of varnish."

"I've refinished more than enough pieces around here. Slow process." He continued sanding the wood table, back and forth, in a clockwork fashion. "You're welcome to look around while you're here." Joshua nodded toward the shelves, packed with remnants of old homes.

As Finn explored, he passed piles of windows and doors stacked like cards, old mirrors and faded paintings that had once adorned the walls of grand homes.

In the back, a movement caught Finn's eye. Tucked into a corner where the light didn't reach, a shadowy figure in a yellowed mirror snapped into focus before fading from view. Finn couldn't see details, only the outline of a face without definition. But the silhouette, even in the dark, seemed familiar, a vague memory that surfaced somewhere in his brain—but where? He stepped back, although he didn't know why, and turned to go. He picked up speed as he found his way to the front of the shop.

"What's the rush?" Joshua peered over his glasses as he rubbed a cloth on the table.

"I need to leave." He opened the door, ready to flee, then turned back to Joshua. "Who is in back? He looked familiar to me."

Joshua shook his head. "No one, son. You're the only person who's been in here since yesterday."

HE NEEDED to get to the dock and clear his head. It's possible Joshua was a senile old man who'd forgotten about the visitor in the shop. Or . . . Finn didn't want to go there. The second option meant something he wasn't ready to face again.

He still had enough daylight to work for an hour on his boat before the light would die and he'd head back to his empty apartment.

He grabbed his tools and earbuds and headed toward Bertha, ready to drown his problems with loud music and elbow grease.

He lowered himself to his hands and knees and chipped at the old, cracked varnish. *Scrape, scrape, scrape.*

As he slid the tool across the deck, peeling the varnish like a second skin, he turned to see Megan and Harrison strolling along the dock.

His timing was abysmal. He buried his face and turned up his music, hoping they wouldn't stop.

"Well, well, look who we have here," Harrison bellowed. "If it isn't the tug-of-war champ."

Finn pulled out his earbuds and glanced at Harrison's knee wrapped in a brace. He hadn't noticed him wearing any brace before. "How's the knee?"

"The pain still comes and goes. If I need further treatment, I'll send you the surgeon's bill." Harrison laughed.

Finn bent down to scrape. Hopefully, they would get the hint and leave.

"We're taking the speedboat out tonight." Harrison dangled the idea in front of Finn. "You want to come?" Everyone in town knew about the Brinks family's racing boat. Harrison liked to show it off on weekends, zipping across the lake, a rooster tail of spray behind him.

"Nope." Finn stepped on Harrison's invitation. "But thanks." He wasn't sure why Harrison was inviting him, but the last thing he wanted was to be a third wheel. Finn's eyes flicked to

Megan, who stood quietly behind Harrison. "How do you feel about that, Megan?"

"He's trying to convince me it's the smoothest ride on the lake." Megan gripped the bag she was holding, her knuckles white.

"And fastest." Harrison smiled. "It makes a sailboat look like a rowboat. Excuse us. We're going to head out while it's still light."

Harrison walked ahead of Megan as she slowly turned to go. Finn kept his eyes glued to the floor as he ran his fingers over the peeling varnish.

Finn grabbed his headphones and turned up his music to drown out the gurgling motor of Harrison's speedboat. He had a job to do. That's all he cared about now.

An hour later, the low rumble of a motor approached as Finn cleaned up his tools, satisfied with the small section of deck he'd scraped clean. Although he'd barely made a dent in the stripping process, the scraping and sanding had worked off his frustration.

As soon as Harrison pulled his boat into the slip, Megan hopped out and darted down the dock.

Megan's voice echoed in the distance. "Good night, Harrison."

"Wait, you're leaving so soon?" Harrison's voice bellowed across the water. "You're not still mad at me, are you? I was just fooling around."

Finn didn't want to hear this conversation. He didn't want to care about Megan's white-knuckled fear or the reason she was bolting from Harrison now.

Let it go. But somehow, he couldn't.

As she rushed past his boat, her eyes flicked over to him and then angled away. Her face was drained of color.

"Everything all right?" He wiped his hands on a towel.

She passed him, then her body froze. "He was playing

around. Stupid jerk."

I told you so would have felt so satisfying, but he held back. She was as rattled as a spooked horse.

"What do you mean?"

"Trying to scare me on purpose. He thought it was funny that I was afraid. He didn't even care—" She narrowed her eyes at Finn. "Don't even say *I told you so* unless you want to get hurt."

Could she read his thoughts that easily?

He picked up his scraper and wiped it with the towel. "I know better than to rub it in."

Harrison finally reached Megan and caught her arm. "You weren't scared of a boat ride, right? I've never lost anyone yet." He attempted a forced smile that looked like he'd just had a dental procedure.

"I told you I wasn't comfortable." Megan glared at him and pulled her arm from Harrison's grip. "Stop touching me."

Harrison's cheeks flushed red. Clearly, he wasn't used to women refusing him.

"Can't you take a joke?" he retorted. "Or are you always this dull?"

Finn stepped onto the dock, fists clenched, no longer able to hold back. "Can't you listen to what she said? She asked you to stop. Apparently you need your hearing checked." He didn't want Harrison to touch her again.

Megan put out her hand to stop Finn. "I can handle this. I don't need your help."

Harrison smirked. "Now who needs their hearing checked?"

Finn gritted his teeth. He wanted to wipe Harrison's smug smile right off his face. This guy irritated him to his core.

Harrison gripped Megan's arm again. "Come on back, beautiful. We'll go one more round on the lake. I'll be nicer this time. Promise."

"I said let go. And don't call me that."

Finn's hands rolled into fists. *Don't get involved.*

But when he glanced back and saw Harrison trying to pull Megan toward his boat, something in him snapped.

He whipped around, a tiny spark of emotion fanned into flame. "Let her go now."

Harrison dropped her arm. "What are you going to do about it?"

Finn stared down Harrison as he moved into his personal space.

"Is that a threat?" Finn stepped closer, their faces inches away.

"Finn, stop," Megan pleaded.

"Yeah, it is," Harrison spat in Finn's face. "Because if we get on the boat, then she'll listen."

"Not if I can help it." Something broke in Finn. He grabbed Harrison by his polo shirt and pushed him backwards. He hadn't meant to shove so hard, but Harrison stumbled and then landed on his hip. The fall knocked his designer prescription sunglasses off his face. They bounced on the dock once and plunged into the lake. He reached for them, but it was too late.

Harrison blinked like someone had struck him. "Do you know how much those cost?" he said through gritted teeth. "You're going to pay for this." Harrison squinted his eyes. Without them, he was like a blind man. He crawled on his hands and knees, peering into the water. No way he'd find them in the murky lake.

"Why did you do that?" Megan pulled Finn over to the side. Angry lines formed between her eyebrows.

"Because he deserves it. The way he treated you was uncalled for."

"I can take care of myself." She leaned forward, whispering in his ear as Harrison wandered to his boat to find another pair of glasses. "The Brinks family doesn't forget a wrong. You'd better go."

"I'm not leaving you here alone."

"Go, Finn. It's not good for you to stay."

"I'm not going without you," Finn whispered. "I don't trust this guy." Finn grabbed Megan's hand and held her gaze. "You deserve better."

Her eyes flitted from Harrison to him. The conflict washed over her face.

"If I leave with you, he won't trust me."

"Promise me you won't go with him."

She paused. "I promise I won't. But I can't go with you, either."

He had already lost this argument, but he didn't want to let go of her hand.

"Meg—"

"Go," she whispered, "for me." She looked into his eyes, then gave him a quick kiss on his cheek. The brush of her lips warmed his body.

Still reeling from her touch, Finn ran his hand through his hair, frustrated she would ask him to leave now.

Harrison finally returned, looking like an angry animal. His message was clear. *Get lost.*

Finn didn't want to go, but the way her eyes pleaded left him with no choice. He'd made his first enemy in Wild Harbor.

CHAPTER EIGHTEEN

FINN

Finn spent the night fighting sleep until early morning, his mind stuck on ugly memories. When he finally drifted off, his dreams turned dark, triggering ghosts in his past.

It was time to call his therapist again.

The first time this happened, he had been in the Coast Guard, working a tragic accident on the lake involving a drunken boat driver. Finn had been the rescue swimmer who'd discovered the victim's body. With greying hair and a full beard, the man had been thrown from the boat when he'd crashed into another craft.

From that point on, Finn's grief collided with tragedy, tripping something in his brain. The doctor called it PTSD. Finn called it a nightmare that wouldn't end.

He'd endured countless dreams about pulling drowning victims out of the water since then, but every time, the face of the man changed. Last night, it had been Harrison. It was only when he woke with a start that he realized his twisted memories were playing out with new faces, each one as gruesome as the last.

That was the strange thing about trauma. It wasn't a onetime journey, but more like learning to survive the crash of waves when he was swimming. Every time he thought he'd made it through, another wave pummeled him in the dark. It was the incessant force of each unexpected crash that made grief so hard to deal with. Every blow knocked him down again.

The morning alarm blared a high-pitched beep that woke Finn with a start. He rolled over like a dead weight and pressed snooze. The day bore down muggy, making his head swim.

He sat up, rubbing his forehead, and noticed a message on his phone from Megan. He'd turned off his ringer, exhausted from last night's ordeal.

Megan: I have news.

It was a one-sentence statement that told Finn everything he needed to know. She had snagged prized information from Harrison.

The news left him deflated. She didn't need his help after all. He had risked his neck for her. Couldn't she at least recognize his sacrifice?

He pulled on a shirt and willed himself to forget last night, to wipe away the kiss she had brushed across his cheek.

It was a distraction. Nothing else. She knew the quickest way to twist his arm.

Finn finished dressing and washed his face in the sink. His feelings for her left him only one option: He needed to put up some shields. Find new people to hang out with. Maybe even get some furniture for his apartment.

But that's not what he desired. He wanted *her*.

His phone buzzed with a message from Matt about meeting at the French Press at seven.

Finn grabbed his bike helmet. *Perfect timing.*

"The Brothers" were Matt's small group of friends. It would be the perfect distraction to take his mind off last night's debacle.

As Finn entered the café, a group of guys gathered in a private back room where a sliding barn door could be closed for privacy.

Few people were up this early, giving their group the needed space and privacy for their meeting.

"Welcome, Finn." Matt slapped him on the back. "Meet the brothers. You know Alex and Max already." He pointed to two other guys. "Cam is a high school buddy, and Noah is the other barista here."

"Thanks for letting the new guy come. This isn't like joining a fraternity, right? I'm not going through some initiation ritual?"

"Nope. Not at all." Cameron leaned back in his chair. "The only rule is that what happens in the Brothers' circle, stays in the Brothers' circle. We don't share what we talk about with anyone."

Finn nodded. "Makes sense."

Matt sat down. "Everyone has a chance to share what's going on in their lives. We don't keep secrets, because it hurts the integrity of the group and erodes trust between brothers."

Finn shifted in his seat as he grabbed the coffee carafe on the table and poured a cup for himself.

Alex pushed the creamer toward Finn. "I used to be the new guy in town before you showed up. Let me warn you, these guys won't let you keep things private. They nail you to the wall with hard questions."

How in the world was he going to talk about Megan with her brother sitting next to him? He knew the answer: avoid the topic. Finn shifted uncomfortably in his seat, second-guessing his decision to attend.

"Who wants to start?" Matt said.

Max brought another carafe of coffee to the table with a pile of scones on a tray. "Okay, guys," Max said. "Breakfast of champions is served."

Max placed the food in the center of the table and sat down on a chair next to Matt. "What do we have on the agenda today?"

Alex grabbed a scone. "I'll go. I wanted to share some big news." He hesitated and rubbed his hands together. "I finally bought Lily a ring."

Matt lit up with surprise. "What? Congrats, man."

"That's awesome," Cam added.

"Please don't say a word. Especially you, Matt." Alex raised his eyebrows to show he meant business.

"Your secret is safe with me." Matt held up his hand, pledging to keep the secret. "One of my brothers is going to become my brother-in-law. That's amazing. So, what do you have planned for the big day?"

"Can't tell you yet. I'm still figuring out the details, but it will involve the beach."

"Did she pick out the ring?" Cam asked.

"No, I wanted her to be surprised. Is that bad? It's an antique diamond from Joshua."

"Not at all," Matt said. "You've always been good at surprising Lily with something that's perfect for her."

Cam took a bite of scone. "So, when are you going to pop the question?"

"You know Lily. She doesn't want a big, staged proposal. Something quiet and more intimate. The worst part is keeping my nerves in check."

"You're nervous after being on TV?" Noah asked.

"It makes me sweat to think about it." Alex brushed his forehead.

Matt took a swig of coffee. "She'll say yes. I'd bet money on it. And we'll be the first to celebrate with you."

"This calls for another round of scones and coffee. Let me refill our cups." Max and Noah dashed to the kitchen while the guys discussed their week at work.

Matt turned to Finn. "How's the job at the paper going?"

"It's been busy. Dale loaded me with assignments from day one."

"What do you think of working with Megan?" Matt's voice was casual, but there was an undercurrent of something else underneath.

Finn felt his lip twitch as he paused. He wasn't about to give anything away. "She's talented. I have a lot of respect for her."

Matt squinted, like he was trying to decipher a code. "Is there something I should know about you two?"

The other guys laughed. Finn's mouth went dry. This guy didn't mess around.

Cam leaned forward. "Matt's just being an overprotective big brother."

Max refilled their cups. "Why don't you take it easy on the new guy?"

Matt doused his coffee with cream. "I just got this vibe from you at the festival. Nice stunt, by the way."

"What do you mean?" Finn could feel the perspiration forming under his collar.

"Making her go on a Ferris wheel ride with you."

Were his feelings that obvious? "To be honest, I can't figure her out. One second she acts like she can't stand me, and the next, she's a totally different person. Her mixed signals are confusing."

Matt laughed. "Sounds like my sister. Listen, if she acts like she can't stand you, she probably feels the opposite. It's a protective instinct. The only question is, how do you feel about her?"

Finn shifted. Matt had him cornered. "I like her. More than I should. You have any advice?"

Matt crossed his ankles. He didn't seem surprised. "Don't force it. She'll let you know whether you pass the test."

"Good morning, Finn." A familiar voice barked his name, peeking through the door. "I thought I heard your voice."

Dale stood in the doorway, his usual large coffee in one hand. He waved Finn over.

"Excuse me for a minute." Finn left and joined his boss outside the room.

Dale picked up a sugar packet and tore it open. "I was thinking about something this morning, but wanted to talk to you in private, away from the office. Do you have a minute?"

"Sure." Finn turned to see his friends immersed in a discussion. He wouldn't be missed. He closed the door and sat down at a small table with Dale.

"How do you think things are going at the paper?"

"Is there something wrong with my articles?" Finn had the sense Dale was about to drop a bomb.

"No, no. The articles you've sent me are top-notch. So much better than Larry's—not that I would tell him that—but I'm glad he made a career change. Makes my job easier. Both you and Megan are my top writers on staff. Your writing is sharp, concise, and clean. Every editor's dream."

"That's a relief. I thought there was something wrong, and you were trying to let me down easy."

"Oh, no. I see potential. But I wanted to get a feel for how your adjustment is going."

Finn ran his finger around the top of his coffee cup. "For the most part, good."

"What's the other part?"

Finn didn't want to admit his feelings for Megan.

"Is it Megan?" Dale stirred his coffee. "I sense you two aren't getting along. Your new office in the hallway was the first warning sign."

Dale had it half right. Megan was the problem, but not in the way that he thought. "Got any advice for the new guy?"

"I've let Megan do things her way since she started, and she's never given me any trouble. She's a hard worker and loyal. But with you, I'm not sure. That's why I wanted to talk to you." Dale glanced over his shoulder before leaning toward Finn. "I'm thinking about retirement. Personally, I'm not ready yet. But in order to transition out of the paper smoothly, I need to set up my successor. That means helping my staff accept that person as second-in-command, so when I phase out, it's smooth sailing."

Dale was letting him down easy. He had hoped by the time his boss was ready to exit, he'd be more established in Wild Harbor. Maybe even ready for a promotion.

"You want me to accept whoever takes over the editor-in-chief position? Is that what you're asking?"

Dale cleared his throat. "Not exactly." He paused. "I want you to become the new editor-in-chief."

Finn set down his coffee cup. "Excuse me?" Anticipation stirred in his stomach.

"I believe you have the potential to be a great editor. How do you feel about taking over this role?"

"Um, I'm speechless. I can't believe you'd consider me since I'm so new. But I'm not sure how the staff would take it."

"The staff . . . or Megan?"

"Both, but especially Megan. Her heart is set on it."

"Has she told you so?"

"Not in so many words. But she's a talented journalist and has worked here since college. Few people would commit years to their hometown paper unless they have a bigger goal in mind."

"I agree, but Megan wants to be near family." Dale took a swig of coffee, like he needed to be convinced.

"Yes, but she's also crazy talented. She could write novels or work remotely as a journalist for bigger outlets. She's dedicated to covering a small town. That speaks volumes about her loyalty."

Finn wasn't sure why he was giving Megan so much praise after they had clashed so strongly in the beginning. But his feelings had softened toward her, rounding out the prickly edges that had stirred their conflict early on.

"Sounds like you want her to be the editor-in-chief!" Dale laughed. "You're basically giving me all the reasons I should hire Megan and not you."

Finn took a sip of coffee. "I'm flattered. I really am. But she's a better fit."

"Finn, don't discount yourself. The paper is in financial trouble, and you're the guy to help us out. Why do you think I brought you on in the first place?"

"I didn't mean it that way. I'm humbled you're considering me for the promotion. But you should think about this decision. If you decide I'm worthy of the position, I'd like to request one thing. Speak to Megan privately first. Don't announce it in a big staff meeting. Tell her before you share the news with anyone else. That's my only request."

Dale nodded. "That's wise. I don't want her to quit, either. Although that would be your problem, not mine." He gave Finn a slap on the shoulder and chuckled. "I'm glad you're interested in the position. Just between you and me, I think you're the right one for the job. But until I decide, let's keep this conversation a secret. No letting the cat out of the bag early. Got it?"

"Yeah." Finn forced a small smile. "I'll keep it on the QT." He already felt like he had betrayed Megan's trust by hiding Dale's intentions. He swallowed hard. If it was good news, why was he not happier about it?

Finn already knew the answer: He understood what this would cost him. No matter how the news was presented, he doubted Megan would accept it easily. Not getting the job would crush her. But Dale's mind seemed made up, and there was nothing he could do about it.

≈

FINN BALANCED his laptop on his knees in the hallway as Megan poked her head out her door. "You busy?"

He stopped typing. "Are we ever *not* busy?"

"Nope. Need a break?"

"What's up?"

"News." She motioned for Finn to come in.

Finn had waited all morning to hear the news about Harrison, but Megan hadn't ventured out of her office once. It was a relief, actually. His conversation about the editor-in-chief position brewed like a storm in the distance. The more he tried to avoid thinking about it, the more it plagued him. How long until she knew about Dale's decision?

She shut the door behind them, a sign that she didn't want anyone interrupting their conversation.

"I'm assuming your evening with Harrison didn't go as badly as mine."

"He called me after I went home. I patched up things between us by making you seem like a jerk." She sat on top of her desk. "Hope you don't mind taking one for the team."

Finn shrugged. "Smart. Did he fall for it?"

She nodded. "I'd steer clear of him for a while. He's got a lot of money and power in the community, and he's not afraid to use it to his advantage."

He could already see how this was going to be a problem if he took over Dale's job. "What did he tell you?"

"Confirmed what I knew." Megan smiled, a look of triumph on her face. She pulled up the notes on her phone. "It's true his father received a large payment from SCI. Mayor Brinks

accepted the substantial gift in return for getting their relocation green-lighted. He even voiced support in a town council
meeting, citing the financial impact on the community. He told
the town council that luring them to move here is too good of
an opportunity to pass up."

"Wait a minute. How does Harrison know all this?"

"He helps to manage his dad's money and noticed a large
deposit from SCI."

"How much did he get?"

"Harrison didn't say, but he hinted it was a significant
amount."

"So, now what?"

Megan hopped off the desk and circled around to her
computer. "I've been working on the article all morning." She
flipped her monitor so he could see the words on her document.
The Truth about SCI.

"It's not done, but I think I need the green light from Dale
before I proceed. The fallout from this is not going to be pretty."

Finn squinted, reading the article. "Do you have enough
evidence? You need to find someone else who can corroborate
it."

"I've been trying to get additional evidence all morning.
People either know nothing or won't say. One more witness
would make it more credible."

"Does anyone in the office know about this story yet?"

"You mean other than you?" She shook her head. "I've intentionally waited to tell Dale until I can get some additional proof.
He's pretty chummy with Steve. If I get one more witness, his
journalistic values will win out. It's a matter of legitimate public
concern."

"Does Dale want to deal with a bribery scandal that will put
him on the wrong side of the mayor?"

She shrugged. "I wish I knew. I'm really putting my job on
the line with this article. Not to mention setting up my family

for some blowback." She furrowed her brow. "I just don't want people to blame them for something I did. I take full responsibility for the fallout."

"Just be careful, okay? Don't present it to Dale until I've looked it over."

A knock sounded on the door. Megan hurried to close the window on her computer. "Come in." She sat down at her desk, looking unruffled.

Dale opened the door and glanced from Megan to Finn. "Perfect. I need to talk to you both. Got word that the Bellevue Masquerade Party is happening this year after a five-year hiatus. The Bellevues are using the event to raise money for a charity. The perfect feel-good story. I'm going to have you two cover it."

"Why don't you have Finn cover it? He's proved himself in the last few weeks and doesn't need me looking over his shoulder."

So Megan didn't want to attend with him. Her rejection stung.

"Why not together?" Dale shifted his attention to Finn. "We need two reporters on the ground covering the masquerade's history and why the Bellevues are resurrecting it. Our photographer is out of town that weekend, so I'll need you to take pictures. Megan, you'll need to cover the interview with the host and hostess. We've never had so many new readers taking an interest in our stories or advertisers wanting to buy ads. Do you know what that means? We're on the cusp of turning things around. The summer festival article hit a record for the paper. After summer, we can assign individual stories, but until then, I need you working as a team."

Cheri peeked her head in and pointed at Dale. "You have a phone call. Line one."

"Excuse me." Dale bolted toward the door, stopping before he exited. "I'm done with this conversation. Work it out or else."

Megan slumped in her chair.

Finn leaned forward. "I'm sorry if he's putting you in an awkward position."

"No. I'm fine." A hint of reluctance settled across her shoulders. It was obvious she didn't want to be coupled with him at the party.

"How about this?" Finn paused. "Can I make it up to you? Buy you lunch? Agree to write your next five articles? Grovel at your feet?" Anything to lighten her mood.

Megan laughed. "Hmm, I could think of some kind of repayment. Plus, I owe you a date. But groveling isn't necessary. How about Chinese? I've been craving it all week."

"Sounds great, but only if you agree to one thing. You won't eat it here. We'll go out and sit at the park by the channel."

She rested her chin on her hand and gave him a smile that made his knees weak. "You drive a hard bargain, Mr. Avery. But I suppose I can agree to it." Why did she always have this effect on him?

His thoughts already raced ahead to lunch. For once, he'd have her to himself.

CHAPTER NINETEEN

MEGAN

A muffled knock startled Megan into the present. Finn stuck his head in. "The food is hot. Do you want to walk there?"

"Is it noon already?" She checked her cell phone. 12:30 p.m. "I've been absorbed in these stories and lost track of time." She closed her laptop and hopped out of her chair. "I'll meet you downstairs just so it doesn't look like—" She abruptly stopped, glancing at him.

"Like we're going somewhere together?" He smirked. "Got it. See you there."

Megan pulled out a desk drawer to find her mirror. She looked at the compact, then dropped it back in her drawer.

She didn't really care what Finn thought of her. She glanced at her face in the mirror. Okay, maybe she cared just a little. It was a weakness, all this caring so much.

She fixed the flyaways in her hair that always stuck out no matter how much she smoothed them down.

When she checked again, her eyes seemed brighter, her

cheeks pinker. There was no denying her body's physical reaction.

For better or worse, Finn was doing something to her.

His attempt to rescue her from Harrison and play the knight in shining armor had softened her feelings toward him. She shouldn't think about her lips brushing his skin. The way his hand felt in hers.

She wanted more than a date with Finn. She wanted to get to know the man underneath the tough, take-charge exterior. The guy who made her feel safe, who stepped in when she was threatened. Like it or not, her walls were crumbling.

"Going somewhere?" A low voice jolted her as she dropped the compact in her drawer and slammed it shut.

She turned to see Harrison standing in her office doorway. "What are you doing here?"

He put his arms out. "I don't get a warm welcome?"

No way. She pasted on a smile. *Get rid of him. Fast.*

"Sorry. Where are my manners?" She gave him a wooden hug. She hoped it felt like hugging a cactus.

He reeked of expensive cologne and starched shirts. The scent roiled her stomach.

"This is a surprise. What brings you here?"

"You. I had a last-minute lunch cancellation and wondered if you had plans."

"Uh, well, I kinda do."

"Kind of?"

She nodded. If he knew who she was meeting, she'd be in trouble.

"I almost never have a lunch hour free." Harrison tossed out the invitation while he ran his hand through his sun-bleached hair. "What will it take to talk you out of it? I can be very persuasive."

"I made plans with . . . a friend." She wasn't about to give away who this friend was.

Her phone vibrated in the background. She glanced down at Finn's name on the screen.

Hold on, Finn. Gotta brush off this guy.

"Who is it?" Harrison narrowed his eyes, trying to read the screen.

Megan grabbed her phone and tucked it in the waistband of her pants. "Not important." Why hadn't she worn pants with pockets today? A deep, well-placed pocket was a girl's best friend.

"Could you reschedule with this friend? I want to make up for my behavior last night and apologize for some things."

Megan folded her arms. "You don't have to explain anything about last night."

"No, I was a jerk. What happened between Finn and me was inappropriate. I wanted to apologize to him while I'm here." He glanced down the hall. "Any idea where he is?"

"He stepped out." Megan said the words carefully. The phone vibrated again, this time next to her hip bone. It had slipped from her waistband and was awkwardly inching down the interior of her pants.

If she could send him a quick text, she could notify him about Harrison interrupting her exit strategy. But right now, she couldn't even reach her phone. Not with Harrison in the room.

Dale stopped in Megan's doorway. "Harrison Brinks, what are you doing here?"

"Trying to convince this beautiful lady to go to lunch with me. So far, she's giving me the cold shoulder, even though I have all the information she needs about the upcoming masquerade. I just came from one of the planning meetings."

Dale turned to Megan. "Perfect timing for your next story. Go with Harrison. You can count it as a working lunch. He'll take you somewhere nice. Won't you, Harrison?" He turned to Harrison and gave him a wink.

"No less than the best." Harrison's teeth gleamed.

"Then it's settled." Dale shook Harrison's hand. "You kids enjoy yourself."

Megan shifted her weight. "But I—" She desperately wanted a minute alone to rescue her phone, which was currently lodged somewhere between her hip and thigh.

"No buts." Harrison held up his hand to silence her objections. "Your boss just told you to take lunch with me. That means you're mine for the next hour." He smiled and held the door for her. "After you."

Megan bit her lip. She only hoped that she could explain the situation to Finn before someone else did.

"How was lunch?" Cheri asked as Megan bolted through the doors of the newspaper office after lunch.

Megan was already searching for Finn, wanting to apologize for being a no-show. She stopped at Cheri's desk, peeking down the hallway where he normally perched on his metal chair. *Empty.*

"Oh, it was fine." Megan peered into Dale's office, but the door was almost shut. Where was he?

"I heard folks spotted you at DeSoto's." A curious smile played on Cheri's lips.

"How did you—"

"Agnes Bellevue ran into my sister on the sidewalk on her way out of the restaurant. She was gushing about the lobster bisque and mentioned she spotted you with Harrison."

Agnes was the town's biggest gossip. A millionaire's wife, she often went to DeSoto's with her socialite friends. Megan personally loathed the woman. She was known for spending her days lunching for hours, spreading more gossip than doing anything worthwhile. But she was also one of the paper's biggest supporters, especially financially.

"My sister wondered if you have a new boyfriend." Cheri chomped on a piece of gum. "She was itching to hear some juicy gossip."

"You set her straight, didn't you?" A tension headache throbbed behind Megan's temples.

"I told her I didn't know. Then Finn walked by, so I asked him."

Megan's stomach dropped. "You did what?"

"He was standing near my desk, filling up his water bottle."

"What did he say?"

"He didn't know about your lunch with Harrison. Then he left after that."

Megan screwed her eyes shut and tried to rub her headache away. So far, it wasn't working. "Where did he go?"

Cheri shrugged. "He didn't tell me."

Megan turned to leave. She had to find Finn and explain this horrid mess.

"Wait, before you go." Cheri held up a shiny pink fingernail. "One of your sisters called too." Cheri handed her a sticky note. "Call her as soon as possible."

She had finally rescued her phone from her pants when she excused herself to the ladies' room at the restaurant. She wouldn't make that mistake again. From now on, she was only buying pants with pockets.

Megan bolted down the stairs of the building. She'd call Finn first, find out where he was, and then return Lily's call.

When she tried Finn, his phone went to voice mail. She switched to texting.

Megan: Where are you? We need to talk.

She waited for a response as she climbed into her convertible. If she had to guess, he was at the dock, working on his boat.

She drove down Main Street and then turned onto Harborside Drive, craning her neck to find him. Her phone rang, and she answered it with a practiced motion.

"Hey, Megan." Lily's voice was urgent. "What is this about lunching at DeSoto's with Harrison Brinks?"

Megan rolled her eyes. "Oh great, you've heard too?"

"Cheri told me. I called the office because I couldn't reach you."

"My phone took a trip down my pants. Don't ask."

"I wondered what was going on. Don't tell me Harrison Brinks asked you out."

"He did, then convinced my boss it was for business reasons."

"I heard Harrison pulled out all the stops."

"Agnes needs to mind her own business. She's the one who started this mess."

"That *is* her business . . . making sure the whole town knows."

DeSoto's was the hub for rich people, the fanciest restaurant in town, with a waterfront view and a ridiculously expensive menu. Harrison had insisted on a four-course meal, even though all Megan had wanted was a salad. The food had been wasted on her. All she could think about was Finn.

"Why were you trying to reach me?" Megan rubbed the tense spot over her brows.

"As long as you promise you won't tell."

"Okay." Megan's nerves were frayed. She needed to find Finn.

"Alex accidentally revealed some information about Finn. At their guys' group, Finn admitted he had feelings for you. He asked Matt for advice."

"Matt knows? Oh, great." Megan's head throbbed more.

"Don't worry about Matt. You need to decide what your plans are with Finn."

"I know, I know. But first I need to take care of something else."

"What?"

"Trying to find Finn and explain why I stood him up for lunch."

Lily paused. "Wait. You had *two* dates for lunch?"

"Not dates. At least, not with Harrison."

"Then why do you need to explain?"

"There's been a misunderstanding."

"Finn knows about Harrison taking you out for lunch, doesn't he? Except he doesn't know how you feel about him."

"Bingo. When he found out I was at lunch with Harrison, he left the office. I feel sick about it." Her fingers stroked her forehead. Her headache was growing worse.

"What exactly is going on between you and Finn? Has he expressed any interest in a relationship?"

"He hasn't told me in so many words. But then again, I've pushed him away every chance I get. He's my coworker. Off-limits. No office romance ever works out . . ." Megan stopped herself before going further.

"Did something happen between you two?" Lily let the silence hang in the air as Megan sat in her convertible, the sun beating down on her shoulders. Her sister wasn't about to let the subject go.

Megan released the air in her lungs like a deflated balloon. "I didn't want anything to happen, but I got caught up in the moment."

"Are you saying what I think you're saying?" Lily was a mind-reader with her and Cass. "You kissed him, didn't you?" Lily laughed. "I'm proud of you!"

"For what? Shouldn't you be giving me a lecture about my

poor decision-making skills right now? It was rash, and I'm not even a rash person."

"Meg, it's about time. I'm glad you finally let someone kiss you instead of doing something stupid, like whacking them with your purse."

"Oh, Lily. I'm an idiot who's fallen for someone who is completely off-limits, and now, the mayor's son is involved, and I don't even want him near me."

"I'm enjoying this more than you know. My sister is part of a love triangle!"

"I'm not in a love triangle. I'm in trouble. You've got to help me out of this."

"Me? You need to get out of this hot mess on your own. Knowing Agnes's connections, the whole town is going to think you're dating Harrison."

"That's exactly what I'm afraid of."

"Then you need to set things straight. Tell Finn how you feel and be upfront with Harrison. For both their sakes."

Megan closed her eyes and rubbed her temple. Her aching head unsettled her stomach. She could explain everything to Finn. She just didn't know how. Her brain was mush.

"You're right." Megan nodded. "I'm going to track down Finn and talk with him."

"Call me if you need anything."

If Megan was going to tell him the truth, she needed to do it now. Otherwise, she might not be brave enough later.

She hurried to the place where his boat was usually docked and noticed the slip was empty. On the end of the dock, she took her shoes off and dangled her feet in the water. She'd wait all night if it meant she could explain the truth to Finn.

An old sailboat made its way toward her. She smiled and waved, her heart drumming loudly, but Finn didn't see her. His gaze shifted toward something else in the boat.

Megan craned her neck to get a closer view. That's when she

saw it: Scarlett stood next to Finn, wrapping her arm around his waist.

Megan took a step back as the realization unfolded in front of her. Finn wasn't alone.

She felt the heat rise to her face as she backed away. She didn't want Finn to see her there, foolishly waiting for a dream that would never happen.

CHAPTER TWENTY

MEGAN

"Meg, are you okay?" Cassidy put her hand on her sister's arm as they walked into Bella's, a local boutique, intent on finding accessories for the masquerade party. After calling in sick for a few days and working from home, Megan couldn't avoid Finn any longer. The masquerade was quickly approaching, and she had no choice but to go.

"You seem like you're on another planet," Lily added as they filed down the aisle.

"Dreading this weekend." Megan lagged behind her sisters' pace.

She should just get over Finn. If only it were that easy.

Finn was sweet and charming, but she had stood him up for lunch. Why wouldn't he choose Scarlett after what she'd done? He was clueless about her feelings for him.

"You can't keep calling into the office and telling them you're working from home forever," Lily pestered. "You're going to have to face him sometime."

"I know. I just don't want to yet."

"You're avoiding the inevitable." Cass ran her fingers across a silky black dress. "Aren't you covering the masquerade with him on Saturday?"

"Not *with* him. I'll cover my part, and he'll cover his. We don't have to be together. In fact, Harrison already asked if he'd see me there."

"Don't tell me you said yes." Lily stopped her sister.

"I didn't say yes." Megan bit her lip. "But I didn't say no either."

"What?" Cassidy put down the dress she was holding up.

"Why are you both looking at me that way?" Megan held her hands up. "I told him I had a job to do, but we could meet up at some point."

Lily covered her eyes. "Are you trying to lead Harrison Brinks on? Because you're doing a good job of it."

"I don't want to be alone if Finn shows up with Scarlett on his arm."

"So Harrison's a decoy to make Finn jealous? Brilliant plan, sis, just brilliant." Lily shook her head.

"It's not that simple." Her sisters didn't understand. She was attending an event where nearly everyone would attend with someone, except for her.

Lily grabbed her sister's arm. "Instead of denying your feelings, why not try actually admitting them? At least then you'll stop hiding from Finn."

"That's easy for you to say. Everything worked out perfectly with Alex."

She bolted ahead of her sister, blinking back the emotions flooding her eyes. It didn't help that Lily's love life was going incredibly well. Alex checked every box: loyal, loving, kind, and handsome to boot. He was Prince Charming in a tool belt. She had gotten her fairy-tale ending.

But Lily's happiness only highlighted Megan's despair. Had

she done something to get kicked out of the *happily ever after* club?

Or perhaps it was something almost too painful to admit— that she wasn't the type of girl men could truly love. Too much baggage. She loved her job, but it couldn't erase her pain. So she hid behind beautiful essays and wooed people with her words. But in real life, she wanted to hide in the bathroom before people figured out the truth. She wasn't the confident woman behind the computer. She was an imposter. A fraud. A woman whose body had betrayed her. Who would want her?

Megan picked up a black half-mask, the kind that looked like she was heading to Mardi Gras instead of one of the finest mansions in Wild Harbor. Even after a five-year hiatus, the Bellevues assigned a formal dress code along with a masquerade mask. Men in tuxes, women donning ball gowns with fancy hats and long gloves.

"You're so lucky to go. I can't believe I'll be stuck at work." Cassidy ran her fingers across a pair of black satin gloves. "At least we can help you find a mask and some jewelry."

"What are you wearing on Friday? This dress is gorgeous." Lily touched a red flowing number. She pulled it off the rack and draped it against Megan's body. "A showstopper if it fits." Lily was making chocolates for a wedding and wouldn't be attending either. Megan was the lone member of the Woods family going to the formal affair.

"I'm not wearing a dress. Just my black jeans with a blouse. I'm a reporter, not a guest, so I'm exempt from the dress code, except for the mask."

"You are *not* wearing jeans." Cassidy grasped her sister by her shoulders. "No way. We're finding you a dress." Cassidy immediately perused the racks, combing through the dresses.

Megan slumped. "I don't see the point."

Lily joined the search. "You'll feel less down in the dumps if you wear this. If Finn shows up with Scarlett, you might as well make him wish he was there with you. Wait, what about this one?" Lily pulled out a black silk dress.

Megan paused, her eyes sweeping over the garment in Lily's hands. It looked like something a movie star would wear. Not her. "Okay, hand it over. But if it doesn't fit, I'm wearing jeans."

"If it does?" Cassidy asked with a mischievous grin.

"Then it's a deal."

THE DRESS FIT like a silky second skin, draping her curves to her ankles. Megan wasn't even sure she'd know how to walk in it. She was terribly uncoordinated in formal dresses and stiletto heels. She tottered like a baby learning how to walk.

She sunk into the couch and popped an antacid tablet, hoping it would ease her stomachache. Her troubles couldn't be solved by a pain reliever.

Her problem was Finn.

As much as she tried not to care about him, she did. More than she wanted to admit.

She stood and smoothed the dress across her hips, taking one last look in the mirror. She knew what she had to do. Get her work done, and somehow, avoid Finn.

She grabbed her sparkly black clutch and headed out the door. Ready or not, it was time to get this night over with.

The masquerade was held at the estate of William and Agnes Bellevue, one of the wealthiest families in Wild Harbor. When Megan had attended seven years ago, she'd snagged a last-minute ticket from a friend who couldn't attend. It had been so unlike her to agree to a date with Tyler after having met him only a week before. A year apart, Tyler and Finn had a remarkable physical resemblance. The same hair, the same jade-stone eyes. So when Finn had shown up in Tyler's place, his face concealed by a half-mask, dressed like every gentleman there, she hadn't even suspected it wasn't Tyler.

As she pulled into the Bellevue Mansion's sweeping entrance, the memory of her last time here rushed back. She was facing the same man she had met seven years ago, and her emotions were just as confused as before.

A valet stepped forward, his eyes sweeping over her. He cleared his throat. "Madam, do you need any help?"

Megan shook her head and dropped the keys in his hand.

"Then feel free to head into the gardens."

She adjusted her dress as she stepped out of the car, tugging at the waist as if it would somehow magically expand. She wouldn't be eating much tonight. With her last-minute purchase, she didn't have time to alter a dress, so she'd chosen one off the rack. She took a step and wobbled on her heels. It was like walking on stilts.

The gardens were next to the carriage house, a massive six-car garage with living quarters on the second floor that were bigger than her childhood home.

"Madam, you'll be needing this." The valet picked up her mask lying on the passenger seat. "It's a masquerade. The one requirement of the Bellevues."

"Yes, thank you." She slid the mask over her eyes as he drove away.

The party had already started as guests mingled on the garden grounds, which overlooked the lake behind them. As she stepped through the gate into the garden, people chatted, their laughter dancing in the air. The lights hanging over the garden twinkled as the sun sank over the lake, turning the night sky into a watercolor display. Servers weaved between guests, carrying silver trays of fancy hors d'oeuvres and fluted glasses. A fountain trickled in the center of the garden as women sparkled in fancy dresses and expensive stilettos.

As Megan stepped into the crowd, people turned their heads,

taking a second glance as she made her way down the curving garden pathway.

She didn't belong in this crowd. These people were the socialites of Wild Harbor, people who knew the Bellevues because they had money and power. Harrison Brinks belonged to this world, not her. She didn't run in the same circles and couldn't imagine living with such extravagance. Designer dresses. Wrists and earlobes dripping with diamonds. Manicured properties and meticulously designed gardens. They were the privileged and pampered while she was an imposter.

She rotated slowly, seeking an escape, when someone's eyes burned into her. She gazed over her shoulder to see Finn staring at her from across the garden, a drink in his hand, his eyes locked on hers.

He moved toward her, his look holding hers, like the promise of something sweet. She couldn't move. Everything in her froze as she watched him approach, more handsome than she had ever seen him before.

A fluttery feeling rose in her stomach. He looked good in his tux, and it made it all the harder to pretend she didn't care.

The light caught his green eyes and sculpted cheekbones, and suddenly the fluttering in her body rose higher. Her breath caught. Everything that she was feeling was out in the open, exposed. It's like Finn's presence stole the air from her lungs.

"I wondered if you'd come." His eyes held hers.

She could barely form words. "Wouldn't miss it."

She wanted to explain everything, but she couldn't do it. Not here, when so many people were watching their every move.

"You look . . . amazing." His eyes swept over her, taking in her hair last.

"My sisters talked me into it. I wanted to wear jeans. Do you think everyone can tell how awkward I feel in this dress?" She glanced around.

"No. You're stealing the show. When you walked in, people couldn't help but notice. You're stunning."

If these words had come from Harrison, she would have passed them off as nothing more than flattery. But Finn wasn't the type to offer them so easily unless he meant them. Something blazed between them, making her heart race.

She needed to smother these feelings like a wet cloth over a lit match. Snuff them out before she burned even more.

"Are you here with someone?" She couldn't even bring herself to say her name. *Scarlett.* The effect was like biting down hard on her tongue.

"No. I'm here—with you." He grinned. One meant just for her. It woke every nerve in her body.

Slow down, heart. Keep breathing.

Tonight, she had to hold herself together, to pretend like her feelings weren't spiraling out of control. She dodged his eyes, hunting for an escape, afraid he could read her feelings if she held his gaze for too long. She grabbed water from a server who strolled by.

"How should we begin?" Her eyes swept the crowd, an attempt to tear her mind away from his overwhelming draw. The memory of tackling him was almost too strong to resist. She'd do it again if they were alone.

Focus on the job.

"Maybe I should talk to the mayor and get a few quotes? Or perhaps, the Bellevues?"

She was already making calculations in her head of who she should talk to, trying to avoid his eyes still pinned on her. Live music floated in the air as couples paired off for dancing.

"Meg . . ." Finn whispered, an urgency in his voice.

She pretended not to hear him. It was a desperate attempt to keep him at arm's length, to not turn and crumble completely.

He touched her bare shoulder, and it sent a shiver across her collarbone. She shifted toward him, reluctantly opening her heart to his invitation. For once, his face was stripped bare of his usual confidence. "Before I lose track of you for the evening, can I have one dance?"

She paused as doubts rose to the surface like bubbles in a fluted glass. Now wasn't the time to drill him with questions. She held his gaze, then nodded. If she spoke now, she'd either ruin the moment or say something she regretted. She had a journalist's instincts, and her head sometimes overruled her heart when it came to love.

Something told her to let go of the questions and trust Finn. *For once.*

He led her to the dance floor, and her heart flip-flopped as his firm grip grasped hers. She couldn't remember the last person who'd made her feel this way.

The thought of falling for Finn both attracted and terrified her. She wanted to both smother him and simultaneously run away. Did love always inspire such opposite reactions? She had never been crushed by so many overwhelming emotions at once.

When she looked up to see if he felt it too, she saw the answer in his eyes—the longing to know her and to be known by her.

He led her to a corner of the garden where couples swirled and swayed, unaware of anyone but the person they were dancing with. For once, no one seemed to stare at her or Finn. Each couple found their rhythm with their partner, melding their bodies into one swaying figure, their faces shining toward the other.

As Finn wrapped his arms around her waist, and she leaned into him, she could smell the dizzying scent of his aftershave. Fingers stroking her back, his hands sent a shock of electricity down her spine. Being this close to another human plummeted her under deep waters. But this time, she didn't have any fear.

Love wouldn't pull her down as the waves rolled in. Instead, it would hold her.

"Well, if it isn't Megan and Finn." A familiar voice pulled her out of a sweet dream. She wanted to wave it away, but the voice kept calling her back.

"Ms. Woods." A finger poked her shoulder. Harrison stood next to her, breaking up her dance with Finn.

She glanced at Finn's face, reluctant to pull away from his embrace. His eyes held hers.

She finally turned to face Harrison. His jaw clenched, the muscle slightly bulging on his sculpted face.

Finn's hand lingered on her back, a clear sign he didn't want to let her go. He was putting a stake in the ground, but Harrison ignored it.

Harrison's eyes flicked to Finn's, storms brewing behind his steel-grey irises. "I want a word with the lady."

Finn slowly released her, but his look promised more. "I'll find you later."

Harrison touched Megan's arm. "I want to introduce you to a few of my friends, people who might be good connections for future articles, especially if you take over as the editor-in-chief, eventually."

He was dangling a carrot in front of her, and he knew it.

She hadn't ever mentioned the promotion to him. But Harrison understood what drove her in life, and like it or not, he thought like she did. The need to achieve was her weakness, and now he was using it to drive a wedge between her and Finn.

"Would you like to meet them?" He touched her elbow, pulling her away from the man who'd captured her heart.

Harrison's hand remained firmly grasped around her arm, even while Finn didn't take his palm off her back. Finn's arms were a soft place to land, a safe space where she felt held. She could stay here forever, couldn't she?

But doubts lingered in the back of her mind. He still hadn't explained his intentions with Scarlett.

She tried to avoid the questions in Finn's eyes as she left him. She didn't want to end their dance, but her feelings were scaring her.

"I'm sorry. I should go," she whispered before Harrison led her away.

He didn't respond. He didn't have to.

She knew what he was trying to tell her without saying a word. He wanted her to stay.

It took everything in her to walk away.

CHAPTER TWENTY-ONE

MEGAN

Harrison introduced her to a dizzying number of people during the night. Raucous laughter, decadent food, and the thrumming of a loud bass swamped her senses. Couples danced, men unbuttoned their collars, and drinks flowed as the night music swelled. Still, nobody left or took off their masks to head home. Every guest seemed ripe for revelry. Everyone, except Megan.

She faked a smile, pretending to be interested in strangers' witty banter with clever comebacks and a few sarcastic jokes. Her eyes flitted across the garden, trying to pin down the one person she cared about. Only the shifting moon reminded her that time was slipping away for one more dance with Finn.

"You're charming every guy here," Harrison whispered as he turned his attention to her. "Including me. Do you know what kind of power you have?"

"I'm not interested in power." She took a swig of water. The only thing she was interested in was where Finn had gone. She had lost him in the crowd.

Harrison placed his hand on the small of her back as he introduced her to a prominent business executive. It was obvious from people's stares that they thought she was Harrison's latest prize. She moved a few feet away from him. Harrison shifted toward her again, intent on sticking with her. She certainly didn't have the means or the influence that most people here did. She couldn't figure out what Harrison's motive was, but she suspected it was not love. Probably nothing more than physical attraction.

Her sisters had warned her she was the type of girl men would always look at twice, even though she had never cared for her looks. Her hair was too thick, her eyes too dark, her body too soft and curvy. She wanted Lily's light hair and Cassidy's tall, model-thin frame. Megan was more comfortable in jeans and a T-shirt than schmoozing with Wild Harbor's elite.

Her eyes roved the crowd, looking for the one person who made her feel like herself, maybe even a better version of herself.

Finn. She could desperately use his advice on how to escape from Harrison now, who seemed focused on monopolizing her time.

Her head was swirling from the noise, the press of the crowd, the pulsing beat. She needed to step away, catch her breath, and figure out a way to escape this place. If only she could find Finn. She hadn't seen him since Harrison had whisked her away.

Peals of laughter soared over the music, spurring Megan toward the exit, away from the throngs of people. A sea of black masks were swallowing her, couples swaying and embracing, the swell of music and the scent of heavy perfume.

Harrison pulled on her arm, stopping her. "Another dance?"

Her stomach clenched. She had already danced with him once, and it had only confirmed the sick feeling in her stomach.

She couldn't stand him. What was she doing here? She pushed away from his grip.

"I need to go to the ladies' room. I'm not feeling well."

"What?" he asked, leaning closer. The music reached a fever pitch, competing with the chaos of the crowd. "The ladies' room." She pointed toward the restrooms.

"But you're mine when you come back." He gave her a sly smile before she rushed off.

Finally. If she could slip away and sneak to her car, she'd head home, even if that meant leaving Finn without a last dance. She'd send a text letting Harrison know she'd left. Chances were good he would hardly notice.

As she zigzagged through the crowd, she caught sight of Thelma, one of the few friendly faces from Wild Harbor. When Thelma's husband had died, he'd left her money stashed in well-planned investments. Thelma now had means, but she never acted like it. She still shopped at the thrift store, just like she had before she'd realized she had a fortune.

"Honey, you look like a million bucks in that dress." Thelma glanced over Megan's gown. "It's no wonder you caught Harrison Brinks's eye."

"Thank you. But that's the thing. I don't even want Harrison to notice me. I'm not really his type."

"Well, he doesn't think so. He's been glued to your side all night, except for that moment he stole you from Finn's arms. Did you see Finn keeping an eye on you the rest of the night?"

She spun around trying to figure out where he was. "I haven't seen Finn. Do you know where he is?"

"Got tired of waiting and left. Went that way." She pointed toward the exit, back toward the walled entrance where the valet had taken her car.

"I was afraid you'd say that."

"Why?" Thelma's eyes brightened. "What do you need?"

"Thelma, I need to find Finn. If you see him, will you tell him I'm looking for him? Just don't tell Harrison, okay?"

Thelma mimed zipping her lips closed.

"Thank you, Thelma." Megan nearly bolted from the crowd toward the exit of the garden, where Finn had last been seen. It was probably hopeless now, but she wanted to search for him one more time before she left the party.

As she walked outside the walls of the property, away from the noisy crowds into the darkness, she suddenly could breathe again. The music still lingered, but it was more like a gentle ballad, the deep bass melting into the background of the night.

A deep breath of cool air filled her lungs. She was alone for the first time in hours, finally escaping the noise that had assaulted her senses.

Her shoulders relaxed, the tension releasing from her whole body. She should have come out here hours ago.

Out of the shadows, Finn emerged, striding toward her, his gaze sharpened on hers. She didn't know where he had been or how he'd found her, and she didn't care.

She only knew that as much as she should turn away, she couldn't. A different kind of desire overtook her. She was not only struck by his broad shoulders and the sharp outline of his face, but by how much she wanted to be near him and back in his arms. She was like a moth to a flame, but this time, she didn't look away.

"I was searching for you." Her voice was hushed, afraid that someone would eavesdrop on their conversation. It was as if the entire world dissolved, with only the moon as their light and the music to fill the gaps. "Why didn't you come find me?"

"What about Harrison?" He stopped in front of her, near enough for the air between them to be magnetic.

"I'm done with Harrison."

"That's not what he thinks."

"How do you know?"

He glanced toward the garden wall where the crowds mingled on the other side. "A guy can tell. He can't stop touching you. It's so obvious, Meg."

His comments stung. "You're reading into things. I'm not Harrison's type. I don't have the connections, the means, any of the things that most of these women have. Why would he be interested in me when he could have any other woman in town?"

"You don't know?" He rubbed the side of his jaw. Then he dropped his hand and looked at her in amazement. "It's because you're beautiful. Intelligent. You speak your mind—"

"I'm not sure that's a good thing."

"It is when it's a sign of confidence, someone who knows what she wants. He's not a dummy. You're the most extraordinary woman here tonight. But I can't stand seeing him all over you." Finn clenched his fists. "Guys like Harrison don't stick around. But if you ever need anything, I will always come for you."

His words rumbled through her body. "You shouldn't make promises like that."

"After our first kiss, don't tell me you didn't feel something between us."

She had tried to forget his lips on hers. To tell herself that he didn't really have feelings for her. She'd justified it, explained it away, rationalized it from every angle. Yet, she still couldn't forget.

"I was caught up in the moment." She swallowed back a wave of emotions. He would not pull her walls down. She had been taken by him, but she wouldn't allow her feelings to show.

"I don't believe you."

She lifted her chin. "I know what I feel."

"You didn't feel anything while we were dancing?" He

removed her mask to look into her face. He gently slid it over her hair and then removed his own.

Suddenly all her emotions were uncovered, laid bare, stripped of all pretense. She wanted to make excuses. Tell him she felt nothing, but something stopped her. She knew he'd see through her.

"The truth is," she whispered, "I didn't want you to let go."

It was all she needed to confess. He stepped forward and took her in his arms. His hand slipped to her face as his lips found hers. This time, she didn't pull away, but melted into him, letting herself fall into the most delicious dream. His hands slipped to her back, and she felt like she was drowning, her pent-up desire unleashed in one kiss. Her hands found his hair and slid down to his neck.

The sound of feet rustled close by, and it was all she could do to pull herself back into the present, away from him. She wanted to stay in his arms, but the urgency of being caught set off an alarm bell in her head. She forced herself to pull away. It took every ounce of energy to let go, especially since he was reluctant to stop.

She stepped away as someone rounded the corner. It was Agnes Bellevue with one of her friends, Marla Trueblood.

Agnes halted mid-step. "Excuse me. I didn't realize anyone was out here."

Megan hoped the darkness hid her burning cheeks. "I had to catch my breath. Get away from the crowd." The corner of her mouth twitched. Of course she needed to breathe after that kiss. Megan rubbed the back of her neck, hoping no red, blotchy patches were giving her away.

Agnes looked between them. "It's dark out here, don't you think? A good place to hide."

"You haven't seen Agnes's dog, have you?" Marla interrupted. "A small white bichon frise? He escaped from the house, and we only just noticed. Agnes is distraught." She patted Agnes's shoulder.

"I'm so sorry, but we haven't." Not that Megan would have noticed a dog during that kiss. She probably wouldn't have noticed a herd of elephants.

"We'll keep an eye out," Finn added.

"Thank you. I'm just so concerned. I hope we find my little munchkin soon." Agnes started to turn away, then stopped. "Oh, Megan, I think Harrison is looking for you. You may want to let him know where you are, just so he doesn't get worried. Or would you like me to?"

"No need to tell him," Megan shot back.

"If you insist." Agnes forced a smile. Megan couldn't tell if she suspected more than she let on or if she was merely trying to help. But either way, Megan couldn't stay there with Finn. As much as she wanted to be alone with him, it was too dangerous now.

Megan watched the women leave, then turned to Finn. "I have to go. This is too risky. I'm sorry."

"I'm the one who's sorry." He took her hand, trying to stop her so he could steal another moment.

He cupped her face in his hands and kissed her one last time.

She didn't want this to end, but the stakes were too high now, especially since Agnes had found them together.

His last embrace unleashed a floodgate, but Megan slowly wrenched away, propelled by an urgency to leave. Tonight had changed everything.

"When will I see you again?" he asked as she pulled away.

"Monday at work." She took slow steps backward, trying to control her racing heart.

"That's not the answer I wanted to hear."

She knew he wanted more time. But now, her only thought was to flee. "It isn't safe for us to be seen here."

"Nothing good is ever safe. Let me come with you."

She hesitated. She was good at running from what scared her. Hadn't she been doing it her whole life? But this time, she didn't want to leave him.

As he put his hand out, she accepted the invitation.

For once, she wasn't going to run from fear.

CHAPTER TWENTY-TWO

FINN

After leaving the masquerade, they headed to Joshua's cabin, where they sat on the porch swing, watching fireflies and talking until the early hours of morning. They didn't have to worry about interruptions. About Agnes or Harrison. Or even their future together. He wouldn't bring it up.

She leaned on his shoulder, and he wrapped his arms around her. He could do this forever.

For the rest of the weekend, Finn couldn't stop thinking about Megan, especially that kiss.

It left him longing for more, like having a taste of a rich dessert, only to have it taken away after one bite. He wouldn't let anyone take Megan away from him now.

As Finn swept into the office on Monday morning, Megan was bent over her computer, focused on another article. It was back to business as usual.

She offered him a smile. "Hey."

"Hi." He held out coffee for her. Anything to make her smile.

"Wow. Thanks, I needed this, especially on a Monday. By the way, could you read my latest story?"

Finn didn't know what to expect from her, but it wasn't this. She was hyperfocused on ticking off her to-do list. It was so typical Megan, it drove him crazy.

"I don't even get a special hello?" He set down his computer bag.

"Oh, I'm sorry. What did you expect?"

He tried to hide the sting of disappointment. "More than the usual coworker small talk. Maybe even a repeat of Saturday night?"

"Since we're at work now, we can't really . . ." She let the words hang in the air.

"Kiss? It's fine." It wasn't fine. He could tell she didn't want to talk about it. "What's up?"

"I have more info about the SCI story. I think this could change everything."

He knew the article was important, but he also hadn't seen her since the masquerade party. The story could wait.

She pushed the computer toward him.

He ignored it and kept his eyes on her instead. She was beautiful even when she was trying to hide from him. "I'll read the story. But first, I think we need to talk." He wanted to get things cemented in their relationship. If they were going to make things work, they had to stop pretending their attraction didn't exist.

She avoided his eyes as she pulled a brightly colored sticky note off a square stack.

"Okay." She took out a pen and started making a list. "What do you want to talk about?"

"I think you know." He placed his hand on hers, and her eyes held his for a second.

She pulled away. "I'm not sure I can talk about this here."

"We can't avoid it."

She lowered her voice. "You know this would never work." She went back to writing on the tiny square paper.

"But why not?" Something flared in his tone. He hated when she closed him off like this. "You need to give me one good reason." He pulled the sticky note off her desk so she couldn't ignore him.

She sighed. "Give me my note back." She put her palm out.

He shook his head. "You need to talk to me first."

She leaned across the desk and tried to swipe it from his hands. He yanked it away from her.

"Fine. You want reasons." She stood. "First, I think it's a bad idea to date someone you work with. It makes things complicated."

"What about *not* dealing with this thing between us? That makes things even more complicated."

"If one of us gets promoted down the road, how will the other person handle it?" She leaned against the wall.

The editor-in-chief position. Of course. He had pushed it out of his mind, intent on not dealing with the problem until later. Funny how she never stopped bringing it up. The issue wedged them apart.

"Meg, we can work this out." He came around the desk and took her hands. Something softened in her eyes. "Just give me a chance to prove to you it could work . . ." He wrapped his arms around her when there was a knock.

They both pulled away when Dale hurried through the door before they could continue the conversation. As much as he liked his boss, the guy's timing was lousy.

"Can I come in?" It was more of a statement than a question, since he had already entered. "I need an update on the sailing regatta. The mayor predicted we'll have the biggest crowd yet. How's the practicing coming?"

He looked from Megan to Finn. They both froze. Megan's eyes dropped to the floor.

Finn didn't want to embarrass her, but someone had to explain. "I'm doing it alone."

"Alone? I asked you both to do it."

Megan held up her hand. "I've tried going out on the water several times. I got sick on my ride with Finn and didn't fare much better on Harrison's boat."

"Harrison Brinks?" Dale narrowed his eyes. "Why were you with him?"

"You'll understand when you read this story. I hadn't told you about it yet because I needed to get Harrison's word first." She turned her computer to Dale so he could read the SCI story. "Harrison's been a major source of information revealing a bribery scandal in our community. He was the one who confirmed that SCI gave his father money."

Dale skimmed the story and shook his head. "You're suggesting that the mayor accepted a bribe?"

"In exchange for giving SCI a no-bid contract on a city renovation project."

"But why would the mayor's own son reveal that?"

"He agreed to share it confidentially. Harrison and his father haven't been on the best of terms lately."

Dale scratched his head. "Megan, I can't print this. You don't think he'll know it was his son who disclosed this information? What would it do to the Brinks family?"

"I don't understand. This is a matter of public concern."

"You've only got Harrison's word against his father's. You need more solid evidence. It's wrong to make this kind of judgment without more proof."

Megan crossed her arms. "The truth needs to be public. People should know."

"Maybe this comes as a surprise to you, but I don't believe that all news needs to be in the paper. Some issues can and should be worked out in private or in a court of law. Printing this story would tarnish his reputation before he's been tried in court."

She pointed a finger at Dale. "You're just worried because he's your friend. Even though he's done something wrong, you're protecting him."

"We're not a big-city newspaper. We don't aim to destroy people or air their dirty laundry. This is Wild Harbor. We cover little league games and Grandparents Day. Our articles honor local citizens who volunteer and those who served our country on Veterans Day. We present the positives more than the negatives. Instead of always showing the tragedies, we work hard to show the ways we're building up our community. This is not the type of reporting we're known for. Harrison should talk to his father first."

"The citizens have a right to know."

Finn put his hand out to calm the heated debate. He didn't want Megan saying something she'd regret. "Maybe there's a better way to handle this."

"Like what?" Megan asked, her face flushed.

"Talking to Mayor Brinks personally." Finn reached to touch Megan's shoulder. "See what he has to say."

"I've tried. He won't talk to me." Megan shifted away from his hand. "Honestly, Finn, I can't believe after everything that's happened, you're taking his side."

"I'm not taking anyone's side." He wasn't trying to draw lines in the sand, but her look accused him of it.

Dale shook his head. "There are no sides. We won't print this news until we know more."

Megan's mouth fell open. "I thought this newspaper values truth."

"We do, but we also value people." Dale pointed at her computer. "I don't want to set a precedent like this before I retire. If Finn takes over for me and feels differently, then that's his call. But I won't."

"What?" Megan turned to Finn, the shock etched into her face.

This wasn't how she was supposed to find out. He hadn't even agreed to the position.

"Wait a minute." She turned to Dale, her voice laced with anger. "You've talked to Finn about taking over as editor-in-chief?" The way she ignored him, as if he wasn't even in the room, stung. He'd hidden something important from her, and the tension in the room turned explosive.

Dale nodded. "Finn hasn't agreed to anything. But yes."

She turned to him with a steel glare. "You kept this from me? Why didn't you tell me?"

"Dale hadn't decided. I didn't even know if I wanted the position."

The accusations in her eyes nearly undid him.

"But you knew I did, and you didn't even bother to tell me." She blinked rapidly, trying to hold back the tears.

"Meg . . ."

"Don't." She backed away from him and then snapped the lid of her laptop, shoving it inside her bag, followed by a few crumpled papers. She kept her chin down, eyes averted, searching through desk drawers.

He couldn't let her leave like this. Not after everything between them.

"Let's talk about this. Don't go," Finn pleaded. He touched her arm and she recoiled instantly, like fire had burned her. He wanted to explain how he had fought for her, how he'd asked Dale to consider her for the job. But she'd never believe him now.

"I can't stay," she choked out. She darted past him without finishing her sentence.

Finn tried to follow. "Take a few hours, and when you return, we can talk through this—"

She stopped. When her eyes finally met his, they were glassy and lifeless. Tears rimmed the bottom. "No, I mean, I'm not sure I can work here anymore."

"Megan . . ." He reached to stop her one last time before she walked out the door. But as she darted away, he realized he couldn't keep her from leaving.

As the workday wound to a close, Megan didn't return, nor did she come back the next day. She refused to answer Finn's calls or messages. At five o'clock, he drove over to her apartment and knocked on the door. She couldn't ignore him if he showed up at her doorstep, could she?

Aspen swung the door open, drying a glass while a cooking show blared in the background. "Oh, hi." She tried to sound casual, but Finn sensed the tension as something sizzled in the background—the smell of spicy sausage cooking on the stove.

"Is Megan here? I need to talk to her."

"She left."

"Do you know when she'll be back?"

"She's been gone since the day she walked out of the paper. I asked her where she was headed, but she didn't want to tell me. Afraid you'd come around here, eventually." Her expression was guarded.

"If you had to guess?"

Aspen shook her blonde curls. "I don't know. She only told me she was leaving. I think she knew . . ."

"What?"

"That if you came here, I'd cave and tell you. This was her way of protecting everyone. If I were you, I'd wait and give her space."

"I need to talk with her. It's important."

"Finn, it's Megan we're talking about here. She's not going to let you explain anything." Aspen tilted her head as if this were painfully obvious to everyone except him.

"Could you at least text me if she returns?"

"What could you possibly tell her that would change her mind now? You kinda blew it by keeping secrets."

"She told you?"

Aspen nodded. "Her sisters know too."

Finn rubbed his forehead. This was going from bad to worse. Her whole family had probably heard the news, including Matt.

"Do you think she'll come back for the regatta?"

He wanted to see her there, to prove something to her. If there was any chance she'd go with him, he'd beg her. But he knew the chances of that happening now were zero. The trust he'd worked so hard to build had shrunk to nothing.

Aspen shrugged. "Your guess is as good as mine."

By Saturday, Finn had given up on finding Megan. Wherever she was, she didn't want to hear from him. That much was clear. He only hoped that she'd return in a week for the regatta. He didn't know why that mattered, but he wanted her there.

Defeated, he sat down on one of the few chairs he had in his empty apartment. He still hadn't found furniture for his place or properly moved in. Instead, he'd spent every spare moment on the lake, regaining his sea legs, preparing for the racing event. This was the first time he'd seriously gotten back to the water since he'd left the Coast Guard. When he ventured out on his boat, the sound of the waves soothed him like a lullaby. In those moments, it was just him alone in the world.

Until this week, he had wanted to teach Megan how to find that same peace.

But now, Finn struggled to imagine how he was going to

repair this rift between them. He couldn't fix their relationship any more than he could take away his PTSD.

He'd been foolish to believe she could fall for him after everything he'd been through. Why would she want someone who was broken by his past?

As he poured his coffee, he noticed a note lying under his apartment door. He picked up the folded paper and opened it. A shaky cursive hand wrote:

Meet me at the dock this morning at nine. I have something for you.
Your friend,
Joshua

Finn had forgotten about Joshua's offer to go out on the boat. He immediately grabbed his keys and left for the marina. With everything happening in Finn's life, he could use some time with the old man. He wasn't sure what it was about Joshua, but he seemed to draw people in, like a butterfly to flowers. Perhaps it was his unassuming nature. He knew when to say something and when to let silence hang in the air, stirring deep.

As he walked down the dock, he saw Joshua waiting, pensively looking at the lake, as if the old man had all the time in the world.

Joshua's right hand rubbed a spot on his arm almost imperceptibly. His wrist had a deep scar, the shadow of what had once been a severe wound. When Joshua saw him, he put his hands in his pockets, the scar disappearing from sight.

"Beautiful day to be on the lake." Joshua's eyes drifted toward a distant space on the horizon.

"You looked deep in thought." Finn drew up next to the old man's shoulder. "I'm sorry to interrupt."

"Yes, thinking . . . praying. It's all the same to me now. Life can be one long prayer, if you let it."

Finn had never known how to pray, really. When his parents had taken him to church, someone had always prayed in loud, monotone syllables. He'd never thought of prayer as anything more than a public speech to God. His parents only prayed before dinner. Then when his brother had died, the prayers had stopped and so had attending church. His mom had confessed privately that Dad was mad at God, and they were taking a break from church. What had started with a few Sundays turned into a five-year break. Possibly forever.

Now, his parents had found a new Sunday morning routine involving brunch and a morning news program. Grief had slammed the doors shut to faith.

He wondered how Joshua had learned to exist this way, to just be with God. It was like breath and air.

Finn couldn't help but wonder at this man who was so unlike anyone else he'd met. He spoke in mysteries, but was simple and unassuming in his appearance.

"Are you ready to work on the varnish? I brought a few tools." He nodded toward a small bag sitting on the dock.

"Is that what you were referring to in the letter?"

"All in good time." He walked toward Finn's boat and gave a nod. "I take it this is the one. She's a beauty, but you're right, she needs some work." He stepped into the boat with an agility that was unusual for an older man. Then he leaned down and touched the flaking varnish. "With a lot of elbow grease, she'll be as good as new."

"I'm glad someone thinks so. My dad said I'd made a foolish decision buying this fixer-upper. I can't please the man."

Joshua nodded slowly, his eyes clouded over as he lowered to his knees. "Take this." He handed Finn a small brown package. Don't open it until later. The explanation is inside."

Finn rustled the package and felt a hard object.

Joshua resumed his scraping. "Does he talk about Tyler?"

Finn ran his hands through his hair. "I didn't think you knew."

"Word gets around." Joshua scraped at the cracked varnish, forcing it to break away from the wood.

"Unless Dad brings it up, Tyler's a taboo subject. Almost like he never existed. He's closed off that part of himself. His way of dealing with grief." He couldn't believe he was confessing this to the old man. In his parents' house, grief was hidden and dangerous. Nobody wanted to talk about it.

"What's your way? Refinishing old boats?"

Finn couldn't deny it. "Probably. I should have gone to more counseling. Boats aren't cheap."

"But distraction is." Joshua scraped some more. "It's what most folks do to take away pain. Trouble is, you have to face your problems sometime."

Finn joined him on his hands and knees, scraping alongside the old man. "My parents won't talk about Tyler. So I've dealt with it myself. Pushed it away. Ended up with PTSD. I tried going to support groups. All it's done is make the hurt worse." Finn scraped harder.

His brother's shadow followed him everywhere—in every decision he made, every job he worked, each failure or triumph. He wanted to be rid of his ghost, to break free from trying to live up to his memory. Everyone expected Finn to become what his brother never would.

"Death can change a man. Sometimes for good. Sometimes not." The varnish flaked off as Joshua scraped in long strokes.

"I get that Tyler's death changed my dad and me. I just don't know what to do about it."

"You can't change what's broken." Joshua paused. "Acceptance might be the hardest thing of all."

"You're talking to a guy who quit the Coast Guard because I couldn't handle another rescue. I thought that Tyler's death would somehow make sense if I were saving lives. But after pulling bodies from the water, I realized I can't save anyone. Not even myself."

Finn scraped the varnish harder, clenching his teeth. He didn't want to stir up memories from his past. He fought the tidal wave of sadness building in his chest, years of pent-up emotions waiting for the dam to break.

Joshua stopped, then touched Finn's arm. "No one can save themselves. At some point, we all end up on the bathroom floor searching for God."

Finn pulled back and shook his head. "Then where is he? That's the question I can't let go of. Where is he when everything falls apart?"

Joshua paused, his eyes flashing with light. "Right there in the darkness."

CHAPTER TWENTY-THREE

MEGAN

W hen Megan had escaped for her spur-of-the-moment trip, her sisters dropped everything to go. They traveled to a beach an hour north, staying at a quaint bed-and-breakfast along the lake. But even the gorgeous Victorian home and idyllic private shoreline decorated with bright rainbow umbrellas couldn't revive Megan's spirit.

She wrapped her beach towel around her shoulders like a blanket. Tears stung her eyes as the wind whipped her hair. If only this beautiful setting could spark joy in her. Thank goodness for sunglasses. She wiped the corners of her eyes, avoiding her sandy fingers. She scanned the people on the beach, children squealing as waves pummeled them with frigid water, couples holding hands, kicking waves as they strolled barefoot along the shore.

They all reminded her of what she couldn't have—a complete family. She thought she had accepted a quiet life until Finn came along. When she was with him, hope took root in her heart and teased her, dangling a dream she could never have.

"Are you done for good at the paper? Like, this is it?" Cassidy asked.

"I haven't turned in my resignation, but probably."

"What will you do when you get back?" Cassidy asked, popping another chip into her mouth.

"I have no clue. I've never even thought about other jobs in Wild Harbor." She rested her chin on her hand and watched as two kids jumped waves in the lake, oblivious to the world around them.

"I can always use help at the chocolate shop." Lily reached into Cassidy's bag and stole a chip.

"Thank you for the offer, but making chocolates is your thing. I'd probably screw up an entire batch. I'd rather be—" Megan still couldn't say the word *unemployed.* "—in between work."

She had always imagined that the jobless were too lazy to work or must have done something wrong. For the first time, she realized how judgmental and cruel that kind of blanket statement was.

Now, she was the one out of work. No matter how much she tried to convince herself that her unemployed status was a badge of honor because she had stuck to her journalistic values, she knew the truth. Finn hadn't been honest with her. He had beaten her at her own game, snagging the position she wanted while hiding the truth. If she hadn't fallen so hard for him, she might have seen this coming. Too late for that.

Apparently, she hadn't really known this man that she had been so willing to give her heart to. She scratched at a scab on her leg, ignoring the sting of reopening an old wound.

She should have kept him from chiseling away at her rock-solid fortress and worming his way into her life. But she had opened up and trusted, and now, her heart was paying the price.

What a fool.

It was only a matter of time before the whole town would

hear about her leaving. The truth always spread like syrup on pancakes. Megan's instinct was to hide, but Wild Harbor was her home, and at some point, she had to return.

"I know what you need." Cassidy crinkled up the empty potato chip bag. "A blind date."

Megan nearly spurted soda out of her nose. "Because Jeff worked out so well."

"They're not all like him."

"Before that, it was Mr. Water Ski Instructor."

Cassidy frowned. "I forgot about him. You do have a poor track record."

"Oh, thanks." Megan poked her sister in the side, hitting her ticklish spot.

"Hey!" Cass yelped as she pushed away Megan's hand.

"If you get desperate, there's always Larry." Lily leaned forward in her beach chair to get a better view of Megan. "You'd never have to worry about him cheating on you with one of his clients because they're all dead."

Cassidy snorted as Lily's shoulders shook with laughter. Maybe it was too much sunshine or the fact they'd spent the day lazing about, but something had made them giddy.

"You guys are terrible." Megan cracked a smile. "I'm never getting dating advice from you again." Megan tried to hold it in, but her sisters' laughter continued, and a small half-laugh escaped her lips.

"Hey, I have an idea." Cass stood. "Let's sing karaoke tonight. I'm in the mood for some sappy love songs."

"You'll make all the dogs howl," Megan jabbed.

"Are you saying my singing is bad?" Cass opened her mouth. "You're going to pay for this."

Megan sprinted from her chair as Cass chased her toward the water. Megan ran into the waves just as Cass grabbed her arm, pulling her off-balance. Together they fell into the shallow water, their laughter spilling over like a shaken soda bottle.

Megan's stomach muscles hurt from laughing as she wiped the water from her eyes.

Lily waded into the knee-deep water, shaking her head. "Some people never grow up."

Cass leaned toward Megan, a spark in her eyes. "Lily looks too dry, don't you think?" Cass looked downright devious.

"Are you saying what I think you're saying?" Megan raised her eyebrows.

"Yep." Cass nodded slowly.

"Don't you dare . . ." Lily threatened, but it was too late.

Megan and Cass tackled Lily and pulled her down with them, the three sisters falling into the lake together, their laughter and the sound of the waves drowning out all their cares.

A WEEK LATER, the sisters returned to Wild Harbor with sunburned shoulders and sand clinging to the bottoms of their beach bags. Megan dreaded returning, but she couldn't stay away forever, and Lily had promised to be back for a special date with Alex.

Megan had just stumbled through the door of her apartment, bags loaded on her shoulders, when a text popped up on her phone.

Alex: Very important announcement tonight at seven at the chocolate shop. Can you be there? Don't tell Lily. It's a surprise.

Megan envied Lily's happiness: a thriving chocolate shop and a handsome boyfriend—all the puzzle pieces falling into place.

Tears welled up as she dropped her luggage and sank onto the sofa. She was happy for her sister. Thrilled, actually. Lily had always wanted to be a wife and mom. But the contrast between her sister's life and her own couldn't have been more apparent. She only wished she could be so lucky.

Something pinched in Megan's abdomen, a sharp pain on the lower left side. Megan dug her fist into the throbbing. The memory of her doctor's words hounded her.

"The chance of you ever getting pregnant . . . it's unlikely."

Unlikely. Impossible. She hated those words.

She covered her face with her hands, trying to smother the memory. Not that it mattered now. She couldn't even keep a decent guy, let alone think about marriage and family. At least she'd never have to tell Finn the news.

She rubbed her eyes, angry at her self-pity. That was the real issue between her and Finn, wasn't it?

It wasn't only that he had taken the job she wanted.

She was afraid if she told him her secret, he'd reject her. Her body. Her brokenness. Who she was. And that hurt worse than anything else.

LILY WALKED into the chocolate shop holding Alex's hand, a diamond sparkling on her left hand.

"I have good news!" She held up her hand, showing off the huge gem.

"Woo hoo!" Matt pumped his fist in the air.

Cassidy squealed. Mom nearly smothered Lily with a giant hug.

Only Dad remained quiet, beaming as he sat at a table with Megan.

"I'm just thrilled," Mom exclaimed, giving Alex a bear hug. "I was wondering how long you'd keep us in suspense."

"It's only been a few months."

"But Lily's been waiting for you for years. I've never seen

her so happy." Mom wiped tears from her eyes as Lily approached Dad and wrapped her arms around his shoulders.

"Dad, what are you thinking? I need to know you approve."

Since their dad's stroke, he'd struggled to find the words for things. But this time, his voice flowed effortlessly.

"You got my approval, one hundred percent."

Lily hugged her father and then sat down next to Megan without saying anything.

"I'm so happy for you," Megan whispered as she wrapped her arms around her sister. "You found a good one."

"I want the same for you. You know that, right? Nothing but the best for you, Meg." Lily sprang out of her seat, pulling Megan with her. "I have your favorite chocolate. A key lime truffle."

They walked over to the case where the confections glistened under the light. Lily pulled out a white chocolate truffle filled with a tart key lime filling and placed it in her sister's hand.

Megan cupped the dome-shaped confection.

"Are you going to eat that chocolate or just stare at it?" Lily teased. "Because I have a dozen extras if you need any more chocolate therapy."

"It's one of the few perfect things in my life right now."

"Things won't stay this way."

"Easy for you to say. You're engaged to a home renovation star and living on the beach." Megan leaned against the counter and took a bite of the truffle.

"That might be true now, but it hasn't always been this way. Remember when I broke up with Thomas? It turned out to be the best thing that ever happened to me."

"Please don't spout platitudes. Because if you do, I'm going to cry."

Lily wrapped her arm around Megan. "You don't know how

things will turn out. If I had a magic wand and could make all your problems disappear, I would."

"If you had a wand, I'd make Finn disappear. He's the reason I'm a hot mess."

Lily examined her sister's face. "You like him, don't you?"

"I *did* like him. As in, past tense." She covered her face with her hands as if she could forget about him by shutting out the world. "Okay, I still do," she admitted, defeated.

Lily pulled her sister into a hug. "There will be others. Just wait until they see you in your bridesmaid's dress. They'll be falling all over themselves to dance with you."

"That's not true. You'll be the star of the show. You know what they say about bridesmaids . . ."

"Don't even say it." Lily stepped back and pointed at her sister. "I will not let you throw a pity party for yourself. I'll prove you wrong."

Megan's phone interrupted her sister's lecture.

Harrison: One last chance to sail with me tomorrow in the regatta and be part of the winning team. Please? I'll even throw in a special donation for the paper if you join my team.

Megan exhaled. She'd forgotten about Harrison.

"What is it?" Lily peeked over her sister's shoulder.

"Harrison wants me to be on his team for the regatta. Not that I'll be any help. But he's willing to make a donation, and the paper needs a sizable gift."

"Won't he be competing against Finn?" Lily grabbed a few more chocolates for her family and passed them out. She could overhear Mom already planning her wedding. She yelled across the shop, "Mom, you can't plan my wedding without me!"

"I wasn't planning on going tomorrow, but for the paper, I'd do anything."

"Uh-oh. Your wheels are turning." Lily bit into a chocolate.

"Harrison has a shot at winning. His gift to the paper could spur others to donate. Grandpa would be so proud. Whatever it takes to keep this town's newspaper alive."

"What if Finn wins?"

"I'm no worse off than now. Harrison is Finn's enemy. Can't stand the guy."

"But what about your issues with water?"

"That's still a problem." She placed her hand on her stomach. There was no way around it. "I'll take my motion sickness meds and pray my anxiety stays in check."

Her biggest problem was how she felt about Finn. At least the race would be a distraction.

"Thelma swears that my chocolate helps with everything— her arthritis, anxiety, even dating."

"There's not enough chocolate to fix my problems."

Lily held up a perfect truffle. "Oh, honey, there is *always* enough chocolate."

MEGAN MET Harrison on the dock early the next morning, which was already bustling with people.

"You look lost in thought." Harrison smiled at Megan as he prepped the sails and ropes. "You're not thinking of bailing on me like you did at the masquerade?"

"I told you why I left the party. Not a big fan of crowds."

As far as Megan knew, Agnes hadn't shared any gossip about her and Finn. At least she could breathe a sigh of relief knowing their kiss was still a secret.

She grabbed her bag to locate her phone when she realized it was gone. She felt her pockets. Nothing.

"Hey, I need to run back to my car to get my phone. Don't leave without me, okay?"

"Not a chance," Harrison said, coiling another rope.

She hurried down the dock and found her phone sitting on the passenger seat of her vehicle.

A text from Aspen had come in twenty minutes ago.

Aspen: Finn came by this morning looking for you. He wanted to see you before the race because he has something for you. I may have let it slip that you'd be there today. Don't hate me, okay? He said it was important.

Ugh. As if she needed anything else on her plate today. Her nerves were already frayed at the thought of sailing. Thinking of Finn only made her more jittery.

"Meg." A familiar voice made her jump.

She swung around. *Finn.* So much for avoiding him.

She caught a whiff of his aftershave, the same scent she remembered from their kiss. The memory made her weak. She leaned against the car.

"Hello, Finn." She hated that she could still be lured by his magnetic attraction even though he had broken her trust.

"I'm so glad I found you." He was breathless from running. "Could we talk?"

"Don't you have things to do for the race?"

"I do. But this is more important."

She put her hands on her car and leaned back. "I'm not sure I can talk, Finn. Not after everything."

"Please let me explain . . ."

"I can't. I have to get back to Harrison's boat."

"Wait, you're going with him?" His eyes turned nuclear.

"You didn't think I'd go with you?" A fire had risen in her chest. "You knew Dale wanted to hire you as the editor, and instead of sharing it, you kept it from me, all the while pretending there was something between us."

"Meg . . ."

"You want to know what the crazy thing is? I fell for it all."

"Will you at least listen to my side?"

"No, I will not listen. You fooled me before, and it's not going to happen again." As she brushed past him, he grabbed her arm.

"Please, don't go." He pulled a small box out of his pocket. "I need to give you one thing."

He held the box out for her. She took the faded silk box and opened it. Inside was a translucent piece of green glass. The edges were no longer jagged, but had softened, like pebbles at the edge of the shore.

She turned it over in her fingers.

"What is it?"

"From Joshua. Sea glass he found on the shore. Tradition says that whenever a sailor would leave on a journey, he would be given a piece of sea glass to carry in his pocket until he returned. A reminder that no matter how far he traveled, he'd always come back home."

The story circled in her brain, like a familiar tune. Had Joshua told her this before? She couldn't remember him talking about it, but something about the tale seemed vaguely familiar.

She stared at the color. It reminded her of jade. "Why are you giving this to me?"

"Joshua asked me to pass it along today. He said you'd know why."

She had no idea why Joshua wanted her to take it. She tucked the glass in her pocket and left her hand on it, her fingers smoothing over the edges. "Good luck today."

"We'll need it."

"We?" she frowned. *Please not Scarlett.*

"Joshua volunteered to sail with me. We practiced together this week. The water is like his second home."

She often spotted Joshua at daybreak in his fishing boat, but she didn't know he sailed.

"I hope it goes well." She still fingered the glass in her pocket, wondering what it meant.

Finn looked like he wanted to say more, but he clamped his mouth shut and nodded.

She left him in the parking lot, her thoughts swirling like waves before a storm.

As she sat down in Harrison's boat, she saw one more message.

Finn: I'm so sorry. I wish things hadn't ended this way.

She put the phone away and took a deep breath, slowly exhaling.

Me too, Finn. Me too.

CHAPTER TWENTY-FOUR

MEGAN

It wouldn't be hard for Harrison to make good time on his sailboat. They had moved up to the front of the starting line, in prime position to make it around the first buoy as the leader in the race. Powerful gusts filled their sails, pushing their boat along with a speed that almost took Megan's breath away. Twenty boats clipped along the course, and Harrison's boat led the pack.

Harrison explained the course as he steered. "We need to go from the starting line around the buoy, then return to the starting line and take the lap again. It's essentially a two-lap race. If I can get in front early, we'll be in a dominant position for the entire race."

Megan tried to relax, but she could barely pull her shoulders down from her earlobes. The wind whipped her hair while her heart pounded like a jackhammer. She searched for Finn's boat. He had gotten to the starting line late because of her. The time he had taken searching all over town had set him back, putting him behind from the start. A twinge of guilt twisted inside her, and instinctively, she reached for the glass in her pocket.

It doesn't mean anything. She considered tossing it overboard, but it was a gift from Joshua.

Megan craned her neck for Finn's boat. She could see his craft several boats back, gaining speed, making up for lost time from his poor position at the starting line.

The morning sun beat down on them as they sailed across choppy waters. Megan's shoulders relaxed, although her nerves still tingled on high alert with every bump.

Harrison pointed ahead. "We're going to be turning into the wind, and the sails are going to end up on the other side of the boat. I'll need you to steer while I take care of the sails."

"What? But I don't know how."

"Just follow my instructions. It's difficult for me to attempt both, so you have to help."

Her stomach immediately clenched. Nothing seemed easy around water. She hadn't wanted to touch the boat, but she needed to overcome her phobia of water.

He gave her the tiller. "When I say ready to tack, start turning the boat. I'll release the jib sheet while the boom rotates so that the sail moves to catch the wind on the other side. Ready to tack?"

"Ready." Megan watched as Harrison effortlessly controlled the jib sheet so the sail rotated.

"Turn," he instructed.

For a moment, they lost momentum as they went into the wind.

"More!"

Megan followed Harrison's instructions, but they'd lost speed when the boat had stayed too long turning into the wind.

Finn's boat had moved up to third place and was gaining on them.

"We almost lost our lead." Harrison scrambled back into

place and grabbed the tiller from her hand. He was agitated at losing time.

Megan surveyed their lead and couldn't figure out why Harrison was upset. "We're still ahead."

"It would be great if you could be useful in some way." His voice cracked with frustration.

"Let me try again on this next turn," she yelled. Sweat trickled down her back under her life jacket. Even with the wind, the sun made her unbearably hot.

They sped ahead, making good time, but Finn's boat still moved into second, placing him close enough that Megan could see his face now. He maneuvered the sails smoothly while Joshua steered, steady and focused. The sun reflected the joy in Joshua's face, as his grey hair ruffled in the wind. Their team of two worked together seamlessly while Harrison grew increasingly frustrated that he was losing ground to Finn's old boat.

Harrison adjusted one line as angry creases deepened across his forehead. Finn and Joshua were closing the gap between them. Both boats zipped along, increasing their pressure to maintain speed.

As they neared the turn, Harrison changed his mind and grabbed the tiller from her hands.

"We can't lose time on this turn or they'll take the lead."

"I know what I'm doing now."

"You obviously don't." The edge in his voice made her feel like an idiot.

She shouldn't have agreed to this. In his eyes, she had already failed.

Her body burned under the constricting life jacket. She unbuckled the straps, hoping to get some air for a few minutes. "Please let me try."

He gave her the tiller. "As long as you listen to me." He glanced at Finn's boat on their tail, and then surveyed their sail, trying to measure the direction of the wind.

Megan could see Finn doing the same, calculating their turn.

"Ready to jibe?"

"Ready." She turned the boat away from the wind, but Harrison frowned as they lost speed.

"It's not right," Harrison snapped, then bolted to take over for her, grabbing the tiller while trying to adjust the main sail. She had caused the mistake, and now they were losing more time on the turn. This was a key moment in the race. Whoever took this turn fastest would likely win the race, and Harrison wasn't about to give up.

She tried to move out of his way, but just as she did, the wind caught the mainsail and the boom swung wildly across the boat.

"Watch out!" he yelled.

By the time she glanced back, it was too late. The heavy pole struck her in the head before she could avoid its force. A sharp pain radiated through her skull as she lost her balance and fell overboard into the lake.

She barely had time to take one last breath before her body plunged into the water, sending a cold shock through her limbs as her life jacket slipped off. As she sank under the waves, panic soared through every nerve, and she froze, her dead weight sinking deeper. Suddenly, the need for air sent off alarm bells in her head. Her arms flailed in the water, searching for the life jacket, trying to find the surface. The water was murky, but she could sense light. She kicked hard, struggling toward it, her lungs screaming in pain for a breath of oxygen.

She'd learned to swim as a child, but since the accident, she only swam in places where she could touch the bottom. Her swimming skills were acceptable, but less so in the violent undercurrent of the lake where the boats had stirred up the waters. Why had she been so stupid to unbuckle her life jacket?

As her head broke through the surface of the water, she gasped for breath. A wave choked her, filling her mouth as she sputtered and coughed. Her shoulders burned as she fought to keep her head above the water. At this pace, she wouldn't be able to stay afloat. Panic surged in her chest, pulling her down like a brick as she struggled to swim.

"Meg," a voice cried in the distance.

"Help!" Her head bobbed above the water, aching from the impact of the boom. A stream of blood ran down her forehead, and she tasted it on her lips before she sank under another wave. The sirens in her head wailed as her body fought against the force of the waters. She simply didn't have the strength or skill to maintain this level of exertion.

"I can't—" she screamed, but a wave filled her mouth again, causing her to choke and flail.

She needed air. Her mind erupted, scattered with empty details. She couldn't think about anything but getting more oxygen to her lungs. It was as if her brain turned off and only one thing mattered now: survival. As her lungs demanded oxygen, her body fought the impossible strength of the water. She couldn't do this for much longer.

A carousel of images circled in her mind. *Dad. Sunset. Campfires. Mom.*

Her arms and legs were on fire now, muscles burning, mind shifting sideways as the world spun like a tilt-a-whirl. Her thoughts no longer made sense. Images flashed before her like a slide show. *Sisters. Brother. Grandma. Beach. Running. Home. Bed. Night. Fireflies. Swing.*

She tipped her head toward the sun. The light was her only hope before she sank into darkness. Suddenly, an image of Joshua cut through the screaming in her brain.

He leaned over the edge, holding a hand to her.

She closed her eyes and tried to reach for the vision, but her body became a weight too heavy to hold, and she slipped below the surface instead.

Without warning, something grasped her arm in the dark,

and a powerful arm encircling her waist pulled her to the surface. Her body, weary from fighting, didn't resist, but melted into his strength. Her head broke through the water as light blinded her. Air filled her lungs as something pulled her along. She still hadn't opened her eyes to see who her rescuer was. All she wanted was to breathe, but she had inhaled too much water. She choked and coughed, her body heaving from pain.

"Meg, I'm here."

She could hear his voice, but her brain was spinning wildly, still trying to find enough air to emerge from this nightmare. She could feel herself floating now, the effort of fighting gone.

A body pressed close to hers, straining to swim through the water, holding her up. When she opened her eyes, she knew who had saved her. That's all that mattered now. Her heavy eyes fluttered shut.

"Meg, don't give up on me now."

Her head rested on something soft, and she could feel him tugging her body along.

"I'm . . . tired. I can't—" She couldn't even get the words out. All she wanted now was to sleep, to let her body drift away into a dream.

"Not yet. Stay with me. Joshua's in the boat, but I need your help to hoist you on it."

"I can't."

She felt a hand on her cheek. "Open your eyes. Meg, I need you to look at me."

She willed herself to open them, even though they were weighted by exhaustion.

An image drifted into her bleary vision.

Finn.

"I need you to stay with me," he said in a low voice that sounded like the warmth of a blanket. "You're safe now."

That's when she realized it. He'd come for her, just like he'd promised.

CHAPTER TWENTY-FIVE

MEGAN

A blurry, vague memory blotted out what happened next to Megan. She remembered crawling into the boat and collapsing on the deck, but whether Finn pulled her out or she'd climbed in herself, she couldn't remember. Her memories were murky and fluid, like the sensation of swimming underwater.

When she woke up in a hospital room, her siblings crowded around her while Mom and Dad sat nearby.

"She's awake." Cassidy's voice cut through the soft murmur of voices in her room. Her mom gathered with her sisters on Megan's left, while her father and Matt flanked the opposite side.

Fingers gently stroked the hair from her forehead. Her lips were dry, like she'd spent too long without water.

"What happened?"

Her vision blurred, then the faces of her family shifted into focus like the lens of a camera.

Her mom stopped stroking her hair. "You had a minor accident in the lake. For the second time in our lives, you frightened us to death."

Megan groaned. "I remember falling in the water and then..."

Her eyelids fluttered shut. She didn't want to relive the next part. The memory felt like a car skidding out of control on a slippery road. Then her mind blanked, a dark void blotting out the accident, her body's way of protecting her from the trauma.

"How did I get here? I can't remember anything but falling, then water, and nothing."

Cassidy held her hand. "Finn called 911, and an ambulance met you at the dock."

Fuzzy faces slipped in and out of her mind like a blurred photo. She recognized people, but something distant flickered, a liquid memory that shifted out of focus.

"I saw Joshua when I was in the water. He told me to not be afraid. How was that possible?"

"He was in Finn's boat, but the boat was far away," Matt said. "I don't think you could have heard him."

She rubbed her forehead as if she could make the memories clearer. "I don't understand. Did Harrison pull me out?"

Her family glanced at each other.

"Why are you all looking like that? Just tell me what happened."

Matt stepped closer to her side. "You got knocked into the lake when the boom shifted on the mainsail. It was an accident, but Harrison realized it too late. Thankfully, Finn's boat was behind you when it happened. Finn immediately dove into the water to save you, but you sank so fast he couldn't find you. It was Joshua who circled the boat and directed him. Then Finn pulled you to safety. It was—how should we put it? A tense moment."

"Finn rescued me? Did he lose the race?"

Mom nodded.

"Then who won?"

Her mother patted her arm. "It's not important who won. All that matters is that Finn saved you."

"I want to know." Her dry voice cracked.

Mom handed her a cup of water while Matt spoke. "Harrison won, though nobody really cared at that point. When Finn brought you in, everyone thought he was a hero. He might have lost the race, but he was the real winner."

"So Finn lost all because of me?"

"He saved your life, Meg," Lily confirmed. "I don't think he cared about winning after that."

She could only imagine how hard it was to rescue her after everything he had been through.

She closed her eyes. "Where is Finn now? I need to thank him."

Her mom looked at her sisters, then Cassidy spoke. "He stayed with you the whole time until we got here. He wanted us to tell you goodbye."

Megan's phone interrupted her thoughts. Her family had retrieved it from Harrison's boat after the race. She glanced at the screen, hoping it was Finn. Instead, her former boss's name lit up the screen.

"Are you up for this?" Lily asked. "We can ignore it."

"I can do this." Megan put the phone to her ear. "Hello, Dale."

"Megan, I'm so relieved to hear your voice. What happened out there was the worst thing I've ever seen at the race."

"Just don't plaster it on the front page, okay?"

"We have to cover this. Everyone wants to know what happened. I've been fielding calls ever since the accident. But I don't know who will write the story now that Finn's gone . . ."

"What do you mean?"

"He didn't tell you?"

Her mouth went dry. "No."

"Finn resigned Friday."

"Why?"

"He wouldn't reveal why. Handed me his resignation letter and said he couldn't stay in Wild Harbor."

The realization of Finn's departure hit her like a punch. "But he's your replacement."

"Not anymore. Told me he wouldn't take the job, no matter how much I paid him. Said I was a fool if I didn't hire you as the next editor-in-chief."

"I don't understand. He never said a word to me." She remembered their tense conversation before the race. She had shut him down. Refused to even hear him out.

"You know what else?" Dale's voice pitched higher. "He talked the mayor into making a confession about the payments he accepted from SCI. He mentioned that the paper was ready to print your article, and the mayor either needed to come clean or he'd publicize the article. Steve agreed to turn himself in. I'm sure there'll be an investigation, and the federal grand jury will indict him. It was your article that swayed him."

"But you were never planning on printing the article."

"The mayor didn't know that. Finn called his bluff and told him it was ready to go to print."

Her head was still swimming from the news. Finn was leaving town because of her. The mayor was confessing the truth.

"Dale, you need to stop Finn. The paper needs him."

"I tried, Megan. He won't consider it. The guy is stubborn."

Megan bit her lip. "Then I need to talk to him."

"Good luck. I'm pretty sure he's already left. The regatta was his last event in Wild Harbor. He will email his final article to me tomorrow."

Megan closed her eyes. This wasn't the news she wanted to hear. "I'll see if I can get ahold of him."

"Before you go, I have one question. What will it take to get you back on my staff?"

She laughed. "I'm not even out of the hospital yet, and you're trying to negotiate?"

"I can wait. But the offer is always there."

"Thanks, Dale. I appreciate it."

"You know, kid, I missed you when you left the newspaper. It made me realize you're not so bad to have around."

She smiled, warmth radiating through her. "You're not so bad either, Dale."

She ended the call and sat up, trying to figure out if she was strong enough to leave. As tired as her body was, she wanted to track down Finn.

"What are you doing?" Lily placed a hand on her sister's shoulder.

"I need to find out the truth." Megan flung the hospital blanket off her legs. "Get me my clothes."

"What are you talking about?" Cassidy handed her a bag.

"I don't have time to explain. I need to find Finn." She swung her feet off her bed and tried to stand. Her head felt woozy.

Matt grabbed her arm to stabilize her balance. "Slow down. You can't go until they dismiss you. The shape you're in, they won't let you go yet."

She held her forehead and clamped her eyes shut so the room would stop spinning. "I got up too fast. I'll be fine." She blinked her eyes. "See? All good now." The room swayed, and she grabbed the bed rail for support. "Well, almost. Can you help me get dressed?"

She dumped her plastic bag of personal items on the bed. "Why are you all looking at me like I'm nuts?"

"Because you are nuts." Cassidy's eyes widened. "You're putting on your old clothes? Let us at least grab some clean ones."

"You have a better idea? I can't leave in this." She pulled at the pale green hospital gown that hung on her like a sack.

"Before you strip down, at least let us leave." Matt was already helping Dad exit before Megan changed her clothes.

"You're not going to stop her?" Cassidy pleaded with her brother.

"Nope. Good luck." He waved as he left.

Cassidy sighed. "Meg, give us one good reason we should help you sneak out of here."

"Because I need to talk to Finn. He quit his job for me. That's what he was trying to tell me before the race, but I wouldn't listen. He was nothing but a gentleman, and my response was to act like a jerk. Girls, I want you to help me get out of here. We need a good old-fashioned jailbreak."

SNEAKING out of the hospital wasn't difficult. Her sisters and mom hid her from view as they walked straight out the front doors.

As her mom drove to the marina, Megan dialed Finn's number. The phone went to voice mail. "Finn, this is Megan. Please call me back as soon as possible. We need to talk."

She wanted to say more, but she had to tell him in person, to lay it out in front of him so there were no more secrets between them.

When she picked up her car, Lily insisted on driving. "You might feel fine, but that gash on your head still looks bad."

Lily took the car keys from Megan's hand.

"I'm coming too." Cassidy crawled into the back seat. She couldn't argue with her sisters. They were as stubborn as she was.

"As long as you give us privacy when we find him. I need to have the conversation that should have taken place weeks ago."

When they arrived at his apartment, Megan pounded on the door.

One neighbor, an elderly woman hunched over with age, peeked her head out the door. "Are you looking for the man who used to live there?"

"Yes, do you know where he went?" Megan knew she looked desperate, but she didn't care.

The old lady shook her head. "He packed up and left. Dropped his key off with the manager already."

"Did he mention where he was going?"

"Nope. Said he wasn't sure yet. I was sad to see him go. Nicest neighbor, always helping me with my groceries. I'm gonna miss him."

"Me, too," Megan whispered. Why was it so much easier to admit this to a stranger than to anyone else?

Megan thanked the lady and ran down the steps. Where to now? He could be hours away at this point. She sat down on the curb and put her head in her hands. If only she hadn't been so stubborn.

Something fell onto the cement from her pocket.

She looked down. A piece of smooth glass glistened in the sun.

She picked it up and turned it around in her hands.

The sea glass. Remarkably, she hadn't lost it in the accident.

Joshua. He might know where Finn was.

It was a long shot, but she had to find out.

Her sisters waited in the car as she entered Joshua's shop. A metallic *clink, clink, clink* led her to a room where old stained glass windows danced with light. Glass trinkets coated with dust sat untouched on the shelves.

She wandered past crystal chandeliers, faded oil paintings, and grandfather clocks that no longer kept time. Joshua's place existed out of time, like she'd stepped through a portal into another world, one that felt oddly out of place with the modern world.

She discovered Joshua bent over an imposing oak case, his

hands dissecting the inside of an old grandfather clock. His eyes sparked with light when he saw her, and a smile spread across his face, like a cup of cool water on a hot day.

"Didn't think I'd see you today. Thought the hospital would keep you longer."

"I decided it was long enough." She touched the wound on her head.

He pointed. "You always were a strong one. How is your head?"

"Better. Thanks to you."

"It was Finn who rescued you."

"But you found me."

"Team effort." He turned to the clock. "I'm not sure she'll ever keep time well. But isn't she beautiful?"

Joshua had a way of disarming her. He helped her to stop and see beauty when she was ready to rush ahead.

Megan brushed her hand down the dark oak. "I'd love her in my place if I had the room. Maybe someday."

He wiped his hands on his pants, exposing his arm. A deep scar stretched across his wrist. She reached out to trace it with her finger.

"What happened here?"

He pulled at his sleeve. "Long story. Sometime, I'll tell you the whole thing."

She paused, wanting more from the man of few words. He put his hand in his pocket, hiding the scar.

"Was it painful?"

"At the time. Now, it's just a reminder of the past." He tapped his head. "Some people have wounds you can't see. Don't be fooled. The invisible scars are the darkest."

"Joshua, I don't remember what happened at the regatta. But I know you helped Finn. I don't know how to thank you."

"No need to. I'm in the business of rescuing. Why do you

think I keep all these things?" He waved his arm toward the shelves of trinkets.

She pulled out the sea glass from her pocket. "Finn gave me this. Have I seen it before?"

He nodded.

"It's so familiar, like I've heard the story before."

"That's because you have, the day you almost drowned."

The moment floated into her mind like a bubble. The first accident. Her family crowding around her. Their pink-tinged faces circling her while her dad held her in his arms. She had always assumed Dad had rescued her.

But now a new memory drifted into her mind, a long forgotten one. Joshua had been on the beach that day collecting sea glass and had told her the story about the sailors who carried it. It was a promise to return. A token of trust. She had asked for a piece and he had given her one, reminding her to keep it safe.

Then she'd gone out to swim again, leaving the sea glass on her towel to add to her nature collection. Mom had been watching her swim while Dad played Frisbee with Matt. But her mother's attention had been pulled away when Cassidy had asked for help with her sandcastle. It had only been a few seconds, but that's all it took for Megan to be swept under by a wave. Dad had jumped in, followed by Mom, not realizing Joshua had plunged into the water before them. When Joshua had brought her out, carrying her sagging body, he'd laid her in her father's arms.

She hadn't remembered until now.

"You're the one who rescued me?"

Joshua nodded. "I found the sea glass after I wrapped you in your towel. When I placed you in your dad's arms, it must have fallen on the sand."

"How did I not remember?"

He shrugged. "I never mentioned I found it."

"No, I meant . . . you rescuing me?"

"You didn't need to remember."

She wrapped her arms around the old man's neck. He smelled like fresh balsam and wood smoke.

She pulled away from him, turning the glass over in the light. "Why did you give me the sea glass again?"

"Felt like you needed it." He shrugged. "Can't say why."

"What about Finn? He left without telling me where he went. Do you know where he is?"

"I do, but if I tell you where he is, only go to him if you've decided."

She cocked her head. "What?"

"To tell him everything. To finally be honest. He deserves that, at least."

She swallowed. Part of her wanted to walk away. Let go of Finn. Then sweep his memory from her mind. As if she could.

"I don't know."

"You afraid?"

She paused. Why was running away so much easier than telling the truth?

"Trust me on this." Joshua pointed at her. "If you walk away now, you'll always wonder what might have happened if you'd gone back to him."

"What if he doesn't want to see me? He won't return my calls or texts." She had waited too long.

"He thinks that's what you want. He's doing this for you. Just don't tell him I told you." Joshua gave her a wink. "He needs to hear your story. All of it. Only thing is, he doesn't know it yet."

CHAPTER TWENTY-SIX

FINN

Finn rocked on the porch swing at Joshua's cabin—the same place he'd sat with Megan before she'd tackled him with the cake. The sky was a brilliant deep-hued purple streaked with pink, the dying light soaking the sky in a spectacular glow of rich colors at the end of summer. September's cool evening breeze rustled leaves in the nearby trees.

Finn had planned on leaving town quietly, but then he'd run into Joshua.

"Take a few days and think it over," Joshua had urged him. "Stay at my cabin by the lake. Nobody's using it, and the porch swing's waiting."

The cottage was one last reminder of Megan and how he'd bungled their relationship. He'd finally earned her trust, only to break it by not telling her the truth about the job. It wasn't just the position that had wedged them apart, but that he'd hidden it from her. As far as she was concerned, it was an act of betrayal and the final blow to their relationship.

If he moved on, she could have the job at the paper. Another town, another paper. Without her, what did it matter now?

He'd also worked up the courage to call his dad and tell him the news about quitting.

"You sure about this?" His dad's voice had a tremor in it.

"Never been so sure in my life. It's time for me to do things my way, because I can't live up to the expectations of my brother. I've been doing that my whole life, and it's only made me feel like more of a failure. From now on, I need to find my place."

Finn had finally confessed all the things that he'd been holding back. Things that had wounded and haunted him for years. He'd never realized how much these secrets had shackled him, but releasing them felt like freedom.

One conversation couldn't fix his scars, but it had given him a chance to uncover old wounds and start to heal—something he'd been avoiding for far too long.

The swing creaked as he swayed. Only the sound of the crickets echoed around him.

He'd get up early and hit the road. Time for him to leave his ghosts behind. The shadow of his brother's memory had followed him for so long. Even back at Joshua's shop, his brother's memory had stood in the shadows, waiting for him.

Car tires chewed up gravel on the long drive. An engine died, then the sound of footsteps crunching stone.

"I'm on the swing, Joshua," he called.

A shadow appeared around the corner first, like the ghosts of his past.

"Finn." She stood in the same clothes she'd worn when he'd pulled her from the water. The memory shook him, and he wondered whether it was his imagination.

"I thought you were in the hospital."

Megan stepped closer. "I had to find you before you left."

"How did you know I was here?"

She shook her head. "I'm not allowed to reveal my source. But I couldn't let you leave town without saying thank you."

He remembered her lying on the bottom of the boat after the rescue, her body shuddering from pain, her breath racked with heaving coughs. Even while her wet hair clung to her pale skin and water rolled down her cheeks, she'd looked beautiful. Worth losing everything for.

His imagination wasn't tricking him. She was here. *With him.*

"Can I join you?" She sat next to him, and for a few moments, they swayed in silence, not able to say what was really on their minds as the dying light faded. Only the moon's glow reflected off the high planes of her cheekbones.

She didn't look at him, but he felt the tension of her closeness, of wanting to touch her, but forbidden to do so. He loved her so much that it pierced him like a needle threading through his skin.

She finally broke the silence. "Why did you do it?"

"What do you mean?"

"Quit your job. Leave without saying goodbye. Did you think I wouldn't care?"

"I thought that's what you wanted. Me out of the picture. You'd be free to run the paper. You won."

"That's just it." She turned to him. "I didn't win. I made it a competition and lost you instead."

"Meg," he said softly. "Tell me why you're upset. I gave you what you wanted."

"When we started working together, I saw you as competition, a threat not only to my job, but my heart. So I stayed away. Scared you'd see how I really felt. Protecting myself. But after everything you've done, I've realized that's not who you are. You gave up your job. You were the only one who tore down my walls."

"I'd give you anything."

"But what have I given you? I cost you the race. Even staying here."

"No, you gave me something better."

"What?"

"A piece of you." He touched her face gently, stroking it with a tenderness that made her eyes close. "But I knew you'd never give me all of you. I couldn't stay in Wild Harbor and wish for something I could never have."

"There's something I have to tell you." She pulled his hand down, then twisted the hem on her shirt. "It's part of the reason I locked you out. I promised myself I'd never fall for anyone until I knew one thing."

"What is it?"

"What you really wanted."

Had she understood nothing? "You know what I want."

"No. I'm broken, Finn." She rubbed her forehead, avoiding his eyes. "Because I can't . . . I'm not able to—" Her voice dropped off as she chewed her lip.

"Take your time." He could see the pain etched on her face and waited for her to finish.

"Have kids." She swallowed and looked out at the lake. "I couldn't take that away from someone. So I shut men out before I could get hurt. Before the truth disappointed them. Before they rejected me. I was so focused on what was wrong with me, I wouldn't even give you a chance."

He took her hands in his. "Did it ever occur to you that a man could be one hundred percent happy because he has the right woman? That is where love begins—with you and me."

She shrugged. "Not if you want more than that . . ."

"Spending my life with the right person is the most important thing. Whether or not we have kids, when I grow old, I want you to be the one sitting beside me on the porch swing."

He slid toward her and cupped her face in his hands. "We'll figure it out together. If you're open to it, we can explore other options for building a family. We don't have to know everything right now. We only need to take one step at a time." He traced the line of her jaw with his finger, sliding it down the curve of her neck. "You're the most important thing. That's all I want right now."

She leaned back on the swing, and he looped his arm under her waist, cradling her. Her eyes were lit, and a smile glowed on her face. Maybe he could earn her trust back, a kiss at a time. One hundred percent. All of it.

"I heard your voice when you rescued me. You asked me to stay."

He took her chin and gently kissed her. "You don't know how much I want you."

"And you love me?"

"Since the moment I saw you. I wanted to be your blind date that first night. To show you how a woman should be treated."

"Then I'm asking you the same. Will you stay?"

That was all it took. He answered with a kiss, leaning his body against hers, falling into her, their lips meeting in a tender embrace. He hadn't realized how much he longed to hold her in his arms. His hands were in her hair as he drank her in, not able to get enough of her, like a thirst he couldn't quench.

She pulled back, her eyes zeroed in on his. "So that's a yes?"

He nodded.

She nestled her head on his shoulder. "I fell for you the first time you smiled at me. It was like free-falling off the top of a skyscraper. I wanted to take you with me. I just couldn't admit it."

"It seems there were a lot of things we had trouble admitting." He intertwined his fingers with hers.

"I know." She laughed. "But you realize what this means, right? I can't let you quit the paper."

"I think that ship has sailed."

"Not if I have anything to say about it. The SCI story made

me realize I like reporting more than anything else. To be honest, I don't know if I want to be the editor if it pulls me away from writing."

"I thought the editor's job was your dream."

"That's what I thought too, but I bought into a lie. I believed the editor's job would make me whole, and that no one else could do it, but as soon as Dale offered it to me, I realized I was making a huge mistake."

"What are you going to do?"

"Talk to Dale. Tell him I want to stay as lead reporter. Then convince you to come back as editor."

"You don't have to make that offer. I can freelance for other newspapers in the region. You're the one who said we'd never work well together."

"You proved me wrong, and we wouldn't be competing anymore. We'd finally be in our sweet spots." She wrapped her arms around his neck. "Besides, I don't want anyone else to take you away. You'd make an incredible editor. As long as you're okay with being stuck with me."

He gave her a mischievous grin. "You'll have to convince me."

"That won't be hard."

She leaned into him, angling her body into his, the warmth of her lips enveloping his, erasing all the ghosts of his past.

She was everything he'd ever wanted. Always had been.

"You have no idea how much I love you, Megan Woods."

"And you have no idea how crazy I am for you."

He whispered it in her ear. "Finally."

EPILOGUE

FINN

DECEMBER. THREE MONTHS LATER.

Finn burst into Megan's office, a smile playing on his lips as he rubbed his hands together. Snowflakes were falling outside, blanketing everything in crisp white.

"You really should come outside and see the snow." He wrapped his arms around her, interrupting her typing, kissing the side of her neck.

"As soon as I finish this article." Her fingers tapped the keyboard, ignoring his kisses.

"As your editor, I give you permission to finish the job later."

"You told me the story was due today by five." She looked at her watch. "Which is now."

"But it's Christmas." He opened the blind in her office so she could see the lights outside.

Except for the town's gigantic tree, Wild Harbor's Christmas decorations were finally finished, complete with white twinkling lights and evergreen boughs. It looked like the North Pole had exploded on Main Street.

Plus, the ring in his pocket was burning a hole. Not only burning, but setting the whole thing aflame.

He wanted this ring on her finger. *Pronto.*

Three times this week she had turned him down for a date, excusing herself because of a deadline or a last-minute story to cover. The Christmas season had buried their already over-worked staff. Besides the regular local stories, they were swamped with seasonal festivities to cover, like the winter festival, the holiday choral concert, and the lighting of the town's Christmas tree tonight.

Finn was determined to persuade Meg to leave, no matter if he had to pick her up and carry her out.

"So do I have to pry the computer from your hands, or will you come willingly?"

She turned to him and smiled. "I'd be happy for you to pull me away from this assignment, as long as I can have a kiss first."

"Mmm. You drive a hard bargain, Ms. Woods, but I think you could persuade me."

He leaned over and gave her a tender kiss on the mouth, full and satisfying. He hoped it was persuasive enough.

She grinned. "No more work." She slapped her laptop shut. "I'm all yours."

His heart melted at her words. "If I had known it was that easy, I would have tried this days ago."

"I've put in a ton of hours. Plus, with Lily and Alex's wedding this week, I've really neglected you. You've been so patient. I'm sorry if I've been preoccupied."

He drew circles on the side of her neck with his fingertips. "Some things are worth the wait. You're one of them."

She stood and wrapped a winter coat around her shoulders, a shade of red that brought out her dark eyes. "Do you want to grab some dinner at Brewster's, then head over to the tree lighting? We can get hot chocolate on the way."

"I have something better than that." If only she knew.

"What is it?" Her eyes twinkled.

"I can't tell you just yet. But we're headed someplace special."

"Where?"

He raised his eyebrows. "You'll have to wait and see."

"Well, at least the drive will give me some time to work on things for the wedding. Lily roped me into planning the seating chart for the reception, but it's better than the job she gave Cass, which was floral arrangements for the ends of the church pews. I'm so tired of wedding planning." She rubbed her head.

Maybe this was a bad time to pop the question, but he couldn't stop himself now. He'd made sure all the arrangements for this evening were in place. *It's now or never, baby.*

As they headed outside, the snow-covered shop windows glowed with white lights while evergreen boughs swirled down streetlamps.

He grabbed her hand and pulled her toward the park. "We're not driving anywhere. Let's take a walk instead."

"Will we make the Christmas tree lighting? We don't have much time."

"Don't worry. I've got this. Trust me, okay?"

"I do."

He stopped. "One hundred percent?"

She nodded. "Of course, but why is that important?"

"You'll see."

The tree lighting ceremony was happening behind the newspaper building, where the gigantic twenty-foot tree was set up in the park.

Time was running out for Finn's plan, but he hoped he could coordinate things for the seven p.m. countdown.

"Do we have time to eat?" She squeezed his hand tightly,

running to keep up with his long stride as they turned the corner to the park.

He smiled. She hadn't figured out yet that they weren't headed to Brewster's.

"Do you remember when I won the tug-of-war at the Wild Harbor Summer Festival?"

"Yeah, but what does that have to do with dinner?"

"I won a date with you. Except you never fulfilled your end of the bargain. You ditched me for Harrison. I sat at the park waiting for you."

"In my defense, we've gone to almost every restaurant in town for the last three months."

"Hmm, true. But you still owe me one in the park. Tonight, we're finally going to finish what we started."

He took her hand and helped her up a path to a small covered pavilion. Candles illuminated the path leading to a table and two chairs.

"What's going on, Finn? How did you plan all this?"

"Oh, I have some sneaky elves who do my bidding."

"But it's cold out. Not exactly picnic weather."

"Wait until you see the lights from up there. It will all be worth it."

Especially when this ring was on her finger.

The pavilion was on a hill near the lakeshore, decorated with white lights and evergreen boughs, setting everything off in a warm glow. Frozen pieces, like broken glass, dotted the shoreline while the snow softened the hard lines of the ice.

As they approached their table, a gentleman dressed in a black jacket carried a large package toward the table. He opened the insulated bag that kept their food warm and placed it in front of them, then he quietly disappeared.

Megan glanced over her shoulder. "Are there any other people hiding in bushes around here? Because I'm beginning to freak out."

"I'm full of surprises tonight."

"But how did you make all this magic happen in the last five minutes?"

"That's my secret." He wasn't about to confess that her sisters were in on the evening. He had been planning this for the last several weeks, getting everything in place for the big moment. When the snow had fallen in the early afternoon, draping everything in a white blanket, it had been the perfect last touch. As they ate their meal under the twinkle lights of the pavilion, the entire world looked like a snow globe.

She took a sip of water. "I never told you this, but that day when Harrison took me to lunch, all I could think about was you. Even while he was wooing me over fancy food, I had this sick feeling in the pit of my stomach. I should have walked out and left Harrison Brinks."

"You should have." He gave her a wink. "But you were doing your job. And because you refused to back down from the story, it looks like his dad will go to trial for the bribery scheme. Even by pleading guilty, it's likely he'll serve jail time."

"At least Harrison still made his donation to the paper. I think he felt guilty for what happened at the regatta. I wonder if Steve has some regrets about the whole debacle."

Finn's eyes drifted to the town's Christmas tree. "I'm sure he does. He never thought the truth would come out. He had no idea the power of Edna Long. Or you."

Megan initially hadn't been sure how the town would react to the scandal, but since the news had broken, the community had flooded her with notes of gratitude. If there was one thing this community valued, it was loyalty and honesty, a lost quality in so many places.

"This is the perfect view," she said, picking up a roll slathered in butter. "We're high enough I can see the lake and the Christmas decorations from town, and when they light the tree, it will be even more spectacular."

People were gathering around the tree at the base of the hill, unaware of Finn and Megan in their private pavilion eating dinner together. Finn hoped this would give them the perfect spot to view the tree lighting while offering the privacy he needed to pop the question.

Since Dale had retired at the start of the holiday season, he had taken on a bigger role in the community, leading the Christmas committee that planned events for the holiday season. It had afforded Finn the perfect setup for tonight's plan, since he was able to rope Dale into the scheme.

As they finished dinner, a choir started singing Christmas carols. Finn could see Megan's family gathered at the base of the tree, mingling among the crowd, but Megan didn't seem to notice.

She was finishing the chocolate mousse, licking her spoon with an expression of complete bliss. "This is wonderful. A perfect meal, just in time for the lighting."

Dale stood on a platform next to the tree, looking tiny compared to the gargantuan fir, a microphone in hand.

"Tonight, we're going to count down the lighting of the tree, and then we'll have a very special announcement."

"What's Dale got up his sleeve? Is anyone from the paper covering this?" She pulled out her phone to take notes, always a journalist, no matter the situation.

"I don't think you need to worry about that." He took the phone from her hands. "Believe me."

Dale started the countdown. "Ten, nine, eight . . ."

Finn pulled out the ring and kept it hidden in his hand, waiting for the tree lighting while watching Megan's expression. He hoped that the staff at the newspaper office could pull off their part.

"Three, two, one . . ."

The scene exploded in lights, while everyone erupted in

cheers. The tree sparkled with a dazzling, colorful glow, while silk bows and a silver star adorned the top.

Dale came on the microphone. "This year, the newspaper office is taking part in the tree lighting by providing its own special holiday sign for the event."

Everybody turned to the three-story brick building behind the park where Finn and Megan's love story had begun. On the outside of the building was a message written in white rope lighting.

"Wait a minute," Megan whispered. "It says, 'Will . . . you . . . marry . . . me . . . Meg?' What?" She turned to Finn, who was down on one knee next to her. He held the ring up while she stared with wide eyes.

"Are you asking me now? In front of all these people?"

"They're all impatiently waiting for your reply, including me."

"But you still want to be with me, even though we don't know what the future holds?"

"Meg, I wouldn't have asked you if there were any doubts. There are no guarantees. But I want you to trust me. One hundred percent. The only thing I can promise is that I'll love you—if you'll have me."

"If I'll have you? Yes, of course, I will. I want all of you." She wrapped her arms around his neck, the tears flowing down her cheeks. "One hundred percent."

He pressed a perfect kiss onto her lips.

Her yes was more than words. Everything in her body—the urgency of her kiss, the way they fit together, the tears that flowed down her neck—confirmed her answer.

Suddenly, a crowd of people cheered from the bottom of the hill. He was so focused on her answer, he'd forgotten about the crowd.

She pulled away from him and smiled. "I guess we're not alone."

People held up their phones, capturing the moment. Even a photographer from the newspaper was strategically placed to snap a picture. Dale raised his arms in the air, like a referee after a touchdown. "She said yes, folks! The best news of the year!"

Her siblings waved her down from the hill, their faces shining. "If I don't go down there now, I will never hear the end."

She rushed down the hill and nearly slipped in the snow.

"Whoa, slow down there." Finn grabbed her hand, steadying her. "I don't want you to fall."

She squeezed his hand. "Can I be cheesy and say that I've already fallen for you?"

He stopped her for one last kiss. "Anytime you want."

"Remember when I showed you my childhood poems, including that mushy love poem I almost burned in my fireplace? You stopped me that day, and now, I know why. You helped me believe it was true."

Her sisters rushed toward her as she pulled away to show off her new diamond. As Meg's family surrounded her, admiring her ring, someone emerged from the fir trees. Joshua stepped into the light, a big grin spread across his face. He nodded his head toward Finn, then gave him a thumbs-up before slipping back into the shadows.

The tale of the sea glass may have been birthed from legend, but he owed Joshua. He was the one who had rescued Meg and, in a sense, him.

"Finn. What are you looking at?" Megan's warm hands grabbed his as she leaned into his chest. Snowflakes caught in her hair, crowning her in white. Her face held a smile he loved best, one he could never tire of.

"Nothing," he said. "Only you."

He leaned in for a kiss under the lights of the tree. She laughed before their lips met, his favorite sound in the world.

Even with a crowd around them, the entire world melted away with a kiss.

First it was me.
Then I met you.
Now it's you and me, forever.

∾

BONUS WEDDING EPILOGUE

The story isn't over!

As a thank you for reading this book, get a BONUS wedding epilogue of Lily and Alex's big day (and a SURPRISE you won't want to miss) by signing up for Grace's newsletter on graceworthington.com.

This is a special BONUS EPILOGUE just for you!

Sign up to read the bonus wedding epilogue.

Did you enjoy *Summer Nights in Wild Harbor?*
Leave a review on Amazon.

∾

Read on for a sneak peek of **Christmas Wishes in Wild Harbor**, the next book in the Wild Harbor Beach Series.

Finding love is the last thing on her wish list.

When Mila Sutton returns to Wild Harbor for the holidays, the last thing she wants is love. But she needs a date to Lily's wedding and makes a desperate bargain in the process.

Now Mila is looking for a fake date with no strings attached—

the type of man who will fulfill two requirements to pull off the charade: all fun and no romance.

Enter handsome barista, Max, the perfect pretend boyfriend.

But what happens when Max breaks the no romance agreement and starts to have feelings for Mila?

Can their relationship be something more than a charade? Or will time run out before Max can convince Mila that his love is real?

Order Christmas Wishes in Wild Harbor on Amazon.

CHRISTMAS WISHES IN WILD HARBOR

Sneak Peek of Book Three

CHAPTER 1

MILA

The bride posed in the three-way mirror, shifting her body from front to back so that she could glimpse her figure from every angle.

The dress shimmered in the light, the hand-sewn beading flashing with every turn.

Olivia fiddled with the neckline, pulling the gown up to cover her well-endowed chest. "I'm not sure, Mother. Do you think this dress is the one? I like it, but I only get to choose one dress and I want to make sure I choose the right one."

This bride had been particularly fussy, trying on over a hundred elaborate gowns before she declared this one the perfect dress.

The seamstress had altered the dress to her measurements

perfectly, fitting her every curve without an extra inch to spare. But now her forehead wrinkled like two perfectly sewn seams were threaded through it.

Mila folded her hands together calmly as she watched this saga unfold. This could only mean one thing. The bride was not pleased.

"I'm not sure about it." The bride continued to twirl with a dissatisfied pout that was an obvious distress signal for her mother.

"What is it, darling?" The mother hustled to her side and began circling her back with her palm. "Olivia, is it how it fits? Does it not feel right?"

Brides' mothers were always subject to an enormous level of stress. After all, they were attempting the impossible: creating their daughter's dream-come-true wedding. This typically resulted in high levels of anxiety bubbling over into every single decision, including the all-important choice of a gown.

Olivia's brow deepened. "I'm just wondering if I should go with a full gown instead of a fitted one."

Susan Smith continued to pat her daughter's back as if this was an impending crisis. "Maybe we should go back to the drawing board and try on more dresses. What do you say, sweetheart? We are spending thousands on this dress. We want to get it right."

Mila cleared her throat gently to remind them that she was still in the room. She attempted a cool, unaffected face punctuated by a reassuring smile. She'd dealt with brides like this before. Young women who couldn't decide on a dress, no matter how many they tried on. She was like a preschooler playing in a pile of dress-up clothes. All her hopes and dreams were placed on the dress, expecting it to magically transform her from an ordinary young woman in jeans and a T-shirt to a fairy-tale princess.

"I understand you're having second thoughts about the

dress." Mila used her most soothing voice, a soft, pillowy tone that sounded like something between a psychotherapist's question and a children's lullaby. She needed to strike a balance between reassuring the bride and understanding her concerns. Her business reputation was counting on it.

Mila knelt down and fanned out the train of the dress so that it draped around the bride for a perfect photo finish. The result was critical to a final decision.

"This dress is spectacular on you." Mila swept over the bride's body. "Look at your gorgeous figure. The shimmer of the satin. The hand-sewn details. Now that it's been altered, it highlights your waist and draws the eye to your face. We'll see all the love and radiance you are feeling on your wedding day. You will be the most beautiful bride ever!"

She was going overboard, but some women needed the lavish praise when making a final decision. Otherwise, they would never make up their minds, always flip-flopping between multiple gowns, wondering if the perfect dress existed in the world.

It didn't exist, but Mila wasn't about to explain that. She owned the wedding-dress shop, and her job was to make every bride feel exceedingly special, unique, beautiful.

Convincing the bride to say yes to the dress was the only way she made money. Plus, there was the sticky issue of the refund policy. No dress could be returned after it had been altered. It was a term of the contract that Mila avoided mentioning unless forced to.

Olivia softened under Mila's extravagant praise. "I do like this one." She turned in the mirror some more, checking out her backside. "But is it the perfect one? I'm not sure."

Mila was hoping the bride wouldn't waffle. Because the dress had been altered to her exact measurements, if they backed out now, they'd lose their deposit.

Since the gowns were designer brands, each worth thousands of dollars, Mila ended up taking a hit when a bride backed out. The only thing she could do now was gently remind the bride of her nonrefundable deposit and hope they'd keep the dress.

Mila adjusted the delicate lace strap on the bride's shoulder. "I think this dress looks like it was made for you. After seeing you in dozens of dresses, I can't imagine a more extraordinary choice for your special day."

It was easy to make a woman feel good. Mila had no problem envisioning how beautiful each bride could be on her wedding day. She didn't have to stretch the truth. Every woman was extraordinary in her own way.

The bride beamed under the praise, then her brow furrowed again. "I'd like to see a few more dresses. Ones with Cinderella skirts. Lots of pouf, like a dress made for a ball!"

Mila kept her smile pasted on but was left with no choice. "We'd be happy to show you more dresses, but you've already paid the deposit for this dress, and unfortunately, there are no refunds for that down payment. However, we can let you make a deposit on a new dress, if that is what you want."

"What?" Susan, the bride's mother, nearly choked on the words. "I thought we could apply that deposit to any dress we chose." Her forehead crinkled like a piece of aluminum foil.

Mila folded her hands together, a picture of calm, like the Mona Lisa. "Since the dress has already been altered to her exact measurements, we need to pay the seamstress. That is why the deposit is nonrefundable. Not to mention the dress will be harder to sell since it's been fitted."

"What do you mean I don't get my deposit back?" Olivia's furrowed brow turned into a scowl that matched her mother's. Neither was happy with this arrangement. The bride turned to her mother, her eyes glossy with emotion. "Mother, I have to have the right dress!"

"We'll get the right dress. Yes, we will, princess." Susan

patted her daughter's spine before strutting over to Mila with angry eyes. "We need to take care of this. Now."

Mila had dealt with emotional bridezillas before—and their equally pushy mothers. Everyone was under so much stress that it was difficult to defuse the situation. Nobody enjoyed paying more than they had to, but Mila knew she couldn't keep her shop open unless she had these terms. She'd made the mistake of being too lax before, and the price she'd paid was closing her first shop in her hometown. Now that she had reopened a different store in Chicago, her terms were set. It was a careful balance that made it hard for the pickiest of brides.

Mila's hands remained neatly folded, a placid smile at the corner of her lips. She was the epitome of calm, even if her insides were quaking under the pressure. "If this is not the one, I'm happy to assist and help the bride find a wedding dress of her dreams as long as the terms are understood. So, shall we move forward and look at more dresses?"

Olivia wiped tears from the corners of her eyes, trying not to ruin her fake eyelashes.

"Of course," Susan cooed, rubbing her daughter's back as if she'd just endured a traumatic moment. "Where shall we begin?"

The bride's face blossomed into a full smile. "Oh, thank you! I want to try on as many as possible!"

Mila's lips twitched, but she resisted the urge to claim a victory just yet. After all, the bride was still undecided. "Let me call my assistant, Hadley, and we'll bring you as many dresses as you'd like."

The bride jumped up and down in her gown, clapping her hands, her brown curls bouncing like ping-pong balls.

Mila stepped out of the dressing room and let out a slow exhale of air, like a balloon with a pinprick hole. The mother didn't balk at losing her deposit and the bride was elated to look for an alternative. Hadn't she just saved a precarious situation?

Of course, there was still the bride's altered gown, which

would need to be sold at a discount. All things considered, the situation was still successfully resolved with no screaming matches between mother and daughter. In the end, if the bride was satisfied, that was all that mattered. Every dress eventually found its owner like a happy match.

Except in Mila's case, her own wedding dress still hung in her closet. Unused. Untouched. A sad reminder of a broken engagement, buried deep in the back of her closet. She blinked away the white-hot image.

Hadley stepped into the showroom, where Mila scanned the racks for dresses. "Hadley? We need you in the dressing area." Then she returned to the dressing room where the bride still admired herself in the mirror.

Hadley poked her head in. "You called?" The young assistant had worked at her shop for only a brief time but had become a lifesaver for Mila.

"Yes, bring out a selection of dresses with full skirts for our lovely bride. Size eight."

Her assistant's face twitched as her eyes flitted over the bride's dress. Hadley knew better than to ask. She'd get the story from Mila when they closed the shop.

"Of course. More dresses coming right up."

Olivia stepped into a private dressing room to change, leaving the mother of the bride and Mila alone.

An undercurrent of tension thrummed like a bass guitar string. "Do you need anything while you wait? Otherwise, I'll help Hadley choose some beautiful dress options."

Susan's eyes turned hard as flint. "No." They flitted over Mila's hands clasped at her waist, zeroing in on her fingers. A tiny smile formed on the woman's thin, pursed lips. "I see you aren't married."

Mila could feel her shoulders tighten at the mention of her missing engagement ring. The lady's smile wasn't a token of friendliness, but something more sinister.

"No, I'm not, Mrs. Smith."

"Hmm. Interesting. It's hard to find a good man these days unless you have everything going for you. Olivia was so very lucky to meet her fiancé at her university. I've heard that if you don't find a man by the time you're in your mid-twenties, it's an uphill battle. Virtually impossible. Not that you can't, but you know, dear, all the good ones are taken."

Mila was twenty-six, just over the mid-twenties hump, apparently an old maid by Susan Smith's standards. Was this her way of getting back at her for keeping the deposit?

Mila caught her reflection in the three-way mirror, like a house of mirrors. The terror in her face cut through her frozen expression. "Yes, I'm sure your daughter and her fiancé will make a good couple." She was trying to divert the conversation, but it was so difficult to allow this woman to slice the knife through her.

Mrs. Smith wouldn't let it go. "I just thought it odd. Someone who sells wedding dresses and can't find a man for herself. Does it drive you crazy to see beautiful women trying on your dresses, especially when you haven't had the chance to?"

She wasn't about to explain that she had a dress. A very lovely gown hanging in her apartment right now. Mila chose her words carefully. "It brings me great joy to make my brides happy."

Susan gave her a spiteful glance of satisfaction. "Well, then."

Mila glided to the door, still emanating a yoga-calm vibe as her heart pounded violently. "If you don't mind, I'm going to help my assistant."

When she closed the door behind her, she tipped her chin toward the ceiling, trying to stem the tears in her eyes. She would not let this lady get under her skin.

Most of the mothers weren't this difficult. More often, they were cotton candy sweet, women who wore cardigans and smelled like pumpkin-spice lattes. Suburban moms who had sacrificed countless hours at ball practice and swim meets. The kind of mother Mila had, soft and sweet, like a chewy caramel square.

But on rare occasions, she experienced the dark side of wedding planning, butting heads with overbearing mothers who carried cross expressions like they were martyrs on a sacred quest. They couldn't be satisfied. Not one bit.

Since opening her first shop fresh out of college, Mila had never had a customer who had found her weak spot so easily or quickly. It's not that she minded the single life. She quite enjoyed the freedom with its flexibility to come home at any hour or skip dinner. But when people assumed she wasn't fit to be married, it picked at a wound she'd thought had healed over.

Her scar was an empty finger on her left hand.

She went to the showroom, where Hadley had already picked out a dozen dresses.

"Boy, she's a peach," Hadley whispered.

Mila glanced over her shoulder to make sure they were alone. "The mom or the bride?"

"I was referring to the bride. Throwing a fit over her dress? It looks gorgeous, like it was made for her. Adrienne did a wonderful job on the alteration."

"My professional opinion is that she's suffering from decision fatigue. When you've had too many choices, then you start to second-guess yourself. It's a problem with brides."

"I thought maybe she was gown-obsessed. The type that likes to play dress-up."

"Have you talked to her mother?"

"No, why?"

"She noticed I wasn't wearing a ring and made a jab about me being single. Like it was a criticism as a wedding-dress-shop owner." Mila pulled out a puffy dress with lots of tulle, like a giant marshmallow.

Hadley rolled her eyes. "That low blow all because of a deposit? She probably has more wealth than I could ever dream of."

She held up a lacy skirt that billowed like a parachute. It had a gigantic skirt. "It comes with the territory. Stressed-out brides. Stressed-out mothers. They attack everyone else because they need to take it out on someone, right?"

"I'm sorry, Mila." Hadley scrunched her face in dismay.

"I appreciate the sympathy." She'd be fine. She was always fine, right? Never mind that this woman had twisted a fishhook in her raw wound.

Mila should have been married by now, but a year ago, everything had fallen apart. Embarrassment hovered over her like an invisible cloak. The wedding-shop owner who couldn't keep a man. It still stung.

Mila hung a dress with enormous ruffles on a rolling garment rack. Her shoulder throbbed from lifting the heavy gown. She rubbed the sore spot and tried to stretch her neck to one side. A pain shot down the length of her arm.

Hadley slid gowns down the rack to make more space, while the decadently fat skirts fought for room. "Is your shoulder hurting again? Do you want me to take over with this fitting? Let the mom use me as a punching bag." Hadley lifted her fists and gave a swift roundhouse kick in the air. The carefree exuberance of youth gleamed off her smooth, rosy cheeks.

"You don't have to do that. I'm fine, like an old punching bag that doesn't even feel the kicks anymore. I just wish I could take some time off." Mila stretched her arms in the air so that her petite frame gained an inch of height. Any more stretching and her spine would snap.

"Seriously, you need a break. You've been working so hard for the past several months. Why don't you take some vacation over the holidays? I only have one family event on Christmas Day, so I don't mind working extra."

Mila waved her hand in the air. "No, no. I couldn't let you do that."

Hadley was a golden employee, putting in extra time, even when she wasn't getting paid. Mila couldn't figure out how she had gotten so lucky. Especially since her last employee had cheated her out of significant money.

An extended Christmas vacation sounded divine, but could her dwindling bank account afford it? The thought floated through her mind like the soft flutter of a leaf falling. Hadley was clueless about the financial struggles the shop was facing. Mila had only casually mentioned a few paycheck delays, and Hadley had always responded with a casual wave of her hand. "That's fine. Whenever you get around to it," she chimed, like this was nothing more than a blip on the radar instead of a giant storm approaching.

Mila had struck gold with such a dedicated employee who didn't seem to have a dishonest bone in her body. Hadley had the beautiful ignorance that defined a recent college grad—still hopeful that life would simply work out as planned. It wasn't any surprise that she carried a starry-eyed gleam. Hadley lived with her parents and enjoyed their financial safety net. It simply didn't occur to her that life could come tumbling down with one disastrous turn.

But Mila knew better. Her life seemed to crumble like a sandcastle. No matter how she tried to pat the sand back into place, it just kept slipping through her fingers.

Only a few months before, she had made a devastating decision. Her last employee, Stacy, had needed a temporary loan after going through a messy divorce. Mila, who had a soft heart, had wanted to help. She couldn't stand on the sidelines and watch this girl's life fall apart. Grams had taught her that when people needed help, you pitched in like an Amish barn raising. The whole agreement seemed innocent enough: Give her an advance on several paychecks, and Stacy wouldn't be evicted. She could always pay Mila back later.

Then, without warning, Stacy hadn't shown up for work one day. When Mila had called, she had already switched phone numbers and left town. Later, she'd found out that Stacy had not only taken the money Mila had advanced her, she had also withdrawn a large sum from the business savings account. How could Mila be so dumb? She trusted that people were good, but just like her imaginary sandcastle that kept slipping away, her trust in people was slowly eroding.

She stared at the stacks of bills lying on her desk in neat piles, ominous reminders that she needed this month to be extra profitable or she'd have to make major cuts in the new year.

The vibration of her cell phone jolted her back to the present. Thelma Ratcliffe's number flashed across the screen. She was probably wondering when Mila would be home for Christmas. "Hey, Grams!"

"How's my big-city granddaughter doing?"

"Surviving . . . barely." Mila's tone was light and jovial, but there was a tiny hairline crack under the surface.

"When will you be home? I've hardly seen you." This was Grams's way of trying to twist her arm. An old-fashioned guilt trip.

"I'll be at Lily Woods's wedding in a week. Didn't Mom tell you? We're celebrating Christmas that weekend too. It's a bit early, given it's the middle of December."

"Yes, but that's not enough time with you. What about Christmas Day? I haven't made my holiday fruitcake yet. You love my strawberry jam." Her treats were staples at their family's Christmas celebration.

"I will miss it desperately. Can you mail me some? I'll eat it alone around the Christmas tree thinking of you and all the delightful memories of home."

"Humph." Grams didn't hide her feelings. Her disapproval

was like the frown on a kindergartner's drawing. "Why don't you just stay until Christmas? Or do you not like me?" She could imagine Grams's hint of mischief sparkling in her eyes. She had this pointed, funny schtick down. Humor was her vehicle for truth, and it hit Mila right where it hurt.

"More than anything, I want to be home for Christmas. But I have to get more sales in this month." She sat on the edge of her desk and flipped through her bills, dread creeping up her spine. She could make the three-hour trip on Christmas Day if the weather cooperated. That was a big *if* since both Chicago and Wild Harbor were known for their lake-effect snow squalls.

"Why not have your assistant take over while you go home for Christmas? You're the boss." Grams was a take-charge kind of woman. She'd always run Gramps's life like a drill sergeant before he passed away, and he was happy to let her. It was a win-win for both of them.

"There's only one problem. I can't pay her right now." Grams was squeezing the truth out of her like a lemon. Taking more time off wouldn't help a business that was barely making any progress.

"How are you ever going to meet a man if you never have any time off?" Grams was keenly interested in Mila's dating life, which was nonexistent since her breakup with Jake. Mila had buried herself in work, trying to keep her wedding shop afloat. Meeting a man was last on her list of priorities right now.

"I guess I'm just going to be a sassy single woman like you, Grams." Mila cracked a grin behind her phone. She could dish it out as much as Grams could.

"I might be sassy, but I don't want to be single for long. I'm on this newfangled senior citizen's dating app, and I'm planning on meeting Mr. Right as soon as I get a new profile picture on there."

Mila knew Grams loved Gramps more than anything, but she wasn't one to wallow in her grief for long. Time wasn't on

Grams's side, and she wanted to spoil another man with her affection again. Mila understood what it was like to feel time slipping through your hands.

"How do you know if you haven't met him yet?" Mila couldn't imagine her grams on a dating app, explaining what traits she wanted in a man. Gramps had seemed so simple on the surface, like an oversized teddy bear. She couldn't picture Grams with anyone else.

"I feel it in my bones. But it might be my arthritis too." She knew Grams was humoring her, trying to soften her up for dating advice. Grams had been begging her to return to Wild Harbor ever since she moved to Chicago.

"Do you have a date for the wedding yet?" Grams tried not to sound overly interested, but Mila knew she was fishing for some juicy gossip.

"I'm not planning on going with anyone." Mila opened another envelope, her thumb sliding neatly along the seam as it split in two. She pulled out another bill. *Overdue.* She laid it on the urgent pile.

"You know Jake has a new girl."

The words twisted her stomach into knots, even though she tried to let them slide right off. She needed thick skin, like a cement block wall. "I really don't care to know who Jake is dating."

"Why don't you find someone you can have fun with? Nothing serious. Kind of like prom."

"I didn't even enjoy prom." Mila's high school date had been a friend from calculus class. Instead of making small talk, he'd stared at the other couples and blundered through a few math jokes. A decent-looking kid with the personality of a butcher block.

"I don't know. I'm not looking for fun."

"You sound like the saddest country song I know. Let me give you some help. What if I pay your assistant so you can take some extra time off? Oh, and I'll pay your bills this month too, so you don't have to fret about that."

It's like Grams knew about her financial troubles without even asking. "I couldn't possibly let you do that."

"I'll take it out of your inheritance. Consider it a loan with one catch."

"Is there something behind this?" Mila couldn't help but fall for the bait. She desperately needed a vacation, and her grandma had dangled the carrot, luring her into a bargain.

"You find a date for Lily's wedding."

How in the world would she do that? She was too busy to have a dating life, much less try to meet a man. She didn't even know where to look for one. She had known Jake since high school. Where do you meet a kind, decent bachelor when you worked with brides?

"That sounds impossible." Mila felt the walls of her office squeeze in, like they were about to crush the life out of her. She stood quickly and knocked the bills off her desk. They fluttered to the ground like a flock of paper birds. She knelt to pick them up, the amount due flashing like fire, burning her up, until she was a husk. On her hands and knees, her shoulder cramped painfully. There was no way she could pay these. Even with the best sales month ever, she would still be in debt.

"You just think about it, honey." Grams let the pause hang in between them. "You don't even have to tell me ahead of time. You show up with a date, someone you want to be with, and I'll loan you the money."

Mila sat back against her desk on the floor, a pile of insurmountable bills in her lap. One date and she could start the new year fresh. A shiny prospect of hope dangling like a worm on a hook.

She scrunched her legs to her chest and propped her elbows on her knees. "I'll think about it. But I'm not making any promises."

"You know I'm not asking you to find a husband. It's one date. At some point, you just gotta get back on the horse."

"Horse. Gotcha. I'll see you at the wedding. Guest or not. I'll let it be a surprise."

"And if you find a man my age, I'll gladly take him. Surprise me, honey."

A corner of Mila's mouth curved. "A date for me *and* you? That's a big wish. Although I'm sure I'd have more luck finding someone for you."

Grams laughed, then said goodbye.

All she had to do was find a date. How hard could that be? Mila groaned and put her head in her hands. From where she sat on the floor of her office, the walls still felt stifling, but they were no longer squeezing her like a vise. Grams had given her a way out of this mess.

She hadn't been planning on staying more than three days. But now that Hadley had offered to work, and Grams had made her an irresistible offer, the idea spun in her mind like a wobbly top.

It had been so long since she hadn't worked herself to the bone. Her life was wedding dresses. What would she even do with herself? Time off in idyllic Wild Harbor sounded like a bite of luscious pie.

Her phone rang again. Mila stood and adjusted her skirt. Back to professional Mila. Not desperate Mila making split-second bargains with her grandma.

"Hello, this is Mila Sutton."

"Mila, this is Lily Woods. Do you have a minute?"

"How's the bride-to-be?" Mila relaxed her shoulders. Ever since kindergarten, Lily's sister, Cassidy, had been Mila's best friend—practically another sister. *Inseparable* was how their elementary teacher had described them. Hearing her voice made Mila wish she was already home.

"Okay, I think?" Lily's voice was friendly, but pinched. "I'm so sorry to bother you. I'm sure you're swamped today."

"I have a few minutes. What's up?"

"I've got wedding-dress jitters. I'm afraid it won't fit."

"Lily, your wedding dress is perfect and ready to go. I'm sure it will be fine."

"But what if it isn't? I've gained a few pounds from too many treats this month. I had this nightmare last night that I couldn't even fit into my dress."

Ah, yes. *The bride's nightmare.* Other brides had mentioned that disturbing dream. Usually, in the dream, they had to don their regular clothes or their undergarments. Either option was horrifying.

"Don't worry. You're entirely normal. Every bride I know stress-eats. Adrienne usually gives a little breathing room from the measurements."

"But what if it's not enough? Those buttons on the back won't fasten otherwise. Should I diet this week just to be sure?"

"Don't do that. Yo-yo diets aren't great for your health. I'll be out the day before the wedding to make sure it fits."

"You said Adrienne gives some extra room in the dress?"

"Yep. She doesn't want a bride to feel like she's suffocating in a corset."

"I just wish we had more time." She could hear the worry in Lily's voice.

What if she went up to Wild Harbor a week early? Lily could see if the dress fit, and if it didn't, there would still be time to make a small final adjustment. Plus, it would give her time to decide on Grams's offer and scout the town for a last-minute date. Maybe she could talk one of her high school friends into accompanying her, even though Grams had encouraged her to pick someone she was interested in.

"I have an idea. What if I come home early for your fitting?"

"You don't have to do that. I trust you, Mila. This is your job."

"But wouldn't it ease your mind? My assistant volunteered to work extra over the holidays. Not many brides shop for dresses this time of year anyway, and you don't know how badly I need a break."

Mila heard a loud squeal from the dressing room. Apparently Olivia was having a ball playing dress-up.

She leaned against the wall, her shoulder still sore from her tense muscles. "Now that I think about it, a trip sounds like just what the doctor ordered. What are you doing tonight?"

"Just putting together some table decorations for the reception. But I could work in a dress fitting." Lily sounded relieved already.

"Then it's a done deal. Don't you worry at all. I'll call you when I get close to Wild Harbor."

"I can't believe you'd do this for me."

"For your family, anything." It was true, she loved the Woods family like her own.

Hadley peeked her head around the corner. "Fingers crossed. I think she found the dress!"

"Oh, good! Whatever we can do to send her off as a happy bride. By the way, I'm taking you up on your offer. As soon as we get the dress settled with our bride, I'm leaving town."

"You mean today? I've never seen you so—"

She didn't want to say it. "Impulsive?"

"Spontaneous. You're usually planned so far in advance, you can't fit anything into your schedule. Not even a night out on the town. I'm proud of you."

She didn't know if anyone had ever used the word spontaneous to describe her. Her life generally followed the same pattern every day. Even her wardrobe was color-coded. Mondays were black-dress day. Tuesdays, navy blazer with white pants. Wednesdays and Thursdays she tried to cheer things up with color—an Ivy League green or a flaming red, while weekends were for patterns. Floral Friday and Striped Saturdays. It all made logical sense.

There was no room for vacation in the pattern of her life. It was an anomaly from what was normal.

"After the last several months, I've realized I desperately need a break. Maybe Olivia and Susan Smith were exactly what I needed—the final push to do something spontaneous, for once."

"Who knows? Maybe you'll even meet someone." Hadley wasn't teasing. She lived for the dream of love. She nearly bubbled over hearing every bride's engagement story.

Mila jotted down a few reminders and grabbed the stack of urgent bills. The clock on the wall was nearing five. Normally, she'd work a few more hours after the store closed on a Saturday, but not today. "Oh, I doubt that. I'm not looking for anyone. He'd have to run into me before I noticed him."

"Never say never." Hadley gave her a wink. "Enjoy every minute."

"I will. Call me if you need anything. I owe you for this, Hadley." Mila plucked her black wool dress coat from the back of a chair and grabbed the garment bag holding Lily's wedding dress. As she stepped into the frigid temperatures, the icy wind stole her breath away.

She walked a block, turned toward the parking garage, and saw a man dressed as Santa standing next to a red kettle.

She fished around in the bottom of her wallet, looking for some cash. She usually only carried credit cards, but she hated walking by a donation bucket empty-handed.

A shiny silver object winked at her from the bottom of her wallet. Her grandfather's silver dollar.

Every year at Christmas, Gramps had gifted her a card containing a shiny coin. When she was seven, she'd declared the new coin her lucky charm and hidden it in her purse. Over the years, she had transferred it from purse to purse, eventually forgetting it in the corner of her wallet. She had learned long ago that there was no such thing as luck, but she still couldn't bring herself to toss it.

She dug around in her purse, raking through the bottom, reluctant to give away a memory tied to her gramps, who had passed away a year ago.

Santa clanged his handbell like a clock chiming the hours. "Merry Christmas!" he bellowed in his best Santa-like voice. His beard sat crookedly on his chin while the long white curls of his wig blew into his eyes.

"I'm sorry I don't have more change." She held up the silver coin, giving it a quick goodbye before she held it over the coin slot. Gramps would understand that it was time to let the coin go. Her luck had run out long ago.

The coin clattered at the bottom of the pail.

Santa's face flashed a smile under his fake beard and rosy, frostbitten cheeks. "Thank you, my dear, and may your Christmas wishes come true."

What Santa didn't know was that they already had. She was going home.

Get *Christmas Wishes in Wild Harbor* and fall in love all over again!

THANK YOU!

Thank you for picking up Megan and Finn's story. I loved writing it! It's an honor to have you read this book. My hope is that Wild Harbor is a place you can escape to and that the friends who live there feel like home.

I want to write stories that warm your heart, remind you that you're loved, and take you away to a magical place, if only for a day.

I love hearing from my readers. My email list is the best way to stay in touch and I share stories there that I don't share anywhere else. Plus, every week I include great book deals and new releases! Join it at graceworthington.com.

You can also join me on instagram or facebook @gracewor-thingtonauthor.

ACKNOWLEDGMENTS

I'm forever grateful to my husband, Sam, and my two children for supporting my crazy writing dream and encouraging me when the words don't flow easily.

Every writer needs a good team and I couldn't do it without mine. Thanks to my editor, Emily Poole, and my wonderful beta readers who give me such valuable feedback, Leigh Ann Routh, Joy Martz, Heidi Lanter, Michelle McCubbins, Thelma Nienhuis, and Denise Long. Thank you to Judy Zweifel for giving this story a final proofread and Kristen Ingebretson for the beautiful cover design.

To all my readers, I'm so grateful for you and hope you love this series as much as I've loved writing it.

ALSO BY GRACE WORTHINGTON

Love at Wild Harbor

Summer Nights in Wild Harbor

Christmas Wishes in Wild Harbor

ABOUT THE AUTHOR

Grace Worthington writes clean contemporary romance novels and loves giving readers a happily ever after with heart. She has a degree in English and resides with her husband and two children in Indiana.

Did you know there is a bonus wedding epilogue for this book only available for Grace's newsletter subscribers?

Don't miss the free bonus epilogue of Lily's wedding with a surprise!

Sign up for it at graceworthington.com

Join Grace's newsletter and snag this free bonus epilogue.